BATTL

It was obvio̶u̶s̶ ̶...̶ ̶ ̶ ̶ ̶ ̶ ̶ to surrender willingly, but Angelo had his own straightforward solution to that.

"Gladiator mode!"

The sergeant imaged the transformation through receptors in his helmet, and his *Trojan Horse* went through mechamorphosis, transforming to Gladiator mode, the Hovertank's most powerful. His mecha became a waddling, two-legged gun turret the size of a house. Its main battery appeared, a cannon with far greater firepower than that of the tank or Battloid.

Angelo opened fire, hitting one of the stone columns dead center. It was blasted in two, in a shower of splinters and dust, collapsing and breaking into a thousand fragments. He traversed the barrel and let off another round, blowing chunks from the ceiling.

"C'mon, Zor! *Show yourself!*"

The ROBOTECH™ Series
Published by Ballantine Books:

GENESIS #1

BATTLE CRY #2

HOMECOMING #3

BATTLEHYMN #4

FORCE OF ARMS #5

DOOMSDAY #6

SOUTHERN CROSS #7

METAL FIRE #8

THE FINAL NIGHTMARE #9

ROBOTECH™ #9:

THE FINAL NIGHTMARE

Jack McKinney

A Del Rey Book

BALLANTINE BOOKS • NEW YORK

A Del Rey Book
Published by Ballantine Books

Library of Congress Catalog Card Number: 87-91226

ISBN 0-345-34142-?

Printed in Canada

First Edition: September 198

Cover art by David Schleinkofer

FOR KALLAN AND CAITLIN LOCK,
WITH LOVE FROM UNCLE JACK

CHAPTER
ONE

*Many women were often in the thick of the fighting during the
First Robotech War. They served splendidly and gallantly. But they
were usually restricted to what the military insisted on calling
"non-combat roles," despite the great numbers of them killed as a
direct result of enemy action.*

*By the time of the Second Robotech War, with the Earth's re-
sources depleted and its population drastically reduced by the
First, sheer necessity and common sense had overcome the linger-
ing sexism that had kept willing, qualified women off the front
lines.*

*Nevertheless, the Robotech Masters' onslaught quickly had
Earth on the ropes. It is instructive to consider what the outcome
would have been if the Army of the Southern Cross had faced the
planet's second invasion without half its fighting strength.*

Fortunately for us all, that is not what happened.

Betty Greer, *Post-Feminism and the Robotech Wars*

Lieutenant Marie Crystal made a willful effort to face the camera now as she had faced enemy guns
yesterday.

She drove back her bone-deep exhaustion, the pain of
battle injuries, and the despair of a desperate situation that
even the light lunar gravity couldn't alleviate. She intended
to finish her report with the clarity and precision expected of
a Tactical Armored Space Corps fighter ace and the leader
of the TASC's vaunted Black Lions. . . .

And maybe, after that, she could collapse and get a few
minutes' sleep. It seemed now that she never wanted anything *but* sleep.

In the wake of the disastrous all-out attempt to destroy
the Robotech Masters' invasion fleet, Marie had to shoulder

1

even more responsibility. The chain of command had been shot all to hell along with the Earth strikeforce itself.

Admiral Burke was dead—diced into bloody stew by an exploding power junction housing when the blue Bioroids cut the strikeforce flagship to ribbons. General Lacey, next in line, lay with ninety percent of the skin seared off his body, teetering between life and death.

The senior officer, a staff one-star, was still functional, but he had virtually no combat command experience. The scuttlebutt was that he was being pressured to let somebody else run the show. An implausibly successful Bioroid sortie and the resultant hangar deck explosion on board the now-defunct flagship resulted in Marie being named the new flight group commander.

She went on with her after-action report to Southern Cross military headquarters on Earth.

"Our remaining spacecraft number: one battlecruiser, two destroyer escorts, and one logistical support ship, all of which have suffered heavy damage," she said, looking squarely into the optical pickup. "Along with twenty-three Veritech fighters, twelve A-JACs combat mecha, and assorted small scout and surveillance ships. At last report we have one thousand, one hundred sixteen surviving personnel, eight hundred and fifty-seven of them fit for duty."

Fewer than nine hundred effectives! Jesus! She pulled at the collar ring seal of her combat armor, where it had chafed her neck. She couldn't recall the last time she had been able to strip off the alloy plate and get some real rest. Back on Earth, probably. But that was a lifetime ago.

"As I stated previously, deployment of the enemy mother ships, and their assault craft and Bioroid combat mecha, made it impossible for the strikeforce to return to Earth. Since we were also cut off from L5 Space Station Liberty, and were forced to take refuge here at Moon Base ALUCE, we are making round-the-clock efforts to fortify our position against an enemy counterattack. Major repairs and life-support replenishment are being carried out as well, and civilian personnel have been placed under emergency military authority."

It all sounded so crisp, so can-do, she thought, trying to focus her eyes on her notecards. As if everything were under control, instead of at the thin edge of utter catastrophe. As if the survivors were an effective fighting force instead of a chewed up, burned-out bunch of men and women and machinery. As if the attack hadn't been the most insane strategy, the worst snafu, the most horrifying slaughter she had ever seen.

Recording her stiff-upper-lip report, she felt like a liar, but that was the way Marie Crystal had been taught to do her duty. She wondered if the brass hats at Southern Cross Army HQ back on Earth would read between the lines—if that pompous, blustering idiot, Supreme Commander Leonard, had any idea how much suffering and death he had caused.

She yanked her mind off that track; feeling murderous toward her superiors would not help now.

"Our medical personnel and volunteers from other strikeforce elements are tending to the wounded in the ALUCE medcenter. But facilities are extremely limited here, and I am instructed to request that we be permitted to attempt a special mission to ferry our worst cases back to Earth."

What could she add? There was the natural Human impulse to tell the goddamn lardbutts in their swivel chairs how much hell she had seen. There was the desire to see someone capable, someone like General Emerson, for instance, march in before the United Earth Government council and charge Leonard and his staff with incompetence. There was an inner compulsion to tell how futile it felt, preparing the civilian ALUCE—Advanced Lunar Chemical Engineering —station for a last stand, and getting the VTs and other mecha ready to sortie out again if the need arose.

Forget it; shoot 'n' salute, that was a soldier's duty. Maybe a miracle would happen, and the mysterious aliens who called themselves the Robotech Masters would cut ALUCE and the strikeforce a little slack. If the Humans could just have a few days to get themselves back into some kind of fighting shape, that would change the mix a lot. But Marie had her doubts.

"This completes the situation report. Lieutenant Marie Crystal, reporting for the Commander, out." She saluted smartly, her mouth tugging in a faint, ironic smirk.

The camera tech wrapped it up. "We'll transcribe it and send it out in burst right away, ma'am." She took the cassette of Marie's report.

The Robotech Masters had been having more and more success interfering with the frequency-jumping communications tactics the Humans had been forced to use. To avoid any interference, the report would be sped up to a millisecond squeal of information. Hopefully it would get through.

And when they get it, what then? Marie wondered. *We might be able to sneak one shipload of WIAs back, but for the rest of us there's no way home.*

In the headquarters of the Army of the Southern Cross, Supreme Commander Leonard studied the tape. The smudged and hollow-eyed young female flight lieutenant reeled off facts and figures of bitter defeat with no expression except that last upcurling of one corner of her mouth.

"Mmm" was all he said, as Colonel Rochelle turned off the tape. "We received this transmission from ALUCE eight minutes ago, sir," Rochelle told him. "Nothing else has gotten through the enemy's jamming so far. Looks like they're onto our freq-jumping stunt. The people down in signal/crypto are trying to come up with something new, but so far the occasional odd message is all we can really hope for from Strikeforce Victory."

Leonard nodded slowly, looking at the huge, gray screen. Then he whirled around and threw himself into a seat across the conference table from Major General Rolf Emerson.

"Well, Emerson! How about that!" Leonard pounded his pale, soft, freckled fists the size of pot roasts on the gleaming oak. "It would appear that our little assault operation wasn't a complete failure after all, eh?"

Everyone in the room held their breath. It was a well-known fact that Emerson had opposed the mad strikeforce scheme from the outset, and that there was no love lost between the Supreme Commander and his chief of staff for Terrestrial Defense, Emerson. And everyone had watched Emerson grow grimmer and grimmer as Marie Crystal delivered her casualty report.

Now Emerson looked across the table at Leonard, and more than one staff officer wished they had had time to get a little money down on the fight. Leonard was huge, but a lot of it was pointless bulk; there was some question about how much real muscle was there. Emerson, on the other hand, was a ramrod-straight middleweight with a boxer's physique, and few of the men and women on his staff could keep up with him when it came time for calisthenics or road drill.

Not a complete failure? Emerson was asking himself. *God, what would this man call "failure"?*

But he was a man bound by his oath. A generation before, military officers had violated their oaths. They had served grasping politicians—most tellingly in the now-defunct USA—and that had led to a global civil war. Every woman and man who had sworn to serve the Southern Cross Army knew those stories, and knew that it was their obligation to obey that oath to the letter.

Emerson stared down at his fingers, which were curled around an ancient fountain pen that had been a gift from his ward, Private First Class Bowie Grant. He worried about Bowie only slightly more than he worried about each of the hundreds and thousands of other Southern Cross Army personnel under his command. He worried about the survival of the Human race and that of Earth more than he worried about any individual Human life—even his own.

Emerson gathered up all of his patience, and the perseverance for which he was so famous. "Commander Leonard, the ALUCE base is a mere research outpost, with civilians present. Aside from the fact that by the standards of the Robotech war we're fighting, ALUCE is tinfoil and cardboard! I therefore presume you're not seriously thinking of fortifying it as a military base."

It was as close to insubordination as Emerson had ever permitted himself to go. The silence in the Command Briefing Room was so profound that the roiling of various stomachs could be heard. Through it all, Emerson was locked with Leonard's gaze.

The Supreme Commander spoke deliberately. "Yes, that is my plan. And I see nothing wrong with it!" He seemed to be making it up as he went along. "Mmm. As I see it, a military strikeforce at an outpost on the moon will enable us to hit those alien bastards from two different directions at once!"

A G3 staff light colonel named Rudolph readjusted his glasses and said eagerly, "I see! In that way, we're outflanking those six big mother ships they've got in orbit around Earth!"

Leonard looked pleased. "Yes. Precisely."

Emerson took a deep breath and pushed his chair away from the oak table a little, as though he was about to face a firing squad. But when he came to his feet, there was silence. All eyes turned to him. The general feeling was that no one on Earth was more trusted, more committed to standing by his word, than Rolf Emerson.

No one could be relied upon more to speak the truth into the teeth of deceit.

And this was certainly that moment. "ALUCE is a peaceful, unreinforced cluster of pressurized huts, Commander Leonard. I don't think that anything the strikeforce survivors can do will make it a viable military base. And it's my opinion that by provoking the enemy into attacking it you'll be throwing away lives."

So many staffers inhaled at the same time that Rudolph wondered if the air pressure would drop. Leonard's faced flushed with rage. "They've already mauled our first assault wave; it's not a question of provocation anymore. *Damn* it, man! This is war, not an exercise in interstellar diplomacy!"

"But we haven't even *tried* negotiating," Emerson began, a little hopelessly. An over-eager missile battery commander named Komodo had fired on the Robotech Masters before any real attempt could be made to contact them and learn what it was they wanted. From that moment on, it had been war.

"I'll have no insubordination!" Leonard bellowed. To the

rest of the staff he added, "Mobilize the second strikeforce and prepare them to relieve our troops at Moon Base ALUCE!"

Outside the classified-conference room, a figure clad in the uniform of the Southern Cross's Alpha Tactical Armored Corps—the ATACs—moved furtively.

Zor still didn't quite understand the half-perceived urges that had brought him there. It was a familiar feeling, this utter mystification about who he was, and what forces drove him. It was as though he moved in a fog, but he knew that somewhere ahead was the room where all Earth's military plans were being formulated. He must go there, he must listen and watch—but he didn't understand why.

Suddenly there was a bigger figure blocking his way. "Okay, Zor. Suppose you tell me just what the hell you think you're doing here?"

It was Sergeant Angelo Dante, senior NCO of the 15th, fists balled and feet set at about shoulder width, ready for a fight. His size and strength dwarfed Zor's, and Zor was not small. Dante was a career soldier, a man of dark, curling hair and dark brows, not quick to trust anyone, incapable of believing anything good of Zor.

The sergeant grabbed Zor's leather torso harness and gave it a yank, nearly lifting him off his feet. "What about it?"

Zor shook his head slowly, as if coming out of a trance. "Angie! Wh—how did I get here?" He blinked, looking around him.

"That's my line. You're sneakin' around a restricted area and you're away from your duty station without permission. If you don't have a pretty good explanation, I'm gonna see to it your butt goes into Barbwire City for a long time!" He shook Zor again.

"Oh, Zor! There you are!" First Lieutenant Dana Sterling, commanding officer of the 15th, practically squealed it as she rounded a corner and hurried toward them. Angelo shook his head a little, watching how her smile beamed and her eyes crinkled as she caught sight of Zor.

Like her two subordinates, she was dressed in the white Southern Cross uniform, with the black piping and black boots that suggested a riding outfit. She barely reached the middle of Angelo's chest, but she was, he had to admit, a gutsy and capable officer. Except where this Zor guy was concerned.

She rushed up to them and grabbed Zor's hand; Angelo found himself automatically releasing his captive. Dana seemed completely unaware that she had blundered into the middle of what would otherwise have been a fight. "I've been looking for you *everywhere,* Zor!"

Zor, still dazed, seemed to be groping for words. "Just a second, Lieutenant," Angelo interrupted.

But she was tugging Zor away. "Come along; I want to ask you something!"

"Hold it, ma'am!" Angelo burst out. "Why don'tcha ask pretty boy here what he's doing hanging around a restricted area?"

Dana's expression turned to anger. Like the sergeant, she had tracked down Zor with difficulty, but she wouldn't let herself think badly of her strange, alien trooper. She shot back, "What are you, Angie, a spy for the Global Military Police?"

Angelo's black brows went up. "Huh? You know better than that! But somebody has to keep an eye on this guy. Or don't you think what he's doing is a little suspicious?"

Dana rasped, "Zor's suffering from severe memory loss. If he's a little disoriented at times, that just means we should show him a bit of compassion and understanding!"

She slipped an arm through Zor's, clasping his elbow. Angelo wondered if he were going crazy; wasn't this the same alien who had led the enemy forces in his red Bioroid? Didn't he try to kill Dana, as she had tried to kill him, in a half dozen or so of the most vicious single combats of the war, her Hovertank mecha against his Bioroid?

"I'll speak to you later, Sergeant," Dana said, dragging Zor off.

Angelo watched them go. He had gained a lot of respect for Dana Sterling since she had taken command of the 15th, but she was only eighteen and, in the sergeant's opinion, still too impulsive and too inclined to make rash moves. He tried to suppress his sneaking suspicion as to why she was so protective of Zor—so *possessive*, really.

But one indisputable fact remained. No matter how loyally Angelo tried to discount it, Dana herself was half alien.

CHAPTER TWO

I could never figure out why Leonard, who hated anything alien, would tolerate that wacky experiment where Zor was thrown in with the 15th ATAC—especially since a female halfbreed was CO. One day, I remember, Leonard had been grumbling about putting Zor back into lab isolation and dissecting him.

Ten minutes later the phone rang. Leonard didn't say much in that conversation—it was real brief. And whatever he heard through the earpiece had him sweating. Right after that he dropped the topic for good.

I happened to see the phone logs for the afternoon over at the commo desk a little later. The call had come from Dr. Lazlo Zand, who ran Special Protoculture Observations and Operations Kommandatura. I did my best to forget I'd ever seen that log.

Captain Jed Streiber, as quoted in "Conjuration," *History of the Robotech Wars*, Vol. CXXXIII

"**T**HE REVENGE OF THE MARTIAN MYSTERY *Women?*" Zor echoed Dana.

"Right!" she said excitedly. "Everybody says it's a dynamite movie. You'll love it! And it won't cost you anything 'cause I've already got the tickets!" She showed him the pair of ducats.

They were sitting in a little park outside the big, imperial-looking building that housed Alpha Tactical Armored Corps HQ. Birds were singing, and a fountain splashed nearby. "As a matter of fact, they're hard to come by, and the scalper charged me *plenty* for these!" She frowned a bit, wondering if she was making a fool of herself.

Zor gave a thin smile. "Well then, how can I refuse, Lieutenant?"

An officer in the 10th squad who had seen the movie last night had said that it was romantic as well as exciting. Dana liked the idea of seeing a movie about alluring, captivating alien women with Zor.

She rushed on, "I don't know *what* I would have done if you hadn't said yes!" Then she stopped, looking perplexed. "Only—now I'm not sure what I ought to wear...."

Zor watched her as she deliberated, certain that no matter what she decided to wear she would look beautiful. He tried to sort out the conflicting emotions and veiled impulses that kept him in a state of confusion much of the time. Zor wondered if these feelings for his lieutenant were what the Human beings called love.

In a geostationary orbit some 23,000 miles above the Earth hung six stupendous mother ships—the invasion fleet of the Robotech Masters.

In the huge flagship, which still bore the scars of battles with the Human race both in space and on the surface of the planet, stood the Triumvirate of Masters. They looked down from the vantage point of their floating Protoculture cap— the enormous, humplike instrument that gave them total control of superhuman mind powers and abilities.

Like virtually all members of their race, the Triumvirate of Masters functioned as a triad, each standing upon a small platform attached to the hovering cap. They were males, with hawklike faces that wore perpetual scowls. The severity of their faces was emphasized by scarlike V's of tissue under each cheek. All of them were bald- or shave-pated; their long, fine hair fell below their shoulders. They wore monkish robes, their wide, floppy collars suggesting the tripartite blossom of the Invid Flower of Life.

The Masters usually mindspoke through direct tactile contact with their Protoculture cap, but they chose now to say their words out loud. Shaizan, who was often the spokesman for the Triumvirate, said, "So, you're saying our Bioroid clones are limited in their effectiveness?"

Looking up at him was a triad of Clonemasters, two males and a female, standing under their own, smaller Protoculture cap. All were tall, pale, and slender. They wore tight-fitting clothes vaguely suggestive of the early Renaissance.

Both males wore full blond-brown mustaches and mutton chops, and one of them had a beard; the androgynous-looking female wore her long blond hair in a simple style. The minor differences between them only served to emphasize their sameness of body and features.

The leader of the Clonemaster triumvirate nodded. "Precisely. Their current cerebral composition makes them undependable. They perform adequately as shock troops, but in order to deal with an Invid attack, we'll need clones much more tightly mindlinked to our triumvirate."

And they all knew that the need to deal with the savage, relentless Invid might come soon. The Flower of Life had bloomed on Earth, and where the Flower bloomed, the Robotech Masters' mortal enemies, the Invid, were bound to appear in short order.

It was all so frustrating to the Masters, even though they didn't reveal any emotion. They had traveled for nearly fifteen years—across the galaxy—in search of the last Protoculture Matrix in existence. There were determined to find that source of power that could return them to their rightful place as lords of all creation. And yet, although they were near their prize, they were unable to claim it because of the stubbornness of the primitive Humans below. Unbeknownst to the inhabitants of Earth, the Matrix, sealed under one of three mounds on the outskirts of Monument City, was going to seed.

The Masters' calculations showed that the Protoculture would soon shift from a contained mass, kept in the prefertilized state in which it exuded its incredible and unique forces, and convert into the Flowers of Life that the Invid ingested to sustain themselves.

But the Humans weren't the Masters' only opposition; they weren't the most formidable enemies. The mounds were guarded by invisible Protoculture entities—three strange, mysterious, and sinister wraiths.

The wraiths had manifested themselves once—or rather, they had *permitted* the Masters to perceive them. They were cloaked and cowled fire-eyed specters—ghosts whose power stymied the Masters' efforts to find out *exactly* where the Matrix lay. Without that information, it was impossible for the Masters to use simple brute force to rip the Matrix from the mounds; that would risk damaging the thing they had come so far to retrieve. The Masters weren't sure yet what other powers or designs the wraiths might have.

And now, to complicate matters further, local perturbations were hampering the performance of the Masters' cloned slave populace. "Yes, that might be our problem with Zor Prime," Shaizan was saying. "We've had some trouble with him, almost from the first moment when he was set down among the Humans. His neuro-sensor has been malfunctioning."

Not that Zor Prime, cloned from tissue samples of the slain original Zor, greatest genius of his race and discoverer of Protoculture, hadn't been of some use. Divested of his memories, the clone had been dispatched among the Terrans as an unwitting spy, so that the Masters could see through his eyes and hear through his ears.

The Masters were also hoping that the trauma of being among the local primitives, and being on the planet to which the original Zor had dispatched the Protoculture Matrix so long ago, would spur Zor's memory. Perhaps they could get Zor Prime to tell them why the Matrix had been sent, precisely where it was, and how to get it back from both the Humans and the invisible wraithlike Protoculture entities who guarded the mounds that hid it.

Dag, second among the Masters, had a slightly more prognathous jaw than the others. He said, "It seems the Human behavioral dysfunction known as *emotions* may be responsible for this malfunction."

Bowkaz, third of the Masters, nodded, his brows nearly meeting as his frown deepened. "Yes. These *emotions* destabilize the proper functioning of the healthy brain and the rational mind."

"What is your will then, Masters?" asked Jeddar, leader of the Clonemaster triumvirate—their chief slaves—bowing humbly before them.

"Hmm," Shaizan said, gazing down on him. "You would like our permission to carry out this plan of yours, no doubt."

The Clonemaster kowtowed. "Yes, my lord. We believe it will be our key to a quick, decisive victory. We only need your approval."

The Masters touched hands to their Protoculture cap. Wherever one of the nailless, spiderlike hands touched a mottled area of the mushroom-shaped cap, the mottled area came alight with the power of Protoculture. The Masters swiftly and silently came to a consensus.

The barracks housing the 15th squad, Alpha Tactical Armored Corps—ATAC—was a truncated cone a dozen stories high, of smoky blue glass and gleaming blue tile (the most modern of polymers) set on a framework of blued alloy. It was a large complex even though it only served as housing and operational facility to a few people; much of the aboveground area was filled with parts and equipment storage and repair areas, armory, kitchen and dining and lavatory space, and so on. In many ways it was a self-contained world.

At the ground and basement levels were the mecha servicing and repair stations, and the motor stables filled with parked Hovercycles and other conventional vehicles, along with the giant Hovertanks—the 15th's primary mecha.

Up in her quarters, Dana wasn't thinking about any kind of machinery just then. Agonizing over what to wear for her date with Zor, she flung every skirt, dress, and blouse in her closet in different directions, draping them with lingerie.

There was, no doubt, something in the regs about officers dating privates, but Zor was a different case. He had been placed with the 15th in the hope that military service would help him recover his missing memory, and that exposure to Earth-style social interaction and bonding would sway him against his former Masters.

When it came to social interaction, Dana was more than ready. It wasn't just that Zor was dreamy looking and a little disoriented. There was also the fact that he was alien, as was

Dana's mother. She sometimes wondered if it was blood calling to blood.

Long before she had actually seen him, Dana had felt inexplicable emotions and experienced strange Visions bearing on the red Bioroid Zor piloted. Something within drew her to Zor.

Now, as she hurried into the unit ready-room, which doubled as a rec room during off-duty hours, she tried to set all that aside and concentrate on having a good time.

Decked out in a frilly skirt and silk blouse, she was all set to yell *Hi Zor! I'm here!* Only—it wasn't Zor she found there.

Squad Sergeant Angelo Dante stepped away from the autobar (it was after duty hours, and the cybernetic mixologist would dispense alcohol to troopers who were certified off-duty) and strolled over toward her. "Well, well! Aren't *we* looking awfully chic tonight?"

She tried to act nonchalant; she wanted to enjoy herself with Zor and not start off the evening with another row with Angelo. "Have you seen Zor around?"

In the days before the First Robotech War (after which an almost medieval cluster of city-states had banded in a loose hegemony to fill the vacuum of world rule and form the United Earth Government—the UEG) soldiers had had less autonomy and more discipline, so the old salts liked to say. If so, she would have welcomed a reversion to those old days.

If she kicked Angelo's feet out from under him and mashed a coffee table over his head, Southern Cross Command might not consider the act a necessary disciplinary measure and it could cause sociodynamic strains. Besides, Angelo was awfully tough.

Dana restrained herself, but resolved to command his loyalty—even if it meant inviting the very big, very strong, and quick NCO to step downstairs to the motor stables and have it out—before another day passed. There was no way *two* people could run a Hovertank squad, or any other unit.

Angelo smiled spitefully. "Yeah. I bet if he had seen you

in your prom queen rig, he would have never asked Nova out tonight."

"Nova? Nova Satori?"

Angelo buffed his nails on his torso harness. Dana considered decking him; he was large, but she was used to fighting for everything she had ever gotten, and if she could get in the first shot . . .

"Uh-huh," he said. "Let's see now: something about dinner, and the theater afterwards."

He backed away suddenly as she came at him with clenched fists, ready to spit brimstone and, he could see from the way she held herself, do some damage.

She was raving. "That no-good two-timer! That sneaking *alien*! He's getting more Human every day!"

Angelo was fending her off. "Well now, ma'am, maybe all he needs is a bit of compassion, remember?" That was what she had said to *him*, back when Angelo was about to take Zor's face off.

"You're enjoying this, huh?" she seethed at him. Then she had an image of suitable revenge. She held up the two movie tickets. "Well, I guess *you'll* just have to escort me, big boy!"

Angelo's face fell and he made some odd sounds before he found the words. "Uh, ah, thanks, Lieutenant, but I'll pass—"

"You ain't reading me, Sergeant! It's an order!"

The Clonemasters' update was even more bleak than had been anticipated.

"My lord, our reservoirs of Protoculture power are running dry. The effects of this are being felt throughout the fleet. Our new clonelings are lethargic and unresponsive; the effectiveness of our weapons is limited; and our defensive shields cannot be maintained full-time. If we do not secure a large infusion of Protoculture, we are doomed."

As Jeddar spoke, the humpish Protoculture cap of the Masters showed them, by mind-image, the deteriorating situation in all six of the enormous mother ships. Where the Protoculture energies had once coursed through them like highways of incandescence or arterial systems of pure, god-like force, those flows were now reduced to unsteady rivulets. It was like looking into one huge, dying organism.

Elsewhere in the colossal flagship, six clones—two triumvirates—faced off, five against one.

On the one side was Musica, ethereal weaver of song, Mistress of the Cosmic Harp, whose melodies gave shape and effect to the mental force with which the Clonemasters controlled their subjects. She was pale and delicate looking, slender, with long, deep green hair.

To one side were her two clone sisters, Octavia and Allegra, both of them subdued and frightened by the very idea of *discord*. And across from Musica was the triumvirate of Guard leaders: tall, fit, limber military males who were now unified in their anger as much as in their plasm.

Lieutenant Karno spoke for them. His long hair was a fiery red; he spoke with uncharacteristic anger, for a slave of the Masters. "Musica, it is not your place to decide how things shall be!"

Another, Darsis, looking like Karno's duplicate, agreed, "It has been decided for us and you have no say in the matter!"

Sookol, the third, added, "That is our way, as it has been since the beginning of time!"

Musica, eyes lowered to the carpeted deck, trembled at the heresy she was committing. And yet she said, "Yes, I know that. We've been chosen for each other as mates, and we must resign ourselves to it. But—that doesn't change the fact that we are strangers, we Muses and you Guards."

Karno's brows knit, as if she were speaking in some language he had never heard before. "But . . . what does that matter?"

Musica gave him a pleading look, then averted her eyes again. "I want so much to accept the Masters' decision and believe that it is right, but something very strange within me keeps saying that the Masters cannot be right if their decision makes me feel this way."

"'Feel'?" Karno repeated. Could she have contracted

some awful plague from the Humans when the primitives from Earth managed to board the flagship for that brief foray?

Darsis and Sookol had gasped, as had Allegra and Octavia. "It's madness!" Sookol burst out.

Musica nodded miserably. "Yes, feelings! Even though we've always been told that we're immune to them, I'm guilty of *emotions*."

Madness, indeed.

She saw the repulsed looks on their faces as they realized she was polluted, debased. But somehow it didn't change her determination not to surrender these new sensations— not to be cleansed of them, even if she could.

"I know I should be punished for it," she declared. "I know I'm guilty! But—*I cannot deny my feelings!*" She broke down into tears.

"What's—what's that you're doing?" Darsis asked, baffled.

"I think I know," Karno answered tonelessly. "It's a sickness of the Earthlings called 'crying.'"

If it was a sickness, Musica knew, there was no question about who had infected her with it. It was Bowie Grant, the handsome young ATAC trooper who she had met when his unit staged a recon on board the flagship.

Instead of a mindless primitive in armor, he had turned out to be a sensitive creature. Bowie was a *musician* and he sat down at her Cosmic Harp and played tunes of his own devising—beautiful, heart-rending compositions that bound her feelings to him. *New* songs—songs that wouldn't be found in the approved songlore of the Masters. He had shown an inexplicable warmth toward her from the very start, and he quickly drew the same from her.

Now Musica found herself sitting at her Harp, playing those same airs, as the other five looked on in shock.

Bowie, do you feel this way about me? How I wish we could be together again!

CHAPTER
THREE

There was never any other child born on Earth from a union of Zentraedi and Human. I made sure of that, with the powers at my command. Because, of course, I immediately knew that Dana was the One; Dana was all that was needed. And the plan went forward.

Dr. Lazlo Zand, notes for *Event Horizon: Perspectives on Dana Sterling and the Second Robotech War*

LIEUTENANT NOVA SATORI TOOK A PRECISE SIP OF wine, then consulted the heavy chronometer on her wrist. "Zero hour."

Across from her, Zor gave her a puzzled look. "Something important?"

Although he was good at fighting, there were still so many things he simply didn't understand. Was he, in the terms of this "date," behind schedule somehow? Was he late in initiating the curious physical interchanges the barracks braggarts always talked about? Was there some accepted procedure for abbreviating the preliminaries? Perhaps he should begin removing garments—but whose?

Nova stared at him. "Well...don't tell Dana or anyone else, but the relief force is just lifting off for the moon."

Nova couldn't for the life of her figure out why she was telling him, except that she liked one-upping Dana. She couldn't really put a finger on why she had come along with

19

him to the restaurant either, except that she felt drawn to him—almost against her will.

When Zor was first captured, Nova was responsible for his interrogation. She had felt that he was an enemy then and was suspicious that that still might be the case. But there was something *singularly* attractive about him. He had an agelessness about him even though he looked young, a serenity even though he was tormented by his missing memory, as though he were a part of her. It was as if he, as the expression went, had a very *old soul*.

Zor was thinking along quite different lines. Nova's mention of Dana reminded him that he was supposed to have gone to the movie with her. It had completely slipped his mind; he wondered if bit by bit he was losing all memory functions.

Some curiosity—more of a compulsion, actually—had made him ask Nova to dinner. He hoped that she could tell him more about himself; he might even be able to recover a part of his lost self. But there was more to it than that, motivations Zor Prime couldn't fathom.

He studied Nova, an attractive young woman with a mantle of blue-black hair so long that she had to sweep it aside when she sat down. Like Dana, she wore a techno-hairband that suggested a headphone. Her face was heart-shaped, her eyes dark and intense, lips mobile, bright, expressive.

"Earth calling Zor." She chuckled, breaking his reverie.

"Eh?"

"Promise not to mention it, I said. Dana's got an awful temper; she's going to split a seam when her precious 15th squad gets left out of another major operation!"

"Don't worry. I won't tell her."

Nova shrugged to indicate that it really wouldn't be *so* bad if Dana found out from him and learned that he had found out from Nova.

She said, "No one's supposed to know the relief force is on its way until tomorrow. I really shouldn't have told *you* about it."

The vague compulsions in Zor suddenly coalesced, and

he found himself asking, "How many ships are going? How are they planning to get past the enemy?"

It would all be revealed tomorrow anyway, and Nova's tongue had been loosened by the wine with which Zor had been plying her. "Well, I heard that—"

"*So! there you are!*" Dana howled, rushing toward the table. The pianist stopped playing and silverware was dropped by startled diners.

Angelo Dante followed, embarrassed. *The Revenge of the Martian Mystery Women* had been a debacle, animated camp moron-fodder instead of the sizzling interplanetary romance-comedy-adventure Dana was under the impression they would be seeing. Apparently the officer who had told Dana about it was jazzing her. Angelo had laughed so maniacally that she had slugged his arm and dragged him out of the theater. Then she set out on a mission of revenge.

Now she set her fists on her hips and glared daggers at Zor. "Just who the hell d'you think you are, you double-dealing dirtbag, standing me up so you can take out something like *her*?"

Zor looked very confused and almost queasy. Nova said, "I don't think I like the sound of that last part."

"You're not *supposed* to, you tramp! It was an *insult*!"

Angelo managed to intervene just as Nova was about to vault across the table for a go at Dana, who was waiting to clean Nova's plow before going on to put Zor in traction.

"Now calm down, ladies!" He looked to Zor for assistance; the maître d' was already headed their way. "Hey, Zor, you just gonna sit there like a vegetable or what?"

Zor tried to put his thoughts in order. He couldn't remember why it had been so important to get Nova to tell him those secrets about the relief expedition. Now that Dana had interrupted everything, he could barely recall the impulse that had made him ignore his date with Dana.

"I–I'm so sorry." He got to his feet unsteadily. "I don't feel well. . . . " He lurched from his place, and headed for the door.

"Damn chicken! Come back and die like a man!" Angelo fumed, for he felt that he was about to meet his own fate.

Outside, Zor stopped to catch his breath, leaning on a railing overlooking a garden near the restaurant's entrance. He heard Nova's voice in his head again, "The relief force is just lifting off for the moon."

But then there was another voice, a cold one, speaking directly to his mind. It filled him with terror and hate, and he saw an image of an ax-keen, angry face set against a collar that looked like the Invid Flower of Life.

It said, *Message received and understood.*

At Fokker Aerospace Field, on the outskirts of Monument City, the last units of the emergency relief force were lifting off. The larger warships were being helped aloft by the brute power of a dozen flying tugs. The tugs released their cables as the warcraft climbed above Earth's gravitational grip.

They formed up, making their way out beyond the atmosphere, moving at flank speed, maintaining communications silence. Their ascent was masked by the bulk of the Earth for the time being. Since the Robotech Masters couldn't maintain geostationary position over Monument City and still guard access to Luna, the expedition would have an element of surprise.

To someone of an earlier day, the giant battlecruisers would have resembled prenuclear submarines, complete with conning towers, and bulky thruster packages attached to their sterns. Their estimated time of rendezvous with the units from ALUCE station, barring trouble, was in just under six hours.

At Moon Base ALUCE, Marie Crystal began organizing things for the evacuation, with brave words to the wounded about how they would be on Earth by the next morning.

Home, she thought, and thought, too, of a certain deuce private—formerly a First Lieutenant—in the 15th squad, ATAC. *Sean, Sean! to be with you again!*

* * *

Jeddar, group leader of the Clonemasters, glared at Musica sternly. "What exactly is the meaning of this behavior?"

"Do you realize that you're jeopardizing the very existence of our people?" added bearded Ixtal, the other male in the Clonemaster triumvirate.

Tinsta, the tall, androgynous female, commanded not unkindly, "Child, explain yourself."

Allegra and Octavia watched the scene, not daring to say a word. They had already concluded that they would never be able to comprehend Musica's new, aberrant behavior. They were frightened to death of being contaminated or punished for what their triad-sibling was doing. Off to one side, Karno and the other Guard clones looked on.

Musica sounded as if she was ready to weep again, something with which Allegra and Octavia were becoming uncomfortably familiar. "I'm sorry! I wish I could explain! I don't *mean* to be disobedient, really I don't!"

"Your mate has been selected, Musica," Tinsta said. "And he is Lieutenant Karno. You will submit to this decision."

"The survival of your own people requires it." Jeddar pressured her.

She shook her head, her long, deep-green hair swinging around her face, moaning, "No . . . no . . ."

"Yes!" Jeddar shot back. "Disobedience cannot be tolerated!"

Musica, moaning, seemed to undergo some sort of seizure. Then she slumped to the deck. Her sisters rushed to kneel by her. The Clonemaster triumvirate gaped; finally, Jeddar found words. "This is far worse that I had imagined."

"Has she ceased to live?" Lieutenant Karno asked numbly.

Jeddar replied, "She has fallen into what the Humans call a 'faint.'" A cold current rippled through him. Until this moment, he had been *sure* that his Robotech Masters ultimately would be victorious. But as Musica now knew emotions, so did Jeddar begin to know the meaning of doubt.

* * *

Everything was on schedule, and the relief force was expecting rendezvous with Marie's contingent, when the chilling news came.

"Enemy ships spotted at mark seven niner, closing on us fast!"

General quarters sounded, armor-shod feet pounding the deck as men and women rushed to battle stations. Cannon and missile tubes were run forth from their turrets as the rust-red, whiskbroom-shaped assault ships of the Robotech Masters plunged at the relief force.

Fast-moving and mounting formidable firepower, the assault ships dodged the Terrans' shot patterns and began scoring hits almost immediately. Hulls were penetrated by fusion-hot lances of energy; there were explosions and explosive decompression in the breeched warcraft. Southern Cross soldiers died in flames, in whirlwinds of shrapnel, and in vacuum.

Battlecruiser number three, the *Austerlitz*, disappeared in a furious fireball. Other vessels were taking heavy damage. The Terrans had been taken by surprise, and no one could answer the question, *How could this have happened? How could they have been waiting for us, as if they knew we were coming?*

But the Humans struggled to throw up a screen of AA fire, bring damage under control, and simultaneously launch mecha of their own. In moments the A-JACs, rotors folded for space combat, howled forth from the battlecruisers to engage in battle.

As soon as the A-JACs began their counterattack, the hatches opened in the sides of the assault ships, and enormous Bioroids rode forth to give battle on circular antigrav Hovercraft. The Bioroids deployed for the fight, looking like vaguely human-shaped walking battleships. They swarmed angrily, outnumbering the Human mecha.

"Air Cavalry One to Lieutenant Crystal," the call came over the command net. "I'm breaking radio silence to request immediate assistance. We are under heavy attack and request immediate assistance."

Marie, on the bridge of the destroyer escort *Mohi Heath*, saw the worried look on the face of Lieutenant Lucas, the Aircav commander. She opened her headset mike to transmit. "Roger, Aircav One; we're on our way."

The ships of the patchwork evacuation force went to maximum speed. Marie threw the headset aside and ran for her own A-JAC, and the rest of her TASC outfit, the Black Lions, hot-scrambled.

The Bioroids were enjoying good hunting.

The relief expedition was short on mecha, since so many had been committed to the first strikeforce and many more had to remain behind to guard Earth. So, the enemy assault ships stayed back and let the clone-operated Bioroids ride their Hovercraft, and slaughter the enemy.

The relief force A-JACs and others fought valiantly, but the sheer unevenness in numbers became apparent at once. Bioroids blazed away with the weapons mounted in the control stems and platform bows of their Hovercraft, and with the disc-shaped handguns that were as big as fieldpieces. A-JACs blazed into explosive death one after another.

Lieutenant Lucas, his unit half gone, was calling to ask permission for a hasty withdrawal; there was no point in throwing away Earth's valuable mecha. Then, suddenly, there was a blue Bioroid on his tail, the gun in its control stem spewing annihilation discs. Lucas only had a split second to wonder who would take over (his exec being dead already) and to hope that the strikeforce somehow would survive.

But then the Bioroid disappeared in a flaming ball of gas, and a strange A-JAC bearing a rampant black lion came zooming past. "Crystal, this is Lucas! Crystal, is that you?"

"Looks like this time the settlers have come to rescue the cavalry," she said. She added to her own outfit, "Okay, boys; let's wrassle 'em around some."

But that was already happening. Marie Crystal's Black Lions had come in on the enemy's rear flank, undetected,

and hurled themselves into the furious dogfight. They had
already changed the odds; within seconds they were turning
the kill ratios around. Before fifteen seconds passed, eight
surprised Bioroids had been shot to fragments or utterly destroyed.

But the enemy seemed determined to stand its ground, as
it were, and fight. The Lions, having been mauled so badly
on their first assault only days before, were more than willing to oblige.

Dogfight? Rat race? *Oh, yes!* Marie thought. *Now you
pay! And if somebody asks who your accountants are, you
just say, "the Black Lions"!*

The engagement got even hotter. Marie did a classic
"Fokker Feint," flamed a blue, then raised Aircav One
again. "Lieutenant Lucas! Now's your chance! Head for
ALUCE base!"

It was too sensible a suggestion for Lucas to argue with;
the units still on the moon would need the relief force, and
Marie's pilots were keeping the enemy busy. Lucas disen-
gaged his A-JACs even as the relief warcraft made their
way past the distracted Bioroids to recover Aircav One
and its birds on the fly. He headed for ALUCE at top
speed.

Some of the enemy tried to give chase, and Marie led
several of her A-JACs to stop them. She decided to change
the mix a bit, and went to Battloid mode. Other A-JACs
followed suit, screaming after the enemy with back and foot
thrusters blaring.

The A-JACs launched missiles, and three more Bioroids
got waxed. The rest broke off their chase, to turn on their
tormentors. Aircav One and the rest of the relief force were
already disappearing for their rendezvous with Luna.

The Black Lions hit the Bioroids with everything they
had, driving them back, until Marie judged that the evacuation force had enough of a head start. With the enemy ranks
drastically thinned out and their attack broken, the A-JACs
got in a final barrage that blew one of the invader assault
ships to atoms. As before, destruction of their field-command

nerve center confused and demoralized the Bioroids; the A-JACs took advantage of that to break contact and return to their convoy at max thrust.

Soon Earth loomed huge and blue-white before them.

Very well; I can't stop you. Take the Protoculture from me!
Seal my fate, and seal your own as well!

The original Zor to the Lords of Tirol

THE ROBOTECH MASTERS' ANGER WAS NOT ASSUAGED
by their warriors' excuse that Zor Prime had mentioned
nothing of a second force coming from Luna to catch the
Bioroids in a pincer. If the Masters were not so short of
functioning servants, many clones, both in the command
structure and in the ranks, would have been deactivated and
sent to reclamation.

The Clonemasters cut short the reports and turned to one
another, as they waited fearfully. "Well then," Dag said to
the Clonemaster group leader, Jeddar, "I presume that is all
the evidence we need. We know we can no longer depend on
Zor Prime's transmissions."

Jeddar bowed. "That is correct, Master. He has been
overexposed to the emotional contagions of Humanity. But
there is a matter of more immediate concern."

"And that is?" Bowkaz demanded, looking down at him.

"Taking Musica as an example," Jeddar responded, "we are seeing an upsurge in emotionality and counterproductive behavior similar to what we now know happened to the Zentraedi giants when *they* tried to recover the Protoculture Matrix."

Shaizan declared to the other Masters, "It seems to me that the time has come to begin all-out production of our Invid Fighters."

The Masters' Invid Fighters were different from the mecha of the same designation once used by the Zentraedi giants. But like the Zentraedi's, the Masters' Invid Fighters —more commonly referred to as the Triumviroid—were the most powerful mecha in the Masters' inventory. The clone/fighting machine system had been developed rather recently —by their stagnated standards—and incorporated certain characteristics of the savage Invid with whom the Masters had fought a long and unrelenting war.

The reason there were not more Triumviroids in the Masters' forces was because their production was so costly. But the Masters now faced the choice of either losing the war or launching a crash program to create a fighting force of Invid Fighters—even if it meant cannibalizing their conventional blues, combat vessels, and their own instrumentality.

The Robotech Masters were also constantly aware that their *own* masters, the Triumvirate of the Elders, waited far across the dark lightyears, expecting results. Nearly all of Tirol's remaining resources had been thrown into this expedition to obtain the last Matrix; the Elders, who were left in the shambles of their empire with a mere handful of clones, expected results—and were impatient.

The decision didn't take the Masters long; they lusted for the power of the Protoculture Matrix more than any vampire ever thirsted for lifeblood. They desired immortality and feared death with a terror greater than any short-lived Human or clone could ever imagine.

The Robotech Masters turned to their slaves and nodded as one.

* * *

Supreme Commander Leonard let Marie make her brief report. Leonard was more pleased with the battle as a propaganda victory and a bolster to his influence with the UEG council than he was with it as a military success. But he was pleased with that aspect of it, too—his loathing of aliens bordered on the psychotic.

After she was dismissed, Marie stepped back into the corridor only to discover Dana, Angelo Dante, and Sean Phillips coming toward her.

Marie was still dressed in smudged battle armor, dirty and weary, but she didn't let that stop her from crying out his name and running toward him, as he hurried to embrace her. "Oh, Sean, *Sean*, you came!"

He was the same as she had pictured him a thousand times since leaving Earth, the smiling, roguish ladykiller of the 15th. Sean had been its commanding officer not too long ago, with Dana his untried executive officer fresh out of the Academy. But a certain scandal concerning a colonel's daughter had gotten Sean busted to deuce private in the Hovertank outfit he had formerly commanded.

The romance started when he saved her life during a firefight. Marie had been very wary of his advances at first, refusing to be one more notch on his bedpost. They had fought like alley cats. But in time she had come to believe his declarations of love, and let herself admit that although she had never been in love before, she was now.

"Darlin', I thought maybe we'd lost you," he grinned, to hide all the worrying he had been doing. Sean was used to being the reckless swashbuckler, going into danger while a woman kept the light in the window, not vice versa.

Then he held her at arm's length again, and saw her eyes brimming. "Marie, what's wrong?"

She didn't let herself surrender to tears. But after the long, exhausting mission, the death and the killing, shouldering all burdens and enduring sleeplessness while sustaining the morale of all around her, she laid her head against his chest and let her breath go, running her fingers through his hair. "Oh, Sean, I—I wasn't sure you really...*really* cared—"

He hugged her and rubbed her alloy-clad back, while the others cleared their throats and turned to look at something else, anything else. Then he held her face in his hands to gaze into her eyes. "It's you and me, Marie Crystal. From now on. Always."

In the conference room, Supreme Commander Leonard turned to his subordinates.

"The relief force has the materials and know-how to turn ALUCE into a strategic military base. With it, we will be able to attack the enemy on two fronts."

But Leonard knew he couldn't afford to fight a two-front war, one against those obscene alien invaders and one against the damned meddling council. However, he had come up with what he considered a brilliant strategy for solidifying his place as Supreme Commander: eliminate the one man who could conceivably be tapped to replace him, and whose military genius threatened to eclipse his.

He turned to Major General Emerson with a fulsome smile. "And Rolf, I have a great little surprise for you."

Emerson, already three steps ahead of Leonard, resigned himself. *He's got my range and coordinates this time.*

The 15th was on stand-down, relaxing in the ready-room, when Louie Nichols charged in with his news.

Bowie Grant sat at the piano, playing sadly and brooding over Musica, as he had since he first met her. He had thought of and disgarded a hundred plans for getting back to her somehow, for being with her, for finding some kind of life together with the Mistress of the Cosmic Harp. She had enthralled him—magicked an enchanted ring round his heart, so that he could think of nothing and no one else. If he had taught her what love was, she was also teaching him, even—*especially*—in their separation.

Louie Nichols burst in, babbling and running around in such a lather that Dana, Angelo, and the rest thought they were going to have to kneel on his chest to get him to spill out what he knew. It sounded as if he was about to begin blubbering, but it was hard to tell with Louie because he always wore big, square, tinted tech goggles, day and night.

"Well," he managed at last, "they've appointed a new commander to take charge of ALUCE and open the second front."

Sean stared at him. "Yeah, so? Who is it?"

Louie worked himself up to answer. "Leonard's sending General Emerson!"

Bowie had been playing softly. Now he brought his fingers down hard in discord. The Robotech Masters seemed to have some kind of pipeline into Southern Cross plans, and everyone knew how high the casualties would probably run at ALUCE.

Emerson was supervising the organization of a new expedition to ALUCE. With the original reinforcing group fortifying the lunar base, it was time to get more personnel, combat units, and equipment up there, to expand preparations for the second front.

He heard a scuffle behind him, and his name being called. He turned from his contemplation of the intense activity all across Fokker Base, the readying of the strikeforce he now commanded. His adjutant, Lieutenant Colonel Rochelle, was struggling to hold back Lieutenant Dennis Brown, a TASC Veritech pilot who had once served as aide to Emerson.

"Brown, we've heard enough out of you!" Rochelle was yelling.

Brown thrashed, trying to break loose. "But it's a suicide mission, General Emerson! They're trying to get rid of you!"

"As you were!" Emerson hollered, and Brown and Rochelle subsided. Emerson went on, "It's not for me to second-guess my orders, Lieutenant, nor is it for you. We give orders and see that they're obeyed; we obey the orders that are given us. We see to it that we don't violate the oath we've sworn, not for any personal loyalty or preference. There's no other way an army can function. Thank you for your concern, but if you don't return to your post at once, I'll have no choice but to have you placed under arrest."

Rochelle and Brown had released one another. The lieutenant saluted. "Yes, sir."

"One more thing," Emerson snapped. "No operation under *my* command has ever been or will ever be a suicide mission. I'd have thought you knew me better than that. Dismissed."

Dana found that Bowie simply refused to talk about his godfather being posted to ALUCE. Bowie seemed determined to have the world think he cared nothing about General Emerson.

It was Emerson who had insisted Bowie serve time in the Southern Cross Army, as Bowie's parents had wished it, Emerson claiming that it had nothing to do with personal feelings or his affection for Bowie. Now it was Bowie's chance to hide behind a soldier's code, and the rest of it, to shield his sorrow. Dana, with little choice, let it be so.

At the Global Military Police headquarters, a round-the-clock screening program consumed everyone's time, especially Nova's. The high command was determined to plug the leak in its system. Endless computer reviews and field reports were the order of the day. Anyone who had access to classified information and particularly those had access to long-range communications gear were being scrutinized.

After all, how else could an espionage agent get the word across tens of thousands of miles of empty space?

Zor got off the shuttle bus across the street from GMP headquarters only to find Angelo Dante standing next to a jeep, waiting for him.

"I keep asking myself, 'Now, why's ole Zor-O so eager to see Nova?'" Angelo said, blocking his way. "And what d'you think crossed my mind? Why, Nova's with GMP! Maybe that's why you're bringing her a present, hey?"

Angelo reached to grab the object Zor had tucked under one arm. It turned out to be a classified looseleaf binder whose title sent Angelo's eyebrows high. *"An Intelligence Overview on the ALUCE Base?"*

Angelo grabbed Zor's torso harness again, just as he heard a Hovercycle flare to a stop at curbside behind him. He heard Dana yell, "Sergeant Dante! Let him go!"

Angelo did, as she stalked over to him. "Now hold on a minute, Lieutenant—"

She yanked the binder out of his hands. "You *will* stop harassing this trooper, Sergeant! Grow up and quit playing GMP spy! Now, get lost!"

Angelo's face was a purple-red. He cared passionately about his world and its people and their survival, of course, and his duty. But there was more to it than that.

Why should I care if this guy uses Dana and wrecks her life? It's her own fault and she's just a snotty, pushy teenage know-it-all anyway! Okay, so she's proved she's got what it takes to lead the 15th, but why should I care if she gets what she's got comin' for getting this weird crush on Zor-O?

He thought all that looking down into the pug-nosed, freckled face and regretted making such a jackass of himself at the movie. Without warning, he found himself wondering what it would feel like to hold her tenderly, the way Sean had embraced Marie Crystal the other day. Then Angelo Dante violently suppressed the thought.

"Yes, ma'am," he said through clenched teeth. He saluted, about-faced and marched to the jeep. Tires chirped as he accelerated away from the curb.

Dana handed the binder back to Zor without even looking at the cover. "Here. Sorry about that, but Angie's such a—"

"Thank you." Zor took the classified book, turned and went up the steps toward the main entrance, barely having registered her presence.

"Hey!" She started after him, but just then a hand closed around her elbow.

If she had been only a little hotter under her high military collar, she would have turned around swinging. But she reconnoitered first, and saw who it was. "Captain Komodo!" she said in bewilderment. "What's the matter, sir?"

Komodo was a man of about five-ten, with a powerful build, of Nisei descent. Just now, he was sweating and a little wild-eyed. "Lieutenant, I need a favor!"

Most people in the Southern Cross knew who Komodo was. After the Robotech Masters' first attack on Moon Base One, Komodo had violated Emerson's ironclad wait-and-see orders to launch missiles at them, ending Emerson's hopes for negotiations.

Emerson had wanted him court-martialed for firing the goading shot in a war nobody wanted, but Leonard, ever the alien-hater, had had Komodo decorated for prompt and brave use of personal initiative, and transferred to fire control on a battlecruiser. Still, the word on the scuttlebutt grid was that Komodo regretted what he had done and he had made mention of his wish to redeem himself.

Now Dana let herself be pulled off to one side by the captain, not sure how anything fit together with anything else anymore.

In a small park near GMP headquarters, Komodo finished, "So I thought you could help me, Lieutenant."

Dana looked him over carefully. "And Nova's the one for you, huh?" According to the captain's story, he had only talked to her a few times, and always in the line of duty. *But when did love ever let reality stand in its way?* she sighed to herself.

Captain Komodo chuckled self-consciously. "I'm assigned to go with General Emerson to ALUCE," he explained.

"And you figure you might not make it back, so you want her to at least know you exist before you go?" Dana said with a blunt, uncharacteristic *need* to hear his answer.

She paced a few steps up and back while Komodo gave a sighing laugh and admitted, "I suppose she could never want *me*."

"Let's have no defeatist talk, Captain!" Dana responded.

Maybe Komodo could serve as a distraction and pry Nova

and Zor apart—and maybe not. Still, it was the only card she had to play, short of letting Angelo—who seemed to despise the alien for reasons she couldn't understand—put Zor in Intensive Care.

She took Komodo's arm. "You can't give up the ship before you've fired your first salvo, Captain." They both laughed, walking back toward the GMP HQ.

They left the trees just in time to see Sean Phillips go racing by at the wheel of a jeep, at breakneck speed. He was roaring with laughter, and Marie Crystal, in the ninety-percent seat, was laughing, too, one arm around his shoulders. He turned a corner on two wheels.

"There's living proof, Captain," Dana said, frowning. "If *that* sorry sack can win a female heart, *anybody* can." Her words didn't seem to fortify Komodo.

The appalling workload at GMP and the presence of Colonel Fredericks, her CO, had kept Nova from seeing Zor when he showed up to return the ALUCE documents. So, Zor had left the binder for her, wrapped in plain paper, and she had claimed it when at last she knocked off for a few hours' sleep.

Somehow, she couldn't see what she was doing as compromising Southern Cross secrets. She did not even *think* of Zor as a security risk. She could only think of those huge, oblique, elfin eyes, the face like a classical sculpture's, the tumbling lavender locks of hair that fell past his shoulders, the hypnotic fascination he held for her.

At the door of her billet in the Bachelor Officers' Quarters, she found a lush bouquet of pink, black, and red roses, wrapped in silver-and-black striped metallic paper. The sight of them took all her fatigue away.

Nova Satori pulled them close to her body, inhaled them, and carried them into her billet. That scent—she drew it in deeply and wished she could lose herself in it, could live in the Heart of the Rose forever. To be with Zor, somehow, someday, seemed so hopeless.

I thought love was supposed to make you happy?

* * *

In the dimness of a bend in the hallway, Dana patted the sweating Komodo's shoulder, as they watched Nova's door close from their concealment.

"That completes the first part of the operation, Captain: the softening-up process!"

Inside her rooms, Nova set down the ALUCE binder and the roses side by side. There was a note in the flowers, printed in block letters: FROM AN ADMIRER.

She held up the other note she had gotten that day, the one Zor had tucked into the ALUCE book. *I can't begin to thank you, Nova. Every bit of information you give me restores more of my memory, more of me.*

Then she realized all at once that she had violated the regulations she was sworn to enforce. *What have I done?*

So the screwball contredanse continued. Dana tried to convince Komodo that his flowers were the cause of the lovesickness he saw on Nova's glum face. Meanwhile, Nova determinedly snubbed Zor and resisted his every effort to get in touch—yet she felt dangerously drawn to him.

It had Nova so distracted that she screwed up, and flagged a VT pilot named Dennis Brown—a former aide of Emerson's, yet!—who had been scheduled to go to ALUCE and was now held back as a security risk.

She hunted the lieutenant down out on the flight line to apologize. He merely shrugged it off. He looked her over for a few moments and decided she could be trusted to hear the truth.

"Maybe it's all for the good. You have the computers and you aren't blind, Nova. Leonard's weeding out all the officers who aren't loyal to him personally, like some Roman emperor sending all his rivals off to distant provinces. Thanks to you, though, at least one of us'll be here to keep an eye on things: me."

He really *was* thanking her! Nova summoned up a grateful smile and resolved to bury Brown's name and file where few in the GMP would ever notice it.

At the far end of the flight line Dana, watching from behind a shuttle's huge tire, whistled. "Man, that Nova knows how to play the field!" Captain Komodo fought off an attack of terminal disheartenment.

CHAPTER
FIVE

THE 15TH'S READY-ROOM WAS DARK. MOST OF THE troopers were out on pass or on ATAC guard duty or dozing. A few, like Robotechnofreak—another term for it was "mechie"—Louie Nichols, were taking care of maintenance or tinkering with their Hovertanks down on the motorstable levels.

Bowie Grant sat playing the piano softly. Sometimes he went into the melodies he had played for Musica, and the ones she had played for him. But tonight he kept coming back again and again to the ones Emerson had taught him as a child, when the General introduced him to the piano and fostered Bowie's love of music. Bowie played his own compositions, the early ones that had made Emerson so proud. There was no one in the dimness of the ready-room to hear the music, or to see his tears.

Below, though, in a long, black military limousine parked under the open windows of the ready-room, there was an audience.

Major General Rolf Emerson sat in the back seat with the window down, listening. He didn't recognize the alien tunes, though he suspected what they meant; he knew each note that Bowie played from their shared past, however, and understood those completely.

Emerson's efforts to contact his ward had been rebuffed, and the general respected Bowie's right to be left alone.

Perhaps I never should have made him enlist; perhaps he shouldn't have had to serve, Emerson reflected. *But then, it would be a better Universe if none of us had to. But it's just not that kind of Universe.*

"That's enough. Take me back," he told his chauffeur, hitting the button that raised the window.

Take me back . . .

This time it was a *cascade* of roses, tumbling down onto Nova in a fragrant red avalanche the moment she opened the closet in her billet to hang up her cloak. Suddenly she wasn't bone-tired anymore, not even with the liftoff of Emerson's strikeforce less than forty-eight hours away.

She let the roses shower around her, giggling and gasping, and tried forlornly to understand all the conflicting emotions and impulses that were starting her own private war. She was knee-deep in flowers.

There was a note taped to the shelf: *Depot 7 at 2100.*

At the elegant Pavilion du Lac, Marie Crystal pushed away her fourth sidecar. *If Prince Charming doesn't get here with the carriage soon, Cinderella's gonna be too stinko to care!*

Might even serve him right, she thought. She had blown half her savings on a drop-dead white satin evening gown, and the most expensive perfume she could find. Her walk was very different than it was when she was in uniform; she had seen men panting, admiring. And rather than cut a swath through the local male wildlife, here she sat, waiting for her Romeo.

She went out onto the balcony to get a little fresh air,

sighing in the moonlight, thinking of Sean, smelling the orchids there.

She had been shot out of the sky and he had mechamorphosed his Hovertank, risen up in Battloid mode to catch her burning, falling Veritech. He had sworn he would love her, and no one else, evermore. Had held her to him as his Battloid had held her VT to it. Had made her love him.

You beast! You toad! I've never been in love before....

Below, hiding behind a column on the portico, Sean grinned and got ready to go surprise her.

Marie had shown up early for their dinner date, and she had decided to see how long it would take her to lose patience. It hadn't taken long; he was barely late at all. *But I've kept her waiting long enough*, he thought guiltily, and got ready to run up the steps to her.

A voice behind him called, *"Seanie?"*

It was Jill Norton, an old flame, all decked out like a green-sequined sea goddess, throwing herself at him to hug him. "It *is* you!"

She locked her lips to his, and he had to wrestle her in order to crane his head around and look up at the balcony. Marie was giving him the kind of stare that preceded homicides.

Just like Cinderella, Marie lost a glass slipper on the winding stairs. In fact, she lost both of them. She pushed her way in between Sean and his latest trollop, about to leave, but spun around suddenly and grabbed him by the front of his suit.

Before he could move, she kissed him as hard as she could—she put all her love and all her wanting and all her hurt into it. Sean was starting to think he might survive the encounter when she pushed him away and rocked him with a slap that almost took his head off.

In the poorly lit corner of Depot 7, Dana practically had to put an arm-bar on Komodo to get him to show himself and approach Nova. As he walked over, he kept turning around to make sure Dana was still in the shadows for moral support.

However, his worst fears came true when he turned to Nova and got a backhanded fist, knuckles cocked, that sent him whirling onto the cold duracrete facedown.

"Stay away from me, Zor!" she shrilled. "You hear me, Zor?" But inside, she feared that she might really have hurt him.

Komodo pushed himself up partway. "Lieutenant Satori, I hear you." He wiped blood from his mouth.

"Oh my god! Captain Komodo!"

He levered himself up. "Zor, eh? Now I get it!" He lurched off into the blackness, sobbing, running nearly doubled over, as if she had given him some eviscerating wound.

She looked around and saw Dana standing, a small pale figure, under a nearby worklight. "I might've guessed, Sterling. Now do I have to part that little blond puffball hairdo with a loading hook, or are you going to tell me—"

She was interrupted by her own wrist comset. The only way she had been able to get some time to herself for the depot rendezvous had been to sign out for a purported tour of the GMP patrols, to check up. So she was on duty.

"Lieutenant Satori, we have a report of an individual, thought to be a woman, driving very erratically and recklessly in a military jeep."

Nova was on her Hovercycle and away before Dana could get a word in edgewise. Dana went and vaulted into the getaway jeep that was waiting, Lieutenant Brown behind the wheel. Dana knew Brown from his brief instructor days at the Academy, and Brown was an old close friend of Komodo's.

Accosted by Komodo, Brown had explained why Nova had come to see him: not a matter of passion, but rather of apology. Then, he joined in on the plot to get Komodo and Nova together, and volunteered to act as chauffeur.

"Go!" Dana howled, pointing at Nova's disappearing Hovercycle as it vanished through the loading bay doors.

"Don't turn on the light, Zand. Just sit down."

Rolf Emerson's voice was soft in the darkness of the office in Southern Cross HQ, but it still filled Zand with fear.

How had he gotten in? Not only were there guards and surveillance equipment, but Zand himself had hidden powers that should have prevented any such unpleasant surprise.

And yet, there stood the Chief of Staff for Terrestrial Defense, in the glow spilling into the darkened office from streetlights and moonlight. "I won't stay long," Emerson added. "Just close the door, sit down, and listen."

Zand did, leaving his office dark. He thought about sounding an alarm; Emerson certainly outranked him, but this kind of unauthorized visit was nothing that even a general's stars would justify. However, there were old animosities between the two, nothing Zand would like to have brought to light. And so he sat, waiting.

"I'm leaving in the morning; you already know that, no doubt," Emerson said, sounding tired. "I just wanted to say this—"

Suddenly he was at Zand's side, his strong hand around Zand's throat. Emerson shook him like a rag doll as the Robotech scientist made strangling sounds.

"You *will* leave Dana alone while I'm gone, do you hear me? If I come back to find that you've tried anything, *anything*, I'll kill you with this same hand and let the Judge Advocate court-martial me."

For all his mild appearance, Zand could easily have shaken off the grip of virtually anyone else; the Protoculture powers he had given himself through dangerous experimentation made such physical tricks simple.

But for some reason, Zand's enhanced powers simply didn't work on Emerson. It was as if the general was immune to Zand's abilities. Emerson knew very little about Protoculture; he had no conscious access to its vast gifts. Emerson had no idea that he was throttling a superman.

He shook Zand. "Do you hear?" Zand managed to nod, breath rattling. Emerson let him go. There would be fearsome bruises on his throat by daylight.

The last time Zand felt Emerson's grip on his throat was fourteen years ago. That was at night, too, when Emerson burst into Zand's lab upon discovering that Zand was running bizarre experiments on the baby daughter left behind by Max and Miriya Sterling. He was exposing Dana to Protoculture treatments and substances from some strange alien plant. Emerson had heard it had something to do with activating the alien side of her mind and genetic heritage. The general was Bowie's guardian, but had been a good friend to Dana's parents.

Zand had believed he would die that night, that moment; Emerson's strength seemed illimitable. Or perhaps it was simply that none of Zand's acquired powers worked in Emerson's presence? Zand avoided him from that time to this moment, and Emerson had made sure, no matter where he was or what he was doing, that Dana was beyond Zand's reach.

Gasping and wheezing, rubbing his throat, Zand tried to make some sense of it. How could a mortal like Emerson block the Shapings of the Protoculture this way? *And in such complete ignorance of what it was that he was doing?* It was as if the overwhelming frustration of it all was some tithe Zand had to pay to win that ultimate triumph, that incredible prize, that he saw promised to him by the Shaping.

It was even more humiliating that Emerson didn't even *realize* with whom he was dealing. To Emerson, Zand was some half-demented Protoculture mystic from R&D, who had deviated from the saner paths followed by Dr. Lang, and ended up deranged.

"I know you've been keeping tabs on her through back-channels and informants," Emerson said quietly. "Don't ever do it again. If I have to come and see you a third time, Doctor, it will be *to take you off the roll call for good*!"

Zand didn't even realize that Emerson had moved away from him until he heard the door open and close. The heir to Emil Lang's Protoculture secrets, and master of new, more perilous secrets of his own, massaged his tortured windpipe. One thing was clear: Emerson was an obstacle that would have to be dealt with first.

Dana Sterling was vital, because she stood at the center of all Zand's star-spanning schemes.

* * *

Marie wove her jeep through the streets and byways of Monument City.

What a little idiot I've been! I knew what Sean was like. I heard all the stories, yet I still believed he'd change just for me!

She ignored lights, ignored speed limits, ignored all peril to herself and others, sideswiping whoever didn't stay out of her way. The night and imminent death drew her on.

Her jeep bounced through an alley and onto an access road that would take her to the cliff overlooking the city. She wasn't thinking clearly about what she would find there, but something told her it would be better than what she was feeling now, and she liked the feeling of the accelerator under her stockinged foot. She only wished she were in her mecha.

It took her some time to realize that a GMP Hovercycle and a jeep were behind her. Over a loudspeaker Nova Satori's voice was commanding her to halt.

Marie stepped on the accelerator.

As the chase barrelled out onto the cliff headland, Nova tried to sideswipe her to a halt. Marie's jeep jounced off a rock, and slewed at the cycle. Marie had an instant's view of Nova's terrified face as she fought her handlebars. Marie hit the brakes and over-corrected, and her jeep went sliding toward the cliff, tailgate foremost.

But Dennis Brown was there first, with Dana belted in the rear and covering her eyes. The VT pilot brought Marie to a stop by letting Marie's jeep slam taillights-first into his own, broadside. The two vehicles plowed along in a spume of dust; Brown's left front wheel went over the edge, and the undercarriage grated along.

The jeep tottered there, but held. Dana and Brown sighed simultaneously. Marie hung against her steering wheel, crying like a lost child.

Dana, Brown, and Nova were still trying to sort things out when the distant sirens and flashing lights caught their attention.

Brown *tch*ed. "It'd sure be bad for morale if we let the Gimps find the hero of the TASCs in this condition." He lifted Marie out of the jeep gently and set her down on the ground.

"But—Lieutenant Brown!" Nova objected, as he slipped behind the wheel of Marie's jeep.

"It's simple," he said, revving the engine. "Frustrated pilot bumped from big mission gets hands on jeep and whiskey, *understand*?"

Nova did; she owed him one. It would be just as he said. "It means the brig, you know."

Brown shrugged at Nova. "A couple days. They need me in my VT too much to do more. Besides, I've got nothing better to do with my time."

He winked at her. "Come down 'n' see me once in a while, huh?"

Then he eased the jeep back and headed off in a spray of gravel. Leaving a high plume of dust and grit, slewing and running flat-out, it wasn't hard for him to catch the posse's attention; the strobing lights and wailing sirens followed Dennis Brown away into the night.

Dana tried to decide what to do or say, with the perplexed Nova to one side, the curled-up, weeping Marie on the other.

In the invasion flagship, the Robotech Masters watched their new production line of Invid Fighters being put through its paces. The mecha resembled oldtime naval mines, spined spheres that looked as much biological as technological. They seemed to be grown of mismatched horn, chitin, and sinew.

The Invid Fighters performed their maneuvers flawlessly. They evaded the fire of multitudes of gun turrets, and when the command came, they turned devastating fire on the turrets with pinpoint accuracy.

"And when they conjoin, they will be an undefeatable Triumviroid," Bowkaz said.

Jeddar of the Clonemasters made his abasing bow. "A Triumviroid, yes, Master. Self-contained and capable of performing the three basic functions of combat: data accumulation, analysis, and response, all within milliseconds."

The very essence of Robotechnology. *Logic dictates that these mecha* cannot *be defeated!*

A weapon as perfect as we ourselves, the Robotech Masters shared the cold thought.

Dawn had brought a break in the clouds; final preparations for the launch of Emerson's strikeforce were being made, last matters on the checklists were ticked off.

Captain Komodo led his unit out at a run. He had indulged his grief and put aside his humiliation; now it was time to discharge his duty, to live up to his oath of service. But a voice calling his name made him stop short as the rest ran on to the personnel elevator that waited to take the battlecruisers' crewpeople to their assignments.

Dana caught up, breathless. "I just want to . . . say, I'm sorry, sorry about—"

He gave her a smile. "Forget it, Dana. Thanks for everything."

The silence that followed was awkward, as they listened to announcements and instructions for everyone who was going to hurry, and for everyone else to get clear. Dana and Komodo groped for something to say to each other.

Then a hand reached out to touch Komodo's armored shoulder. "Captain . . ."

Komodo, pivoting to see Nova Satori standing at his side, looked like a deer caught in headlights. She took his gauntleted hand in both of hers. "I just wanted to say—be sure to come back safely."

It took him a few false starts to answer. "Nova, yes! I will!" He turned, dashing to catch up with his command. "Don't worry about that!"

Dana figured Nova was still not in love with Komodo. But what did that matter when a person might die—when a whole world might?

Dana was about to bury the hatchet with Nova, to tell her what a decent thing that was to do, when both were distracted by another lift-off drama.

"Marie! Come back!"

But Marie Crystal already had a head start, and even weighted by her combat armor she got to the elevator well ahead of Sean Phillips. And anyway, Sean had been caught by Angelo Dante, who gathered him up practically under one arm, and dragged him back.

Angelo hollered at his onetime CO, "Be a man, for god's sake! She's got more important things on her mind, idiot!"

But Sean struggled free at the last moment, as the countdown went for zero and ground crews and PAs bellowed at the ATACs to get to shelter. Sean dashed for the elevator, but he was too late. The doors closed just before he got there. Marie watched emotionlessly—or did she? Just as the closing doors took her from him, her stone-face expression seemed to change.

Sean curled up inconsolably on the hardtop, and let Angelo, Dana and Nova lift him up and bear him away.

In the ready-room, Bowie was by himself again at the piano. He played the songs Emerson had taught him, and the ones he himself had composed early-on.

He heard the first rumbles of prelaunch ignition reverberate across the countryside and the city, as his godfather and guardian readied for battle.

The battlecruisers, destroyer escorts, and other combat ships rumbled and flamed and rose, shaking the ground. The thunderclaps of their drives echoed across Monument City. Dana, Sean, Nova, and Angelo watched the strikeforce draw lines of fire into the blue.

The tumult and the glare of it filled the ready-room windows; Bowie hit a last, hateful note, then sat staring at the keys.

CHAPTER
SIX

It is, perhaps, some ultimate universal justice on the behalf of intelligence (as opposed to physical strength or predation skills) that the secrets of the Universe are open only to those who have left certain outdated belief systems behind.

Or, maybe it's one big—how do the Humans say it?—one big gag.

Exedore, as quoted in Lapstein's *Interviews*

THE ROBOTECH MASTERS, IN THEIR FLAGSHIP, WERE aware of the impending launch of Emerson's expeditionary force; this time there would be no surprises, and the Earth would be dealt a final, crushing blow.

It was imperative that Earth be destroyed not only because the constrained seeds of the Flower in the Matrix below were beginning to sprout into actual blossoms, but also a new and more dangerous element had entered their equations.

The Robotech Masters, nailless hands touching their Protoculture cap, contemplated the cloud of interstellar gas that, in astronomical terms, was so close. To an Earthly observer it would simply be a curiosity, a spindrift that had wandered Earth's way from some impossibly distant H II region. Its aberrant motion could be attributed to a close encounter with a far-off mass of dark matter or to galactic streaming dynamics. The oddities in its internal movements and constitution would be chalked up to some natural phenomenon of density waves.

Just another collection of whorls and billows of dust and phosphorescent gas; just another emission nebula.

But the Robotech Masters knew better and had good reason to be afraid. It was an Invid Sensor Nebula, searching for Protoculture and/or the Flower of Life. The Invid would be coming soon, and so the Masters' time was short.

Long ago, the Invid had been a peaceful species, living out their lives on idyllic Optera, ingesting the Flower and, with the powers it gave them, rejoicing in their contemplation of the Universe. Then Zor, the original Zor, had come to live among them, to learn. He saw in their almost photosynthetic biological processes a by-product that, when isolated, gave him the key to ultimate power: Protoculture.

The infinitely metamorphic Invid were the Apple of Temptation to him, harboring ultimate secrets. Zor was the same to them—especially to the Invid Queen, revealing to them the two-edged bane/blessing they had never conceived of: passion, love.

He understood that the key to the power of Protoculture was the Invid Queen. Zor, consumed with the hunger for knowledge, used her, barely knowing what it was he was doing, and set the course of a tragedy that would stretch across eternity.

The Invid Queen, the Regis, became infatuated with Zor. This infatuation would bring a universe crumbling down with no promise of what would rise from the ashes. Love and Protoculture, Protoculture and love; they were locked forever after in a pattern of exaltation and disaster.

Zor's superiors on Tirol, his homeworld, immediately understood the more obvious implications of Protoculture—its power to penetrate spacetime, to impart vast mental powers, its connection to the fundamental shaping force of the Universe. Like all leaders, they lusted for power; naive Zor was no match for them . . . at least at that point.

Using rudimentary powers derived from the more malign aspects of Protoculture, the overlords of Tirol banded together to subdue Zor mentally, to place an irresistible Compulsion on him. At their direction, Zor stole as many of the Flower seeds as he could from his Optera hosts, and as much Protoculture.

Under his Masters' enslavement, he betrayed the Invid hivequeen, who had taken on a form like his own. Zor left the Regis loveless and full of hate—she who had literally *transfigured* herself, loving Zor so. The rest of Optera Zor laid waste, so that the Flower of Life would never grow there again.

Love and Protoculture; Protoculture and love.

Conquest and dominance were the companion cravings of the Tirolean tyrants' Protoculture addiction. Their giant, cloned Zentraedi worker-menials were transformed into conquering legions; Zor became their savant-slave. He shaped the Protoculture Matrices, and went forth to seed the Flower of Life on other worlds, so their seeds could be harvested for more Matrices.

The overlords of Tirol were transmogrified into the Robotech Masters. Their own race became to them mere objects, plasm to be reshaped and put to the use they chose.

Meanwhile, the Invid, changed by their hatred and suffering, burst forth from Optera to seek the Flower of Life wherever the Masters seeded it, and to slay the Robotech Masters and their servants wherever they found them. The Invid began reproducing with monocellular speed, becoming a teeming horde that daunted even the Masters. A stupendous war roiled across galaxies, but the Masters were content that in time they would win.

The Masters, however, in their arrogance, had forgotten Zor's original exposure to the secrets of Protoculture on Optera, and the expansion of his mental gifts. Little by little, Zor was making patient, microscopic progress against the Compulsion by which the Masters held him.

His breakthrough came in the form of a Vision of what was to be, given to him by the Protoculture. He saw a small, blue-white, unimportant world. A world where Humanity would ultimately obliterate itself, and all life on the planet, in a Global Civil War. There *was* an alternative. It would involve great hardship and suffering for the Human race, but at least it offered a chance for racial survival.

The Vision showed Zor a possible future, wherein a great cyclone of mindforce a hundred miles wide rose from Earth and, high above the planet, transformed itself into a Phoenix of groupmind. The Phoenix spread wings wider than Earth, and with a single cry so magnificent and sad that it wrenched Zor's mind free of the Masters' domination, the bird soared away to another plane of existence.

Zor was then free to work his act of defiance. He dispatched the SDF-1 to Earth, hiding it from the Masters, even as he gave up his life to an Invid attack in a death he had foreseen in his Vision. The last Matrix by which new Protoculture could be produced was gone; the others had all been used up or destroyed in the course of the war, and only Zor had the secret of their creation.

The Robotech Masters, regarding with arctic dread the roving Sensor Nebula that was one of the Invid's coursing bloodhounds, knew little about the original Zor's motives, and nothing of his Vision. They only knew that their fanatic enemies would find them bereft of Protoculture's powers, helpless, unless the Masters triumphed soon on Earth.

And that demanded as a first step the quick and utter destruction of Emerson's expeditionary force.

Aside from some oddities noted in the peculiar nebula drifting so close to Earth, there was nothing to report, the techs said. Emerson worried nevertheless.

The enemy fleet still hung in distant orbit, permitting the expedition room for passage. Emerson's force had already passed the enemy's optimal point for launching assault ships to intercept and engage him. Soon the Humans would be past their closest approach to the invaders, and would be hightailing for Luna. He kept his escort forces deployed and ready for battle, even as his command passed through the leading edge of the nebula.

Once out of the nebula, past the point of greatest proximity to the enemy, the crewpeople began to breathe easier. But Emerson grew even more vigilant.

The Robotech Masters gathered vast amounts of data through their Protoculture cap. "The Humans must be relieved to have passed their zone of likeliest combat without a confrontation," Shaizan conjectured.

"Prepare to destroy them," he sent out the command.

"What're you trying *now*, Louie?" Dana asked the lanky corporal as he bent over the training simulator's guts.

"I'm gonna win back those two beers I owe you," Louie said smugly, fooling with the systemry there, changing some connections, putting in a special adaptor. "You're in for a surprise."

Dana scoffed, "C'mon, Louie! You can't beat a born warrior like me, even with a lot of mechie tricks."

At least he never had yet, even on the *Kill Those Bioroids!* program that he himself had designed for the simulator. She was happy to let him keep trying though; hand-eye training never hurt. She was just sorry the simulator, in the canteen at the local Southern Cross service club, wasn't set up more like a Hovertank's cockpit-turret, or that she hadn't been able to beg, borrow, or steal a simulator for the 15th's ready-room.

The thinking caps did the bulk of the controlling for Robotech mecha, but the tankers inside still had to know their instrumentation the way a tongue knew the roof of its mouth. At the 15th, as in TASC and other units, mock-ups of the cockpit layouts of the particular mecha used by the individual outfit were pasted up in the interiors of lavatory stalls so that the soldiers sitting there could refresh their memorization of their instrumentation during what the brass euphemistically called "available time."

Now Louie, making a final adjustment said, "That's what *you* say." He climbed into the simulator and shocked her by taking off the big, square, dark tech goggles that he wore almost constantly—even in the shower and often when sleeping. It gave his face an open, surprised look.

Dana wasn't sure what to think. Louie was undoubtedly a maverick technical genius. Word was that he had passed up numerous offers for advanced study or research assignments because he liked the action in Hovertanks, but also because he preferred to tinker and modify without somebody breathing down his neck.

Certainly, he had been responsible for one of the major victories of the war when his analysis of the Masters' flagship's power and drive systems permitted the 15th to disable it and bring it down. Even though the other ships had retrieved it and guarded against any recurrence, nothing was taken away from that spectacular success. And *still*, Louie had refused transfer to Research and Development or some think tank.

Now he put aside his goggles and pulled on a wraparound visor, a black and glittering V shape, like something a sidewalk cowboy might wear downtown.

Two jumpsuited technical officers in a nearby booth, discussing Emerson's mission in low tones, suddenly became aware of a furor near the simulator, with TASC pilots and ATAC tankers and others crowding around, exclaiming and cheering. They went over and saw a tall, skinny corporal in black shades blowing away computer-modeled Bioroids with a speed and accuracy unlike anything simulators—or even real mecha—had ever approached.

As the two officers began shouldering their way through the crowd, the kid was waving an adaptor cartridge around and explaining that it was computer-enhanced targeting linked into his glasses, a step up from even the thinking caps.

"I call it my Visual Trace Firing System, or VTFS," Louie was telling them all proudly. "Or if you prefer, my 'pupil pistol.'"

"Mind if I see it?" said one officer, holding out a hand for the cartridge. Louie was instantly wary, and Dana looked the two over as well.

"Major Cromwell, Robotech R&D," the officer said. He indicated his companion. "And this is Major Gervasi. I think we can use this system of yours in our simulation training.

We'll help you upgrade it and give you advice, assistance, and technical resources. Is this the only copy?"

"N-no," Louie admitted, a little uncertain.

Cromwell slipped the cartridge into the shoulder pocket of his jumpsuit. "Fine. If you don't mind, we'll have a look at this one, then. Can you be in my office tomorrow at thirteen hundred hours?"

While stuttering that he could, Louie handed over the visor as well. Dana decided that she couldn't pull rank on two majors, especially ones who worked for the top-secret R&D division.

But more than that, she was experiencing strange sensations, something to do with the mention of research, of Robotechnology, and thus of Protoculture. Something about Protoculture and experimentation . . . It gave her a queasy feeling, sent a jolt of fear zapping through her, brought not-quite-perceived, evil memories. . . .

But she shook it off as Cromwell walked away telling Louie, "We're looking forward to working with you."

Dana smiled affectionately at the goofily grinning Louie. "My brainy boy!" she said.

Outside the service club, Gervasi said to Cromwell, "Good work, Joe. Just what we need, out of nowhere!"

Cromwell nodded. "Send word up the back channels to Leonard and Zand right away. 'Rolling Thunder' is about to get the green light."

Emerson's force was very close to the moon when the Masters' fleet appeared like ghosts all around them, not on the monitors one second, hemming them in the next.

It was what the general had feared. The Masters had penetrated Earth's detection systems before; measures to counter that capability just hadn't worked, and the invaders had bided their time until they could use the tactic to best advantage. That time was now, with the expedition out of combat formation and deployed for lunar approach, with no way back and no way forward.

Emerson was reordering the disposition of his units even as the alien mother ships disgorged scores of the whiskbroom-shaped assault craft. With his battlecruiser *Tristar* at the center, Emerson prepared to fight his way through to ALUCE.

Blue Bioroids came in at the Humans like maddened automaton hornets. The call went out for the A-JACs to scramble, and the expedition's ships began throwing out a huge volume of fire to clear the way for them and hold the Bioroids off.

Once more, Marie Crystal led her Black Lions out in the A-JACs. She was all combat leader, all Robotech warrior now, the regret and hurt from Sean's betrayal savagely thrust aside. Leave love for fools, and let Marie Crystal do what she did best!

The Bioroids and the A-JACs swirled and struck, lighting an unnamed volume of space with thermonuclear lightning and sunfire. The killing began at once, the casualties piled up.

Marie skeeted a Bioroid right off its Hovercraft, so that the circular platform went on, unguided, heading for infinite space. She went to Battloid mode, ordering others to do the same, changing tactics abruptly and taking advantage of the foe's brief confusion.

Assault ships swept in, to hammer away at the larger expeditionary vessels and be volleyed at in reply. Hulls were pierced through and through; blasts claimed Human and clone alike. Space was a maelstrom of plasma-hot beams and blowtorching drives and the ugly flare of dying ships.

Professor Miles Cochran gathered up all of his nerve to ask, "Dr. Zand, the Invid Nebula is so appallingly dangerous—it might even take hostile action against Emerson's force. Are you certain we shouldn't give him some inkling of that? Perhaps it's not too late. . . ."

There had been a tremor in his voice; he couldn't help it. Cochran began to tremble as Zand turned that eerie stare upon him there in the grandiose, forbidden sanctuary of the Kommandatura in a Robotech-rococo chamber deep in the Earth. Zand's eyes were all pupil, with no iris or white at all; his was a gaze no one could meet for long.

Even more unnerving than his eyes was the power radiating from him, which intimidated his handpicked disciples. The power of Protoculture. The outside world might see him as a slightly odd-looking researcher, the UEG's top scientific officer and adviser—a man of normal height and build with an unruly forelock, who dressed in a somewhat rumpled uniform. An egghead. But the seven men and one woman seated around the table knew differently.

The group met in a vaulted room that mixed the technological with the mystical. Side by side with the latest computer equipment and with Zand's own systemry were musty copies of the *Necronomicon* and *The Book of James*, along with talismans and gnostic paraphernalia. There was an enlargement of a satellite photo of the mound in which the wreckage of SDF-1 was buried. Zand sat at the head of the black obsidian table staring at Cochran.

He said, almost delicately, "Do you think I expunged all mention of the Invid, the Matrix, and the Flower of Life from every record but our own just so that you could go blurting it to Leonard and his military imbeciles? Or the fools at UEG? Have I wasted so much time on you?"

Cochran fought against a years-long habit of obedience to Zand, of self-sacrifice to the transcendent plan the scientist had enacted. He and the few others who sat there—Beckett, Russo, and the rest—were the only ones on Earth aside from the man himself who knew just how much Zand had altered the course of history.

"Confrontation is the whole point of the Shaping, don't you see?" Zand went on. "War is the whole point. Do you think Dana Sterling's dormant powers will be released by anything short of the Apocalypse?"

Data on the Invid and the Matrix and the rest of it, gathered from the Zentraedi leaders Exedore and Breetai, and from Captain Gloval, Miriya Sterling, and a few others, had been kept under tightest restrictions. Once Lang, Hunter, and the rest left Earth on the SDF-3 mission, it hadn't taken Zand long to see to it that everyone who knew about that information either joined his cabal, or died.

"The Protoculture's Shaping of history is moving toward a

single Moment," Zand reminded them all. "And that Moment is near; I can *feel* it. I shall take ultimate advantage of that Moment. Nothing will be allowed to stop it."

Cochran, a thin-faced, intense redhead, swallowed. He had a brother in Emerson's strikeforce—who probably would soon become a casualty of the Shaping, but Cochran knew that would not matter to Zand.

To make him feel even more uncomfortable, Cochran was seated next to Russo. Russo was the former senator and head of the United Earth Defense Council. He was the man whose ambitions and prejudices had made him, more than any other Human being, the source of the misjudgments and errors that had cost Earth so terribly in the First Robotech War.

Russo had no ambitions now; he was barely alive. He was a vacant-eyed, doglike slave to Zand, very much a creature of the shadows, like his master.

Cochran managed, "I just thought—"

"You just thought to interfere with the Shaping so that your brother would be out of danger?" Zand cut in. "Don't look so surprised! Why do you think your attempts to get him a transfer all failed? It was because I was giving you a test, a test of loyalty. You wavered, and so you failed. Kill him."

The last words were soft, but they brought instant action. Russo was out of his seat in an instant, pouncing on Cochran. Beckett, on the other side—Cochran's colleague and friend since college—didn't hesitate either, helping Russo bring Cochran to the floor.

Zand's other disciples threw themselves into the fray, terrified of failing this newest test. Even matronly Millicent Edgewick was there, kicking the doomed man. Zand sat and watched, nibbling dried petals of the Flower of Life.

Cochran went down, his chair overturned. His screams didn't last long.

CHAPTER SEVEN

The generals who let us die
so they can shake a fist—
They'd none of 'em be missed,
they'd none of 'em be missed!

Bowie Grant, "With Apologies to Gilbert and Sullivan"

BOWIE WAS TINKERING WITH THE KEYS AGAIN, TRY-
ing not to think about the strikeforce expedition. "Doesn't
that get boring?" Sean asked, leaning on the piano.

"Not really."

"I don't mean you, Bowie; I mean *those* two."

He pointed toward Dana and Louie, who were toiling
over a simulator that looked as if it had been stripped, components lying everywhere. Why they had chosen the ready-
room to work in instead of one of the repair bays or
maintenance workrooms was still unclear, except perhaps
the fact that Dana kept trying to entice people into volun-
teering to help.

Dana had commandeered the simulator from the canteen
on authority from R&D, and neither she nor Louie had slept
that night. On the other hand, as of yet no R&D support
troops had shown up.

"I'm starting to wonder if that Cromwell really wants Louie's gizmo for simulation training," Sean murmured.

"I just—like machines," Louie was expounding to Dana, as he reassembled things. "They expand Human potential and they never disappoint you, if you build 'em right. Somebody with the right know-how could create the ideal society. Unimpeded Intellect! Machine Logic!"

"I didn't know you were such a romantic," she said dryly. *Ideal society? Boy, what a mechie!*

Louie wanted to run the final test, but Dana pulled rank and he yielded amiably. She pulled on a visor, hopped into the simulator, and the computer-modeled slaughter began. It was a quantum leap from the old thinking cap; her score soared.

Elsewhere, the *Tristar*, Emerson's flagship, was fighting a desperate diversionary action, luring the main body of the enemy's forces one way so that the more badly damaged expedition ships could try to limp to ALUCE.

"We can't take much more of this pounding!" Green growled, as the *Tristar* was jarred again by enemy fire.

"I know," Emerson said calmly. "Get me a precise position fix and tell the power section we'll need emergency max power in two minutes."

"Sir," Rochelle said and bent to the task. Green turned a silent, questioning look on the man he had served for so long.

"We're going to generate a singularity effect," Emerson said. They all knew he meant use of the mysterious "special apparatus" given him by R&D in a cryptic transfer that, rumor had it, could be traced to Zand himself.

The idea was to create a small black hole where the ship was, the ship itself being yo-yoed momentarily into another dimension. The singularity would then pull in and destroy everything in close proximity to it. The untested theory and some of the apparatus came from Dr. Emil Lang's research on the now-destroyed SDF-1.

"And then the enemy becomes a brief accretion disc, gets sucked into the singularity, and vanishes forever," Green muttered. "Perhaps."

"We try it or die anyway," Emerson pointed out. To underscore that, another enemy salvo shook the *Tristar*.

Power readings seemed insane, violating all safety factors and load tolerances. Emerson had a microphone in his hand.

"Lieutenant Crystal, you and the other TASCs will lure all enemy forces as close to the *Tristar* as possible, and be ready to get clear on a moment's notice, in approximately six minutes, do you copy?"

"You heard the man," Marie told the Lions.

It was the weirdest mission she had ever been on: sting and run, get the enemy assault ships and battleships and 'roids chasing you. Juke and dodge to keep them from shooting your tail off; somehow keep them from engaging and diverting or delaying you. Protect your teammates but keep moving; do your best to ignore the heavy losses suffered by pilots who had been forbidden, in effect, to turn and give battle. And watch the time diminish down to zero.

As the timer wound down, the area around the *Tristar* was thick with dogfighting mecha, the biggest rat race of the Second Robotech War. The enemy forces were hitting Emerson's flagship almost at will, and it couldn't last much longer.

Then Marie heard Emerson's order to get clear; the AJACs cut in all thrusters and headed away, leaving the field to the milling Bioroids and combat vessels.

Emerson watched the indicators and, when it was time, he threw the switch. Crackling energy wreathed the battlecruiser, seeming to crawl around it like superfast serpents. The tremendous discharge expanded to form a sphere just big enough to contain the ship. The Bioroids' emotionless faceplates were lit up by the radiance of the blaze.

There were cosmic fireworks, then nothing to see as the lightshow was engulfed by the Schwarzchild radius. The Bioroids and vessels closest to the vanished flagship were destroyed by tidal forces. The invaders were sucked into nullset-space.

Those slightly farther away were helpless to escape becoming accretion material, whirling down to and over the event horizon after their fellows. The Masters' mightiest assault force was gone except for a little quantum leakage.

Marie was waiting for the *Tristar*, praying that the last and most critical part of the operation wouldn't be a disaster, when cannonfire rocked her A-JAC. "Damn!" she yelled, pushing her stick up into the corner for a pushover, *imaging* the aerocombat move through her horned helmet even though she was in airless space. *There was one battleship left!*

The other A-JACs scattered as the enemy drove in at them, putting out a fearsome volume of fire with primary and secondary batteries. It was obviously damaged—and so had moved too slowly to be drawn within the deadly radius of the singularity effect.

Now it was practically on top of the Lions, still capable of doing fatal damage to the *Tristar*, should Emerson's ship reappear and be taken by surprise. Marie gave quick orders, and the Black Lions went at the enemy dreadnought like wolves after a mammoth, biting, ripping, coming back for more even though they suffered heavy losses—and luring the battlewagon into position.

But the clones weren't blind to what had happened to the rest of their battle group and fought to keep clear. The Masters' battleship put its remaining power into a run for safety.

But it found another vessel blocking its way. Although the *Salamis* was shaking with secondary explosions and seemed more holes than hull, it closed in on the alien, firing with the few batteries still functioning.

The captain of the *Salamis* and most of its officers were dead. Captain Komodo was now in command, and he knew he rode a death ship. His engines were about to go, and there was nothing he and his crewpeople could do but make it count for something.

Salamis rode its failing drive straight into the enemy's fire.

All engine readings were far into the red; the destroyer-escort trembled. "I love you, Nova," Komodo whispered.

Salamis vanished in brilliance.

* * *

"Okay! Everybody run for it!" Marie commanded. The A-JACs heeded her, zooming away in all directions.

Marie was beginning to think she had miscalculated. Maybe she misjudged the spot or perhaps Emerson simply wasn't coming back. Then an enormous globe of ball-lightning leapt into existence near the enemy, and cometlike sparks flew outwards from it.

Even though the explosion of Emerson's reentry was nothing like the release of energy the decay of a natural black hole would have produced, it was enough to vaporize the enemy battlewagon. In another moment *Tristar* floated alone in space, as Marie laughed aloud and Emerson prepared to rejoin the expedition's main force.

Supreme Commander Leonard put on a self-satisfied look as he passed word of Emerson's victory along to the UEG council, taking as much of the credit for himself as he possibly could. But inside, he seethed. He must have victories of his own!

When he was back in his offices, though, a phone call brought welcome news that turned his day around.

"That was Cromwell from R&D," said his aide, Colonel Seward. "They've completed modifications on that targeting system they got from the trooper in ATAC. Mass production and retrofitting have already begun; they've got their special units on it now."

Then we can start preparation for my attack plan! Leonard exulted. He said to his gathered staff, "Gentlemen, the time has come to strike the telling blow, and capture or destroy the enemy flagship, using both Earth-based forces and the ALUCE contingent.

"Inform General Emerson I want him back here on Earth A.S.A.P. He'll be my field commander on this one."

Run the gauntlet again, Rolf! Your luck has to give out sometime!

* * *

"Listen up, everybody!" Dana's tone was so upbeat that the 15th knew this briefing wasn't just some joystick info-promulgation. They gathered round her, there in the repair bay.

When she had them quieted down from the usual griping and groaning about being interrupted, she motioned to Bowie and said, "Your friend Rolf—that is, Chief of Staff Emerson—has arrived at Moon Base ALUCE with his expeditionary force."

She saw Bowie's breath catch, but then, with deliberate effort, he put on a bored expression. "Oh, yippee-pow. Now we can do some more fighting."

"What's it all mean for us, Lieutenant?" Angelo broke in, seeing that Dana was vexed by Bowie's reaction and wanting to keep things on track.

That somehow triggered the strac side of her personality, the hardnose officer so unlike the wild rulebreaker. She put on her best CO expression and said tightly, "Squad fifteen, Alpha Tactical Armored Corps, will stand-to and make ready to participate in an all-out assault on the enemy flagship to take place in approximately forty-eight hours, Major General Emerson commanding."

She let the gasps and exclamations go on for a few seconds, then cut through them. "*As you were!* Fall out and follow me."

Grumbling, they hopped onto the drop-rack, the conveyor-beltlike endless ladder that carried them down to the motor pool levels to their parked Hovertanks. As soon as they jumped clear of the drop-rack, they saw that someone else had been at work there—at work on their own sacrosanct mecha, in violation of every ATAC tradition.

Odds and ends of components and machinery and one or two forgotten tools were lying around. They gave her betrayed looks, knowing now why they had been given other work details to keep them all off the motor-pool levels.

"They've all been retrofitted and augmented by R&D for extended space combat capability," she recited the briefing that had been given her. "Get used to them. You'll find instruction manuals and tutorial tapes in each tank. We will all run individual in-place drills and dry-fire practice from now until chowtime."

The 15th was only grumbling a little now, because they were fascinated with what had been done to their vehicles. The mecha's lines had been changed only a little, but the 15th could see that the detection and targeting gear was newer and more compact, more long-range. Life-support and energy systems were smaller and much more effective, too. The space saving was mostly due to upgraded firepower and thicker armor.

They spread out, looking admiringly at the tanks but not trusting them yet. Dana herself was uneasy about this sudden mucking around with the 15th's mecha, but she had her orders, and she thought that everything might go all right.

"Good; you're here," someone said behind her. She turned, and found herself facing Lieutenant Brown, decked out in his tailored TASC uniform. "Looks like it's gonna be fun, doesn't it?" he added.

"You're coming along on this party," Dana said, not making it a question.

Brown's handsome face twisted into a droll smile. "Gotta prove I'm not a screwup, don't I?" He looked around and spotted the *Livewire*. "Hey, Louie! Congratulations; I heard you're the one who dreamed up the new targeting systems."

Dana turned, saw that Louie was hunkered over the control grips and computer displays in his cockpit-turret. He didn't respond to Brown's hail. She turned back to the TASC flyer. "Y-you mean the simulator gizmo?"

"They told me it was for simulation training," Dana heard Louie's trembling voice. He was still bent over his controls, his back to them.

Sean was lounging in his tank, the *Bad News*, reveling in its now-enhanced power, checking out the VFTS "pupil pistol" target acquisition and firing system. "First-round kill every time," he assessed; Louie heard him, and groaned aloud.

"Shut up, Sean!" Dana screamed at him, her voice almost breaking.

Something snapped inside Bowie. What if the Robotech Masters had run short of fighters in the wake of Emerson's apocalyptic victory? What if Musica or someone like her was sealed into the ball-turret control module of the next blue Bioroid to find itself in his gunsight reticle?

"I'm through with this!" Bowie howled, veins standing out in his neck and forehead. "There're Humans like us in those Bioroids and *they're not our enemies!* And we're not theirs, can't any of you understand that?"

Dana started to calm Bowie down, but before she could get out more than a few vague, soothing words, she heard a rattle and felt waves of superheated air behind her. Dana and the rest of the 15th turned around and saw Louie Nichols with a thermo-rifle in his hands, its bulky power pack lying on the permacrete at his feet.

His eyes were unreadable behind the dark, reflective goggles, but he was trembling all over. "Those bastards from R&D never even asked me; they just lied, picked my brain, and did what they were planning to do all along. Like *we're* the clones; like *they're* the Robotech Masters!"

He shot a lance of brilliance at the motor-pool wall in a test-burn; alloy melted and small secondary fires started. He figured he had enough power in the rifle to burn the cockpit out of every tank and then go hunting for Cromwell and Gervasi.

"Like we're a bunch of experimental animals," Louie cried at his squadmates desperately, swinging the thermo-rifle's bell mouth this way and that to keep them all back.

He had joined the Southern Cross because he believed in it, but the mind and the products of the mind belonged to the individual, to do with as the individual saw fit; that was the first order of his convictions. Or else, what was the point of all this fighting? Why were the Human race and the Robotech Masters not one and the same?

"We're not just slaves or puppets or lab animals!" Louie shrieked, and put another spear of furnace-hot brightness into a partition, melting it, setting it alight, to keep back an overeager PFC who had been edging toward him.

Lab animals, the phrase registered in Dana and lodged there, because it set off images and reflexes on the very limits of the perceivable. *I know what it feels like to be one!*

Angelo started for the corporal one small step at a time.

"Louie, the balloon's already up. Emerson and the rest go, whether we do or not. All you can do this way is give the goddamn aliens a better edge."

Dana winced at the *aliens* reference and leapt forward to shove Angelo aside, the strange evocations of Louie's words still moving her. She leveled her gaze at berserker Louie.

"Go ahead, Louie." She jerked a thumb at the tanks. "Flame 'em all."

Angelo was making confused, contrary sounds. She went on, "If you can't do it, then I will!" She walked in Louie's direction, only slightly out of the path of the thermo-rifle's tracer beam. The beam wavered on her, away, and back.

Then she was before him, and he turned the nozzle aside. "They lied to us," Louie said, lowering the barrel.

"I know," she answered gently, taking the weapon from him and turning it once again on the tanks.

Angelo stepped into her line of fire. "You swore an oath!"

"So did they, Angie," she said evenly. Dana turned to burn her own Hovertank, *Valkyrie*, first. But she found another figure in her way. Zor gazed at her through the heat waves of the thermo-rifle's pilot.

"I understand this war from both sides; maybe I'm the only one who ever will," he told her. "And humanity mustn't lose, it *mustn't lose*, do you hear me? Listen, all of you: I know what the Bioroid clones feel when they die. I've died before—and I'll die again, as we all will. The difference is in how we'll *live*, don't you see? And for that, I'm willing to fight. And even to kill.

"Dying is a natural thing, sometimes it's even a mercy. But living as a slave—that can make dying seem like a miracle."

He was before her now, almost whispering the words. Dana turned the muzzle of the thermo-rifle up toward the ceiling. Zor pried it from her fingers and deactivated it, just as Louie ran from the motor pool.

"The war must end, *but the Robotech Masters must not win*," Zor said to them quietly, putting the rifle aside.

CHAPTER
EIGHT

Hwup! Twup! Thrup! Fo'!
Alpha! Tact'l! Armored! Corps!
If yo' cain't git yo' mind tame,
Better play some other game!

Marching-cadence chant popular among
ATAC drill sergeants

IN THEIR FLAGSHIP, THE ROBOTECH MASTERS SHOWED
no sign of their dismay as the Clonemasters assessed the
damage they had suffered in Emerson's doomsday victory.

Many of their combat vessels and blue Bioroids were
gone, along with much of the materials that were to have
gone to mecha construction. "We have begun emergency
production of the new, augmented Triumviroid mecha, my
lord," Jeddar was saying, "giving each the power of an Invid
Fighter. It lies within our ability to produce many of these
and they are superior to anything the Humans can field."

The Masters studied the Triumviroid, a red Bioroid similar to the one Zor Prime had piloted. With one of the
horned Triumviroid Invid Fighter spheres in each ball-turret
control module, they would have, in effect, hundreds of
Zors—hundreds of duplicates of their most capable fighter
and battle lord.

"This is our crowning achievement." Dag leered, studying the enormous fists and weapons. "Utterly invincible."

Bowkaz pronounced his evaluation, "The Humans' Battloids will be worthless against it."

And Shaizan contributed, "Finally, the Protoculture will be ours."

The gleaming red armored immensity of the straddle-legged Bioroid loomed above them, so massive that it seemed it could tear worlds apart. The Masters were sure that they were destined to succeed.

There was, however, a tacit silence among them on the matter of the *Humans'* aspirations, which might be contradictory.

The ALUCE forces had rested, repaired their mecha and licked their wounds. At Emerson's order, they lifted off again, to rendezvous with him for what the Human race hoped would be the knockout punch of the war.

Earth and the moon shook to the drives of Southern Cross battleships; the Black Lions and some twenty-five thousand other soldiers looked to their weapons and waited and wondered whether this would be the day they died.

At Fokker Base, Marie Crystal, who had come with Emerson on his harrowing broken-field run back from the moon, prayed for her own soul and those of all the men in her unit. Then she rose, armored like Joan of Arc, and got ready to lead them forth to slay and be slain.

In a mess hall near a launch pad at Fokker Base, there was little for the 15th to do except sit and wait. Their tanks were already loaded, nobody seemed to feel much like talking, and the squeaking and scraping of body armor was the only sound. Serenity seemed to be inversely proportionate to rank: Dana felt the weight of the world on her shoulders, while the latest transferees were trying to bag a few z's on the floor.

They had been listening to the Bitch Box—the PA speaker—drone on for hours. Who was supposed to go where, cautionary notes about final maintenance—and more ominously, chaplain's call and final offers from the Judge Advocate General's office to make sure wills and deeds were in order.

Dana looked out the mess hall window, at the scarred, alloy-plowed spot on a distant hillside where the Robotech Masters' flagship had crashed a lifetime—a month?—before.

"C'mon," she murmured to the PA. *I don't mind dying, but I hate to wait!* "Let's get this turkey in the oven!"

Sean, wandering past seemingly by accident, patted her glittering steel rump. "Easy, skipper."

She spun on him and would have taken a swing at him if he had been closer. Did he think she was so incapable that she needed *his* imprimatur to run her squad? Dana didn't have time to think of anything more subtle or telling, so she barked, "Squelch it, dipstick!"

They were both sweating, teeth locked, ready to punch each other for no good reason—except that they were about to go into battle, to shoot or perhaps be shot by total strangers.

Bowie bounded to his feet, despite the weight of his armor. "Stop it. We only have one enemy, and that's the Robotech Masters. We should be thinking about that." He said it with the uncomfortable knowledge that he couldn't even take his own advice; he, too, was preoccupied, but in a very different way.

Angelo was checking over the mechanism on his pistol. "Think, schmink! Why don'tcha all quiet down and think *mission*?"

"Angelo is right," Zor said quietly.

Louie snorted, "That's easy for you to say, Zor. But us Humans get emotional, especially when it comes to gettin' killed."

Zor didn't rise to the taunt. "You're right: I'm not Human. I wish I could remember more than I do, but I recall one thing clearly. I was far less than I am now, when my mind was ruled by the Robotech Masters.

"I want to destroy them to make sure that never happens

to me or anyone else. I'd gladly give my life to ensure that. If you knew what I was talking about, you all would, too."

Nobody said anything for a few seconds. They had all been in combat too many times to have much tolerance for gung-ho speeches, but something quiet and sure in Zor's voice kept them from mocking him.

"I'm impressed," Angelo said, to break the silence. There were a few grunts and nods of the head, about as close as the 15th could come to wild applause at a time like this.

In their flagship, the Masters gazed down at the Scientist triumvirate. "We observe the Humans' preparations," Shaizan said. "And their apparent intention to use such crude tactics is difficult to rationalize. Do you detect any indication that they are preparing to fight the Invid Sensor Nebula should it attack them?"

The Scientists floated close on their satellite Protoculture cap. Elsewhere in the cavernous compartment, the Clonemasters, Politicians, and other triumvirates stood on their drifting caps and watched silently.

Dovak, leader of the Scientists, answered, "According to our monitorings and intercepts, they plan nothing against the Nebula, but they *are* mounting an all-out offensive against *us*."

The Masters pondered that. Perhaps the primitives below were ignorant of the danger of the Invid. But that hardly seemed likely, especially since the Zentraedi who had defected to the Human side in the First Robotech War would have been well aware of it, and of the Nebulae. Perhaps the Humans were hoping for aid from the Invid.

If so, they hoped in vain; the Invid had a mindless hatred of any species but their own.

In any case, the Humans plainly would not constitute a buffer or third force should the Invid arrive; their civilization and perhaps all life on their planet—except the Matrix— would in all likelihood simply be swept away.

And if they weren't ready for the Invid and in control of a replenished Matrix by then, the Robotech Masters would be destroyed as well.

* * *

Finally the orders came. Dana grabbed up her winged helmet with its long alloy vane like a Grecian crest.

"All right, Fifteenth! Saddle up! C'mon, *move out!*"

Out on the launch pad, Nova managed to steal a few moments from the frantic activity of ensuring a trouble-free embarkation, to meet with Lieutenant Brown.

"I was sorry to hear about poor Komodo," he told her. "I know it was awkward for you but—you made him happy, Nova. Don't ever regret that, no matter what."

She had almost decided not to meet Dennis, fearing that her farewell might be a jinx. She struggled to say something.

"Just take care of yourself until I see you again," he smiled.

"Isn't that *my* line, Dennis?" She felt as if she might start shivering.

He shrugged his armored shoulders. "Nothing to worry about. 'Just another day in the SCA.'" The stock Southern Cross Army crack didn't sound so light, though.

She had a hard time understanding just how she had come to care so much for him, especially in the midst of all the craziness about Zor and the sadness over Captain Komodo. At first it had to do with her guilt over messing up his clearance. Later she admired him for the way he took the fall for Marie Crystal's stunt-driving exhibition, and for his role as getaway driver in Dana's demented matchmaking scheme.

But there was something more to it than that, something that had to do with the indestructible good humor with which he faced every misfortune. She just felt that in some ways he was a kinder, a better person—more compassionate—than she could ever pretend to be.

The warning hooters were nagging. "Gotta go," he said.

He turned to leave, but she caught his wrist. "Dennis, be careful. Do that for me?"

He nodded with a handsome grin. "Count on it. See you soon."

She nodded, watching him as if he were some apparition.

She couldn't quite work up the nerve to tell him, *Come back safe to me, because I seem to have fallen in love with you.*

He was trotting toward his transport, and she had to hurry to reach a bunker. Drives boomed again, and the next phase of the Second Robotech War began in earnest.

The forces from ALUCE came on, unopposed. The Masters refused to react to Humanity's drawing gambit, and played a waiting game. Earth's strikeforce positioned for attack.

Dana found Bowie down in the cargo hold where the 15th's Hovertanks were secured for flight. It took some prompting to get him to open up, but when he did the words came out in a flood.

"Since I met Musica and Zor, I just can't feel the same about fighting those Bioroids! The people in them just aren't to blame! It's like one of those ancient armies where they drove innocent captives in first, to be slaughtered, to gain a tactical advantage!"

"Bowie, I understand. There's nothing wrong with what you're feeling—"

She had put a hand on his shoulder but he shook free, batting it aside. "I'm right on the edge, Dana, and I haven't got my mind right, don't you understand? I can't handle it anymore! I'll let you all down!"

That was serious talk, because everyone in the 15th knew —as all soldiers know—that you don't take that hill for the UEG council, the Promise of a Brighter World, or Mom's fruitcake. No; you do it for your buddies, and they do it for you.

"Bowie, we've always been straight with each other, and I'm telling you: I get those same feelings, too."

"But Dana, that doesn't tell me how to deal with it! Ahhh! So, there it is. Nothing you can do about it, Lieutenant. I'm gonna have to sort this one out for myself."

"I'm only part Human," she blurted. "I, I guess I'm *related* to Zor and the rest, in a way. I don't like the idea of killing any of the clones, either. But Bowie, *think about the alternative. Remember what Zor said!*"

She threw her arms around his shoulders, pressing her cheek to him. "We can't let that happen to Earth, Bowie," she whispered, "and we can't let that happen to the Fifteenth."

A few weeks before, the Masters' fleet would have disintegrated the impudent Human attack. Now it fought for its life, its energy reservoir failing to a point where the battle was horribly even and attrition seemed to be the not-so-secret weapon.

Terran energy volleys and alien annihilation discs crosshatched, thick as nettles, as the Human strikeforce closed in.

The 15th cranked up and sealed their armor, preparing to follow Dana's *Valkyrie* into the launch lock. They got word that their tactical area of responsibility—their TAOR—had been increased by 50%, because the 12th squad had been blown to bits along with everyone else aboard the battlecruiser *Sharpsburg* when enemy salvoes found it.

The earth fleet threw everything it had at the enemy, but the news that came to Emerson, watching stone-faced from his flagship, was bad.

"Missiles, solids, energy—nothing seems to be doing them much damage, sir," Green told him.

There was no sign of the hexagonal "snowflake" defensive fields the Masters had used before, but what Green said was undeniably true. Ordnance and destructive force equivalent to a good-size World War was being tossed at the lumbering invaders, to no avail.

"It might be some kind of shield we haven't seen before, or it might just be their hulls," Emerson replied. But their wasn't much room for fancy changes of plan or pauses to consider now; the huge operation was, by its own size and weight, all but unstoppable.

"Press the attack," Rolf Emerson forced himself to say, trying not to think of the casualties but only of what would happen to Earth if he and his fleet failed. He had seen excerpts from Zor's debriefing, and the monitoring of Zor's comments about life under the Robotech Masters.

"Hit them harder," Emerson said, "and get ready to send in the fighters, then the tanks."

Going in close, risking the furious-bright particle beams of the teardrop-shaped invader batteries, the Earth ships poured down torrents of fire at them. Tube after tube of the heavier missiles, Skylords and such, gushed forth flame and death; racks of Swordfish and Jackhammers emptied, only to be reloaded for another fusilade.

Marie Crystal, ready to lead the TASCs out, sent a silent thought to Sean, to take care of himself.

A close, highly concentrated missile barrage that cost the Terran forces a destroyer escort and the crippling of a frigate somehow opened a gap in the alien flagship's hull. It happened just as the 15th was about to leave the launch lock, and their mission changed in a moment.

There was little G3 operations could add to the standing orders. *Get inside there and disable them! Distract, neutralize!*

The Hovertanks, compact as enormous crabs or turtles with all appendages pulled close, dropped on the inverted blue candleflames of their thrusters.

The rent in the enemy's upper hull was as big around as the 15th's barracks; a gaping, irregular hole, sides fringed with twisted, blackened armor seven yards thick, streaming black smoke and atmosphere like a funnel. It was slightly forward and portside of one of those mountainous spiraled ziggurats Louie insisted on calling "Robotech Teats."

It would still be a tight squeeze for a whole Hovertank squad, and Dana didn't like the idea of being crowded together fish-in-a-barrel style. But there was no telling when the gap would be closed by some repair mechanism, no time to pause and reconsider. At her order, the ATACs dropped slowly toward the hole, for a close pass before paying their housecall.

No Bioroids anywhere, Dana registered.

I don't like it, Angelo told himself.

* * *

"A different tactic now. How strange," Shaizan said, sounding more puzzled than perturbed.

Dag turned away from the crystalline pane, where he had been observing the Hovertanks. "This is an unexpected opportunity," Dag said, as the descending mecha swung slowly past the ruptured hull behind him.

"Yes; I believe it is time to test the new Invid Fighter," Shaizan concurred.

Dag turned and barked, "Scientists! Quickly!"

That triumvirate, having been high among the looping arteries and carryways of the ship's control systemry, descended now on their cap. "Yes, Masters?"

"Deploy our Triumviroid Invid Fighters against those Human mecha out there at once."

"At once!" The Scientists soared off to obey.

Bowkaz, watching the 15th come around for another close pass, closed his thin, atrophied hand into a fist, the spidery fingers unaccustomed to such a strong gesture. "Amazing! These missing links actually think they can triumph against *us*!"

In a large compartment in the flagship, an infernal fantasy landscape had been created. The translucent pink room consisted of high-arching carryways and Protoculture arteries, with clusters of globes that resembled grapes, of all things, at their intersections.

Far below the energizing and monitoring systemry, the Invid Fighters reared, standing in threes, insects by comparison but cyclopean giants in terms of the war raging on the outside.

The Bioroids' chest plastrons were open, shoulder pauldrons raised, helmet beavers lifted to expose the ball-turrets in which their pilots would sit, in yogi fashion.

Dovak's voice came, "Vada Prime, triumvirates of the Invid Fighters, to your mecha! Haste! The Human prey is near!"

Light poured in from the arch intersections where the

grape clusters hung; it illuminated triads of young male clones, the Vada Prime, red-haired but bearing a strong resemblance to the original Zor. They stood, back to back, where the extended chest plastrons of the mecha met like lowered drawbridges.

"Prepare for utilization against the Humans and their blasphemous concepts, their individuality! Obliterate them!"

"Three will always be as one!" one Vada leader chanted. That was the essence of the Invid Fighter systems: the transference of power, awareness, thought—Protoculture energy —back and forth among the members of each triune unit and its mecha, on a millisecond basis. This occurred so that each machine and pilot would be triply effective in the telling moments of combat, which were themselves relatively few.

"One for three and three for one. In thought, action, firepower, and reaction," Dovak intoned. "Remember this, Vada Prime!"

The Vada Prime clones retreated to their globular control sanctuaries, and prepared to hunt down the Hovertanks.

Dana led the 15th in a low approach vector, ready to go down into the hole in the enemy flagship's hull, hoping things went better than they had the last time the 15th entered the Masters' metal homeworld.

But things became complicated even before the tanks could enter; giant figures on Hovercraft rose up out of the smoking abyss of the hull breech. Dana couldn't help but feel dismay when she saw what was ahead. Red Bioroids!

Three, four—six that she could see, and perhaps more in the smoke. She tried not to surrender to despair. *Six red Bioroids!* "New targets ahead," she said, trying to sound confident.

The 15th bore in at the Triumviroids, the downsweep of their front cowlings and the halogen lamps tucked beneath them giving the tanks the look of angry crabs about to settle a grudge. The tanks broke right and left and up and down; they needed maneuvering room.

The enemy split up and jumped them, firing from

weapons in their control stems, and from the disc handguns, lashing streams of annihilation discs this way and that. Dana saw what she feared: they were all as fast and deadly as Zor was, operating in perfect coordination. She fought her recurring image of a complete rout.

Three of them went for a tank that had gone low, like cowboys chasing a wandering heifer, bringing their discus sidearms to bear. Dana saw with a start that the Hovertank was Zor's *Three-In-One*.

CHAPTER
NINE

The politicians who kill troops
But leave no babe unkissed!
They'd none of them be missed,
They'd none of them be missed!

Bowie Grant, "With Apologies to Gilbert and Sullivan"

DANA YELLED, "ZOR, GET OUT OF THERE!"

Zor had the presence of mind to retro, rather than try some fancy maneuver or an uneven firefight. The reds' shots stitched the flagship's hull, passing through the airless spot where Zor would have been. He escaped with only a spider-webbing of his canopy, the effect of a grazing shot.

"That was close, but I'm all right," he said calmly.

An A-JACs unit had found a bowside cargo lock blasted open by another Terran barrage; the mechachoppers zipped in at it like angry wasps, under the same romp-and-ruin orders as the ATACs.

The command came to the Vada Primes from Dovak: "A new enemy combat group is attempting to enter the flagship. Readjust battle plan and destroy them at once."

It took the A-JACs a fatal few moments to realize that they were being attacked by mecha far superior to their own.

One A-JAC was blasted as soon as it came in, going up like a Roman candle. A second, already standing by the opened hull, was riddled and fell apart in fragments. The reds came in, maneuvering and firing in perfect cooperation. The A-JACs' counterfire had no effect on the Triumviroids' battleshiplike armor.

"We're no match for them in these A-JACs!" Lieutenant Brown yelled to the few survivors left in his team. "Everybody pull back! Evasive maneuvers!"

Dana had her own plan of action. She sent her *Valkyrie* leaping high, imaging a change, her helmet sensors picking up the impulses and guiding her tank through mechamorphosis.

Components slid, reconfigured, rearranged; the tank went to Battloid mode. It stood in space, a Robotech Galahad, taking as its rifle the altered cannon that had rested along the tank's prow moments before. She landed on the hull to make her stand, feet spread, rifle/cannon strobing. Angelo and Bowie landed next to her in the same humanoid mode.

Three reds swept in in echelon, their fire well coordinated, promising to sweep the Battloids before them. Angelo remembered what he had learned about the blue Bioroids. He stopped pouring out heavy fire and took deliberate aim.

He hit the lead Triumviroid's faceplate; it shattered, spilling atmosphere and ruin. The thing's Hovercraft began to waver gently, and the red itself went immobile.

"I got one! Hey Lieutenant, go for their faceplates!"

But as Dana looked around to see what was going on, the red's ball turret exploded, the body of its Vada Prime pilot tumbling out into vacuum, breath and blood stolen away in a red mist.

They're humanoids, she saw. *They look . . . just like Zor.*

But she said, "You all heard Angie! Faceplates! And make every shot count!"

Bowie prepared to fire, but a vision of Musica came to him, and he froze. Three more reds came in low over a hull projection, firing so as to scatter the gathering Battloids, and one burst knocked Bowie's tank from its feet.

Dana and a trooper named Royce were almost shoulder to shoulder, putting out a heavy volume of fire, to cover him. The red broke off and banked away.

"You all right, Bowie?"

His Battloid began to lumber to its feet. "I think so."

"Then start shooting, god damn you! Bottom line: *They're* programmed to destroy *you*."

Sean was isolated, his fireteam partner just a conflagration and a memory, the enemy closing in. "Somebody get these 'roids offa me!"

The answer came in the form of an angel of death; the Triumviroid so close to nailing him flew apart in a coruscating detonation. He picked himself up off the hull to see an A-JAC hovering loose. "Huh? I'm dreaming! I'm dead!"

Marie Crystal was on the 15th's freq. "Neither, hotshot."

"Marie?"

"That's right, Phillips, you lucky swine you. You're about four hundred yards from your squad, at one hundred seventy degrees magnetic. Get back to 'em and stay alert! I . . . I don't want to lose you, Sean."

"I won't forget you said that. And I won't let you. What d'you wanna name our first kid?" She could hear the smugness in his voice but didn't mind a bit. His Battloid dashed away at top speed as Dana rallied her command.

Marie switched off her mike. "I won't forget," she whispered. Then she broke left, to try to help suppress the murderous AA fire from the teardrop cannon.

The interior of the flagship was a Hovertank job, and A-JACs, Veritechs—no other mecha had any place in it.

Dana and the first of her 15th leapt right down into a cobra pit.

Her transmissions were patched directly through to Emerson; the ATACs were Earth's best hope now. "General, we're pinned down in the entrance gap by heavy fire from red Bioroids! We're about at a standstill and request assistance—A.S.A.P!"

Emerson was out of his command chair. "We've got to force the enemy mecha back and make that entrance bigger. Any suggestions?"

Green was giving him a dead-level look. "Ramming them is the only way, Rolf."

It didn't even take Emerson a second to make up his mind; Earth could never mount another assault like this, and it was make-or-break time. "Then make ready to use this ship as a battering ram at once."

Emerson's crew acted instantly, and *still* it looked as though it wouldn't be soon enough.

If the enemy mother ship's fire had been as intense as it was when the Masters first arrived in the Solar System, the Human battlecruiser would have been holed and immolated as soon as it came close to the invader. But great hunks of armor and superstructure were blasted away from the enemy ship, and Emerson's flagship was able to stay on course, bearing down on its enemy.

And it provided a welcome diversion, permitting Dana's troops to break contact with the devilishly fast and powerful Invid Fighters and scatter. Even the Triumviroids' power wasn't enough to stop the heavyweight Earth dreadnought.

The wedge-shaped bow drove into the long rift in the invader; the impact sent Bioroid and Battloid alike sprawling and bouncing across the hull. Dana had no idea what power it was that generated gravity on the surface of the enemy ship, but she was grateful for it then—grateful not to be sent spinning into infinite blackness.

With the outer armor breached, the battlecruiser experienced less resistance from the mother ship's internal structure. Bulkheads and decks and vast segments of systemry were crushed or bashed aside as secondary explosions foamed around the cruiser like a fiery bow-wave.

Then Emerson's ship was through, having lengthened and deepened the hull breach to three times its former size, all the way through to the mother ship's port side. As the battlecruiser lifted clear, more explosions from the alien lifted the armor even further, as if peeling back aluminum foil.

Dana got word from the cruiser that the entryway was

clear, and for the moment the reds were nowhere to be seen. She hated the thought of leading her command down there where so many explosions had already gone off, but this was the only chance to go through the opening.

"Let's do it, Fifteenth! Follow me!" The 15th, all in Battloid mode, dashed toward the opening, huge metal feet pounding against the hull, rifle/cannon ready. Angelo was close behind Dana, and then Bowie. Sean Phillips, Zor, Louie Nichols—those were all of the squad that got through.

Several others were annihilated right at the verge of the gap. Still more raced for cover. The sum accomplishment of the biggest Human offensive of the Second Robotech War was to get exactly one officer and one NCO and four enlisted men of ATAC aboard the enemy command vessel.

Aboard his flagship, Emerson was hoping he had given the 15th the margin it needed. No other mecha had succeeded in reaching a position that would allow them to board, and, for the time being at least, none seemed likely to.

Emerson was calling for more diversionary strikes, to keep the Masters busy and eliminate as many red Bioroids as possible, when his flagship was battered by another massive volley.

Colonel Green picked himself up off the deck, checked the incoming reports and called to his commanding general, "It's *another* alien mother ship, sir!" He checked damage readouts. "And we're in no shape to take 'em on, Rolf!"

After the battle and the ramming, Emerson knew that was only common sense. But he said, "The battle plan does not allow for withdrawal at this time—"

A second barrage, even stronger than the first, rattled them all around like dice in a cup. Emerson saw that it wasn't just *one* mother ship coming to the rescue, but at least three. There was no choice; his forces would be utterly obliterated if he didn't at least fall back to regroup.

And there was no time for an extraction mission to recover the 15th; it was committed. Its few young troopers were very likely the last, best hope of Earth.

Marie, back aboard her attack transport to rearm and refuel, heard the announcements and commands over the PA and went cold, as the Earth fleet began to break off contact and withdraw. *Oh, Sean!*

The 15th spotted the two Triumviroids in the corridor ahead of them before the reds spied the 15th. The ATAC Battloids charged almost shoulder to shoulder, unavoidably bunched up, putting out the heaviest volume of fire they could.

A strange thing happened; the enemy mecha whirled and froze. ATAC rifle shots spattered their torsos and faceplates, blowing them out, and the Triumviroids dropped like puppets whose strings had been snipped. The ATACs had had the advantage of numbers and surprise, but it was still a remarkably easy win in comparison to the harrowing battle on the outer hull.

The 15th never even broke stride, but charged on further into the ship, weapons ready. But even as Dana leapt her Battloid over one red's body something occurred to her. *Two—there were only two this time.* And the reds had been working in threes up above. Presumably there was at least one more around down here, perhaps damaged or crushed by Emerson's ramming maneuver.

She had no time to pursue the thought, though, as she led her squad along a curvy passageway built to mecha scale. The deck and bulkheads seemed unremarkable here, but the overhead looked like a big, metallic neural network. No time to stop and study, however.

"Must be kinda familiar, huh Zor-O?" Angelo taunted. "Which way d'we go?"

"I wish I knew, but I don't remember, Sergeant," Zor answered, unruffled.

"I'll just bet ya don't, alien!"

Dana snapped, "Knock it off, Dante! Stay sharp, *all* of you!"

The warning was well timed. A moment later, a diamond-shaped hatch slid open before them and three Trium-viroids leapt into the opening.

But the 15th was so juiced up on adrenaline and the heat of battle that they opened fire instantly. For some reason these enemy mecha, too, were slow in responding, and with their faceplates shot out, they went over like bowling pins.

"Shoot for the faceplates, that's their weak spot!" Dana confirmed, as the ATACs rushed the hatch, covering one another. "If y'get one or two away from the third, it slows them down; if you get a trio, hit them at *exactly* the same moment. Looks like that overloads 'em somehow."

"They have discovered an inherent weakness of our Invid Fighter," Shaizan said tonelessly. It seemed that the single-thinking Human animals were a match for the Three-Who-Act-as-One.

Dag said, "Then, we must reactivate Zor Prime's programming, and resume full command of his mind and actions."

A perfect solution. There could be no chance of malfunction, since Zor was so close to the Protoculture cap.

Bowkaz touched his long, nailless fingers and his palm to a mottled patch of the cap, and the patch shone with radiance. "It is done."

"Lieutenant, somethin's wrong with Zor!"

It was odd to hear concern in Angelo's voice.

Dana and the others stopped and pounded back to where Angelo's Battloid faced Zor's, which stood stiff as a mannikin.

The power of Protoculture coursed through Zor's brain, taking control of every corner of his mind in moments.

Dana shook the paralyzed Battloid a little. "Zor, what's wrong? Are you hit? Answer me!"

Suddenly the *Three-In-One* lashed out, grabbing the enormous alloy fist of Dana's *Valkyrie* in its own, bending it in a take-away hold, threatening to rip it off.

Angelo yelled, "Zor, that's enough!" He had his rifle up, but Dana was in his line of fire.

She worked a quick hand-to-hand trick, rotating her mecha's wrist out of the grip and yanking herself free. "What's gotten into you?"

But Zor's Battloid was already running in the other direction, off toward a side passageway.

Dana only had a second to decide, and no time to sort through her various motives. A part of her simply could not bear to see Zor go off, perhaps blanked out again or suffering some mental seizure, to be captured or slain. Furthermore, he was an important resource to her mission and to the Southern Cross, perhaps her best hope of doing her job in the mother ship and getting her unit out alive.

But she couldn't risk her whole squad trying to tackle one berserk trooper. "Angelo, come with me! The rest of you set up security here and maintain radio contact!"

They had barely started to chase Zor when another threesome of the reds tried to block their way. Dana felt sure the Triumviroids were covering Zor's escape, that he had given them the order to do so.

Dana managed a broken-field run through them, but Angelo took one out with a shoulder block, slamming it against the bulkhead, as the disc guns opened up and the rifle/cannon replied. The passageway was an inferno of close-range firing.

Sean yelled an obscenity as he, Louie, and Bowie set up the heaviest fire they could, distracting the enemy from Dana and Angelo. The Triumviroids seemed to hear an unspoken order, and turned their attention on the remaining troopers. The mecha blasted at each other, blowing holes in deck and bulkheads, brilliant spears of novafire skewing across the small distance separating them.

You look at us and ask why we are slaves. But we look at you and wonder why you are not. What hideous mutation has given you the curse of free thought, and taken away your peace of mind forever?

Remark of an anonymous clone to ATAC trooper
Corporal Louie Nichols

THIS PLACE COULD BE ROMAN! DANA THOUGHT, looking around the compartment into which Zor had disappeared.

It was like some vast gathering hall or ballroom. There was invader systemry around the bulkheads. But set all around the hall/compartment were what seemed to be marble columns in the classic style, supporting entablatures with carved friezes. The ceiling was a smooth dome of polished stone. It made no sense to her, and she had no time to puzzle over it all.

"Zor! Zor, please come out!" The design of the bulkheads was so strange, she couldn't tell what might be a hatch or place of concealment; the columns were too small to offer a Battloid cover.

"We're your friends, Zor!"

Angelo's *Trojan Horse* came double-timing up, having hung back to cover their rear. "Lost him, huh?"

"I saw him come in here."

Angelo raised his weapon. "He can't be trusted. He betrayed us." The punishment for treason in wartime or desertion under fire was obvious. "And I'm gonna give him what he's got coming."

It was also obvious that Zor wasn't going to willingly show himself, but Angelo had his own straightforward solution for that. "Gladiator mode!"

The sergeant imaged the transformation through his spike-topped thinking cap, and his *Trojan Horse* went through mechamorphosis.

Angelo opened fire, hitting one of the columns dead center. It broke into a shower of stone splinters and dust, collapsing and breaking into a thousand fragments. He traversed the barrel and let off another round, blowing chunks from the ceiling.

"C'mon, Zor! *Show yourself!*"

He was right, Dana saw. All her anger at the Robotech Masters welled up; what right did they have to live in such beauty, slave keepers that they were? She went to Gladiator as well, and together she and Angelo Dante stomped about the hall, firing, demolishing the gorgeous entablatures and columns.

Then at random she fired at another bulkhead of rectangular metal. The rectangle crumpled and fell, revealing a space beyond. The hatch fell and through the smoke and flame stepped one lone red Bioroid.

"Zor!" Dana knew it had to be him. All her anger was gone in a moment, and the terrible thought that she had lost him again, perhaps forever, to the Masters, brought out the other side of her personality. Forgetting everything, she hiked herself up out of her seat, and leapt to lower herself from her cockpit-canopy. "Zor!"

"Lieutenant!" Angelo's first impulse was to fire for effect, but before he could do anything, she was in too close, nearly at the Bioroid's feet, arms held up to it imploringly.

"Oh, Zor," she cried forlornly. "Don't you remember me? Have they taken that from you, too?" But the great discus-shaped handgun in the red fist swung to bear on her.

Angelo locked down his controls and rose, to drop from his tank. He couldn't start a firefight and he wouldn't leave Dana to be captured or killed. He chose not to question his own motives as he ran to stand at her side, but he knew loyalty and duty were not his only ones.

Dana was so young and beautiful, so filled with a fighter's spirit. . . . In his whole life, he had met only a handful like her: good soldier, reliable companion . . . someone you could *trust*, could *count on*. In Angelo's vocabulary, those words meant everything.

Zor's voice came to them without benefit of their headphones. It sounded, once more, as it had when Dana had first seen him revealed, near the burial mound of SDF-1. His mindspeech was thin and reedy, higher than it had been a few moments ago, and sounding like someone talking on the inhalation rather than the exhalation.

"Do not move. Surrender or you will be instantly destroyed."

"Zor," she murmured, distraught. "What have they done to you?"

Then light broke from the Bioroid as its head swung back. Its chest and shoulders opened outwards, to reveal the ball turret within it. That, too, opened—and Zor uncurled from a fetal position, seemingly given birth, in blinding glory.

He stood to regard them with contempt, mindspeaking to them. "You have fallen into this trap much more easily than I would have thought, Lieutenant Sterling. You and your command are now captives of my lords, the Robotech Masters."

"I cannot understand the extraordinary influence the female Micronian exerts over Zor Prime's mental functions," Dag told his two counterparts. "Exposure to her emotions is causing departures from several of the clone's cognitive schemata, even here at the center of our power."

"But our control module is at maximum energization," Bowkaz pointed out. "We have near-total manipulation of

Zor Prime. Clearly, it will suffice. What are emotions, after all, but primitive behavioral residue?"

Zor had retreated back into his control sphere, and the discus handgun remained pointed at Dana and Angelo. The two ATACs had removed their helmets and stood looking up.

"Zor, I have to talk to you!" Dana tried again. "You remember me, don't you?"

There was no response, but Angelo noticed that, suddenly, the pistol was wavering. From the shadowy figure of Zor, curled up again in his globe, there was no movement. Dana started walking toward the Bioroid's foot.

"Look out, Dana! He's gonna shoot!" Angelo tackled her just as the titanic handgun fired; the annihilation disc missed, as the two ATACs fell headlong together, but Angelo was quick to understand that it would have missed anyway.

Another blast superheated the deck nearby, but at that range it should have been dead center. Dana and Angelo looked up to see the red's armor re-securing, closing protectively around the ball turret. The red moved spasmodically; more rounds blasted into the deck at random.

Angelo made his decision and ran for his tank. The red continued its disoriented firing, seemingly in conflict with *itself*, until it noticed his main battery coming to bear on it. Dana was just far enough out of the way. Angelo fired, but the Bioroid ducked, barely in time. Zor fell aside as the deckplates beneath his feet leapt up in fire from the sergeant's second shot.

Within his Robotech womb, Zor sweated, moaning, in his trance. He fought himself even more determinedly than his Bioroid fought Angelo, but the internal combat wasn't going well.

Dana swung to Angelo. "You'll never stop him that way! Switch to Battloid mode! And *don't hurt him!*"

Who's she think I am, Wyatt Earp? Angelo wondered. *What'm I supposed to do, wing that goddamn 'roid?* But he went to Battloid and fired his rifle/cannon from the hip. The red dodged, but more slowly.

"Zor's brainwaves indicate a deviance," Bowkaz observed.

Behind him, Myzex, group leader of the Politician triumvirate, spoke from his triad's Protoculture cap. "His exposure to Human influence may have produced an adverse effect on his anterior brain structure."

Dag half turned to the politicians. "You suggest an awakening of dormant racial memory?"

"Possibly, my Master."

Perhaps this was the breakthrough the Masters had hoped for! It might be that emotions were the missing key to the recovery of Zor's mental gifts and, possibly, even to the Inheritance of Acquired Knowledge capacity they had hoped to channel into him by use of their artificial psi abilities. The I.A.K. and the recovery of the original Zor's secrets, a new Matrix—a universe-spanning realm belonging to them alone—it was suddenly all possible.

"The Human disturbance and distraction must be eradicated at once," Shaizan decreed.

Suddenly Zor barreled past Angelo before the sergeant could get off a shot, bashed through another hatch, and disappeared down a passageway.

"Angelo, stay down!" Dana yelled.

"What happened?" Angelo was shaken badly; he had thought his number was up. "He had me dead to rights; why didn't he nail me?"

"I don't know," Dana said, heading back to the *Valkyrie*. "But we have to find Bowie and the others before the aliens do."

Aliens.

The firefight in the passageway was successful for the 15th. The ATACs used what they had learned about the Triumviroids' weaknesses. Without Dana around to object, they had done some fast, straight faceplate-shooting, and even Bowie, seeing that his squadmates' lives were on the line, had made his choice and taken his stand.

But as they stood in the smoking aftermath of the fire-fight, they had realized that it was time to lie low for a while. They had withdrawn to a nearby recycling plant—a gigantic compartment full of moving conveyor belts and organic-looking reclamation equipment. Hopefully Dana would follow their transceiver signals.

Sean picked up two signals that got stronger, until they had to be right in the compartment. He looked up to see two Hovertanks shake loose of the debris and scrap on a ten-yard-wide belt high overhead, and descend on gushing thrusters. Angelo and Dana landed amid a shower of junk and garbage, Dana crying, "Look out below!"

"'Bout time, Lieutenant," Bowie commented dryly.

There were no guards or surveillance devices that they could see. Dana and Angelo and the others hid their tanks in the dark reaches under a big overhead, then the 15th gathered around to do some improvising.

It was clear that they couldn't rely upon Emerson's return anytime soon, and to simply run riot would be to make it just a matter of time before the Triumviroids converged to wipe them out.

"So, what we gotta do is locate the flagship's command center or bridge or whatever they call it around here, then come back with the tanks and take it by force. Everybody, shuck your armor; this is a recon job."

"Secret agent time," Sean sighed. "And where d'we look, in a ship five miles long?"

"The logical place, in view of their setup and systems, is the center of the ship," Louie said. They began climbing out of their armor and checking their small arms.

The ATACs wanted to pack all the weapons they could, but Dana nixed the idea. A lot of throw-weight would only attract attention, and if they got into a situation wherein a few pistols and a rifle wouldn't suffice, they weren't likely to get out of it at all.

Another conveyor belt took them past an entrance deco-rated with a marble arch. They hopped off there, went along a corridor lined with meticulous, hand-done stonework. Angelo, walking point, found himself looking out on a scene that resembled a cross between the Roman Senate and the Borgias' waiting room. There was the same gorgeous artistry, and gleaming floors underfoot. Clones were moving around in small groups, their pastel clothing running toward togalike affairs, or tights with short mantles.

"What's it look like out there?" Dana wanted to know, just behind Angelo but unable to see around him. "Are any of those guards nosing around, or can we keep moving?"

"All I can see are civilians, I guess," he whispered back. He held his tanker's carbine high and moved a step further.

Dana came up and peered out, then told her men, "They don't look like the type to ask questions, out there. We'll just mingle, and make our way along."

"Nothing ventured—" Louie resigned himself.

But the inhabitants of the ship *did* seem quiet, subdued—almost lethargic. The ATACs moved out along an upper thoroughfare that overlooked public gathering places and quiet quadrangles.

They had only gotten a few steps when Dana and Louie saw a small surface-effect runabout headed their way.

Everybody else caught the signals and warnings except Sean, who had been traipsing along more or less on the heels of three attractive females who walked in a bunch. By the time he realized what was happening, the others had taken cover. He was in no position to bolt and decided, in typical fashion, to strike up a casual chat with the gals.

"Um, 'scuze me, Miss—" He tugged her elbow; all three turned as one and went *"Hmm?"* in those eerie, indrawn-breath voices. The runabout of guards was cruising closer.

Sean made idiotic stammerings about having met them before someplace, and maybe they should all do lunch. He laughed unconvincingly, slipped them a couple of winks, sweated.

They were actually quite fetching, triplets with hair dyed orange, blue, and pink to differentiate themselves. They looked at him and listened for a few moments. Sean tried to maintain eye contact and yet watch the guards' slow cruising progress.

Orange Hair turned to her sisters. "This clone's condition is remarkably degenerative, don't you agree?"

"Note the spasmodic facial expressions: neurological breakdown," Blue Hair agreed gravely.

"Let us try to determine the nature of his malfunction before he destabilizes completely," Pinkie put in.

Before Sean could get over his astonishment, they were gathered around him, prying open his mouth, spreading his eye wide to study it, thumping his chest—*feeling him up*.

He had left his torso harness back with his armor, and the three Clonehealers somehow had his tunic open and down around his waist, pinning his arms, and were tripping his feet out from under him in matter-of-fact fashion. He had been walking point, and so he wasn't even carrying a gun.

Their deliberate proddings and pokings sent him into a ticklish laughing fit. *Please, whatever gods there be: Don't let Marie find out about this!*

Dana rushed to the rescue, pushing the women aside. "All tarts pile off!"

"These clones are obviously all infected," said Orange Hair. She raised her voice. "Guards! Seize these clones immediately!"

The runabout came end for end and the guards came roaring back.

"Split up!" Dana cried. "They can't follow us all!" She vaulted a railing with Bowie and Louie bringing up the rear. "Meet back at the tanks!" She ran off down glossy black steps that were mirror-bright and five yards wide.

Angelo dragged Sean to his feet, but realized he had left their tanker carbines leaning against the wall. And there was no time to go for them; shots were ranging around them. They dashed off along the upper thoroughfare; the runabout was following them.

"Y'can't palm yourself off as an *alien*, ya ragweed!" Angelo panted.

"Aw, write it home to your *mother*, Sergeant!" Sean snarled back. They ducked into the first alley they came to.

The guard craft stopped and a cop triumvirate piled out to continue the chase on foot.

The cop/guards split up to search a loading dock at the far end of the alley. Sean and Angelo popped out to jump the middle one, the sergeant punching the lone clone *hard*, making sure he wouldn't get up again. Sean grabbed the guard's short, two-handed weapon to cut down another guard. He pivoted, he and the third guard drawing a bead on each other at the same moment.

CHAPTER
ELEVEN

> *I think the real change in Dana began the first time she had to write one of those letters that starts, "As commanding officer of the 15th Squad, ATAC, it is my sad duty to inform you . . ."*
>
> Louie Nichols, *Tripping the Light Fantastic*

MUSICA CARESSED THE RAINBOW-BEAM STRINGS OF her Cosmic Harp, evoking from it sad tonalities. She had no heart for the tunes the Masters would have her play. The acoustics of her darkened hall made it sound like a cathedral.

Her sisters Allegra and Octavia approached, and she resigned herself to yet another disagreement over her newfound defiance. But Allegra said, "A band of alien soldiers has invaded the core district. We thought you would want to know."

Musica caught her breath. "Have they been injured? Captured?"

Allegra spread her hands in a gesture to show that she didn't know. "Karno and his men have started an all-out search for them. They will be found."

Musica sprang to her feet and walked away. "Don't go!" Octavia called after. "It's too dangerous!"

"I must be alone for a while," Musica said over her shoulder. She thought, *No harm must come to him! Oh, Bowie!*

"You mean your units have permitted the enemy primitives to get away?" Mega, androgynous female of the Politician triumvirate, demanded.

The guard group leader conceded, "Only temporarily, Excellency. But they cannot evade us for long, or escape the ship."

She gave him a frigid glare. "Your incompetence will be punished."

Louie, Bowie, and Dana were not the best mix of talents and traits.

They found what looked like a dormitory, then had to dive under the bedlike furnishings when they heard voices. Peeking out from under the beds, they watched as the Clonehealers (who had been accosted by Sean and had accosted him in return) entered, discussing the matter of the alien invaders.

"I cannot wait to sanitize myself," Spreella said, pulling off her robes, "from the pollution of contact with them." All three undressed, to the ATACs' vast interest, and lay down on beds. Projectors of some kind automatically swung into place. Lights beamed down on the clones and put them instantly to sleep. Little ring-auras danced over them.

A few seconds later, the troopers were wearing the togas, hoods pulled up. They ventured out again, and moved across a rotunda in what looked to Dana like Romeo and Juliet's old neighborhood, except that there were no trellises, no flowers or plants of any kind.

More guard runabouts appeared. The three ducked into the first door they came to and found themselves in a place that made them think of a cocktail lounge. It had softly lit art-shapes of glassy blue panes, and gently turning, unearthly mobiles. There was soft music from something that reminded Bowie a little of a flute. They sat nervously at a table and a female clone placed a strange drinking cup before each of them.

"Drink this, then step through that door to the bioscan chamber," she said, and moved on. Everyone else was downing the same purplish stuff; it smelled fragrant.

They were all thirsty, and hadn't been able to find anything like a public fountain or even a tap. They downed the stuff; it was delicious, a real pickup. Not beer, but not bad, and it cut their thirst.

Dana decided to have a look through that door. "Bioscan chamber" sounded like something the brass hats would want to know about. They went through the door, pistols ready in their belts.

A female nurse-technician clone was there, and the three were directed to put their feet on lighted markers inside capsulelike structures. The nurse manipulated a control component that resembled a small, halved Protoculture cap set on a pedestal, its flat face covered with alien instrumentation that looked like the detailing of a mecha.

Rays played over them, and the nurse informed them that although their dysfunction was far along, there was hope for them. Their mental readouts gave the clone particular alarm.

Bowie and Louie looked like they wanted to bolt, but Dana had the feeling that they were close to something vitally important about the Masters' self-contained world. She followed as the nurse led them into the next and far larger chamber.

The place seemed to be filled with a strange blue mist, a large compartment with scores of glassy, coffinlike containers in rows. Long, transparent cylinders descended from apertures in the ceiling to cast pale light. There were more of the control modules set here and there among the scores of shimmering coffins. The ATACs could see still forms in the glassy caskets.

"Looks like we've found the morgue," Dana murmured.

"These conversion stabilizer units will remedy your malfunctions," the nurse explained. She was used to clones being disoriented when they came to her, but she wondered if these particular three were beyond help. "Observe how this unit is now in complete harmony with his environment."

She referred to a male clone who was revealed as his sarcophagus lid rose. He sat up, blinking, on his elbows.

"His structure was stabilized by this treatment and a simple bio-energy supplement," the nurse went on. "You will now drink these."

She was talking about a sluggish looking stuff in three more drinking vessels that had come down on a floating table. Something in Dana was drawn to the idea of *taking an alien elixir*, of finding out what the strange sleep brought. It triggered some deep memory. She yearned to comply, even while the Southern Cross lieutenant in her knew it would be madness.

The nurse was doing something at a wall unit. Louie suddenly yelled, "Look out, Lieutenant!"

Dana turned. The just-awakened clone was lurching toward her, arms outstretched. He didn't look very stabilized to Dana; he looked like something out of a horror movie, pale and hollow-eyed, the living dead.

Their systems aren't functioning up to par, I guess, Louie thought.

Dana, filled with revulsion, screamed for the thing to stay back and hurled her drinking vessel at it; the glass missed and smashed into a control module. Liquid splashed, the module began sparking and sputtering, and the lights started dimming and brightening.

"More trouble," Louie observed; the see-through caskets' indicators and controls were going haywire. The lids were rising; the clones rose from their resting places.

"Oh, great! The whole graveyard's coming to life!" Bowie yelled.

Dana showed her teeth to Louie with a hunting cat's ferocious mien. "*Here's* your ideal society, Louie! *Here's* your machine dream, your Empire of Unimpeded Intellect!" She seemed about to pounce on him. "Well? How d'you like it?"

The nurse was shrilling something about third stage alerts and out-of-control clones. The three ATACs didn't realize that she meant *them*, not the late risers.

She must have put in a call already, though, because the troopers heard running footsteps coming toward them. Three guards with the submachine gun-looking weapons appeared in a doorway.

"Use the zombies for cover and head for that other doorway!" Dana shouted. Bowie and Louie followed her, weaving among the sluggish, confused clones. Dana was hoping the guards would be busy rounding up the blitzed-out sleepwalkers, but the cop/clones gave chase instead.

The three ATACs ended up out on what appeared to be a public transport platform, like a subway station. Dana, in the lead, took a turn and kept sprinting. They wound through side ways and almost tripped over a parked, unattended runabout.

Dana jumped in, determined to get it working; she hit controls at random and it tore away into the air, leaving Bowie and Louie behind.

Everything she did seemed to make it worse, and in moments she had another guard runabout pursuing her. Dana rode over the rotundas and through the passageways, coming close to crashing every two or three seconds, somehow managing not to kill astonished clones, trying to get back to her squadmates.

She heard the pursuing runabout careen out of control and crash into a wall. As she zoomed out of an alley, Dana's own vehicle tried for a wingover, and she went flying. Resigned to death, she had her fall broken by some kind of awning, and slid through as it ripped. She fell on her rear end on some kind of big disposal chute. It disposed of her, down into a steeply pitched shaft, just as she heard her stolen runabout explode against a distant ceiling.

Her funhouse ticket was good for another ride; she went screaming down into darkness. She came sliding down across an arrival stage, losing speed and uniform fabric and skin, and went shooting off, to bounce off something soft and land in a heap.

"Where did *you* come from?" a calm male clone voice asked.

Dana, rubbing her butt and groaning, turned and said, "You wouldn't believe it."

She found herself looking at a slender, graceful clone with long, straight, steel-gray hair and a very young face. "I am Latell, of the Stonecutters," he said, rising from the peculiar-looking pallet on which he had been sitting and coming to kneel by her. "Are you badly hurt? Is there anything I can do?"

She looked around her. The room suggested a Roman bath converted to use as a clone hospital, but here the beds had no lids. Around the room, the Masters' slaves were lying down or sitting, looking very torpid. "Well, you could tell me what this place is."

"Why, this is the district interim center for purging and replacement."

So, she was at yet another clone spa. "Purging of what?"

He tilted his head, studying her. "The personal consciousness of those who must be rehabilitated, naturally."

A male clone nurse appeared, a twin of the one who had tried to serve Dana the mickey. "You two! Your rest period is now terminated. Resume training."

Latell snapped to attention, then drew the truculent Dana to her feet, afraid that she was so destabilized as to risk punishment. Dana saw it wasn't time to start a dust-up, and let Latell lead her away.

He took her to a chamber where dozens of people—that was how she thought of them—were standing two or three apiece at glowing projection tanks. The clones studied abstract shapes and symbols and hypnotic patterns, which changed and shifted, the clones staring down at them with intense concentration.

"Why are *you* here, Latell?"

"I was found guilty of individual thought," he confessed to her. "And you?"

"Uh, the same."

He looked infinitely sad. "But they've allowed you to keep your permanent body," he observed, too polite to point out what a nonstandard body it was—so rounded and with such an odd voice. "Not the normal procedure at all."

"It's, ah, part of an experiment, Latell."

They were at one of the pool tables. Latell was gazing down at the shapes there, brow furrowed. The shapes began changing, multiplying, going do-si-do. "I'm afraid I must confess: *my* reprogramming efforts haven't been entirely successful—oh!"

He was staring disappointedly at the lightshapes. "The trainer is having no effect. I still have individual thought patterns."

She looked him up and down. "What's so bad about that?"

"You know as well as I. Unstable minds cannot be tolerated—"

He was interrupted as a nearby female slumped against her pool table–trainer and fell to the floor. Dana rushed to her, trying to revive her without success.

She looked around. "Somebody give me a hand, here!"

A female who was twin to the one Dana cradled said frostily, "That is forbidden. Her body will have to be replaced."

So, when one member of the triumvirate got out of whack by the Masters' standards, he or she was either fixed, or replaced. And the triumvirate went on.

Dana showed her teeth in a snarl. "What are you, Human beings or cattle?"

Human? She could hear the word ripple through them with a shiver of disgust. The clones left their trainers and began to converge on her. Latell dragged Dana to her feet, though she fought him.

"You've gone too far," he said. "You must leave."

"Idiots!" she was screaming. "Can't you see what they're doing to you?" Was this how Zor would end his days? But he had been a freethinking Human! To come to this . . .

The nurse had reappeared, with a twin. "This one requires a body replacement. Yes. You, come with us."

The clone grabbed her and Dana let out her rage in the form of a quick footsweep and a shoulder block. The nurses went flying in either direction.

She seized Latell's wrist. "C'mon. I'm getting you outta

here." He didn't resist. He was doomed, whatever he did, and in addition found her fascinating.

Angelo and Sean had guard uniforms to wear over their Southern Cross outfits (though Angelo's was strained to its limits, to say the least), and guns and a runabout, but with the action over, they were at a loss as to what to do next. Parked in a deserted upper-tier plaza, they worried and debated.

A plate on the runabout's dash came alight and a voice said, "Unit thirteen, return to Main Control. Prepare for Override Guidance to return you to Main Control."

Sean checked over his stolen weapon. "Get ready, Angie. We just got our ticket to the target."

Stolen vehicles were the order of the day, only natural for a stranded Hovertank unit. Bowie and Louie had heisted themselves a vanlike craft, and techmaster Louie had quickly figured out how to drive it.

They cruised slowly, hoping to spot one of the others and to get their bearings on either the control center or the tanks. Bowie, riding shotgun, abruptly yelped, "Louie, pull over! Stop!"

"Hah? Whatsamatter? Whatsamatter?" But he did as the other asked. Bowie leapt out and went running after Musica, who had been wandering along as if in a daze.

Louie shrugged. "Why not? We got nothin' better to do."

At Musica's direction, the three drove to the weirdest place they had yet seen in the mother ship. It was like some underground grotto or an ant's orchard.

Glowing spheres, some of them fifty feet across, were *growing* there—at least that was what it looked like. The spheres were held by a network of vinelike growths, alien lianas four and five feet thick, which sprouted dense crops of translucent hairs the width of hawsers.

The vines traveled up to the roof and down to the floor in clusters, where they were rooted in the soil. There, smaller spheres sprouted on single vines, with spores of the mature forms growing in the middle.

Bowie sat and Musica knelt, each looking off in the opposite direction at the tree-broad base of one of the root-vines. Louie waited in the van, some distance off.

"Everyone is looking for you," she was saying. "I was so afraid you'd been hurt or captured."

"It almost happened. It still could, but now I don't care."

She turned to him. "Why do you say that?"

Without looking at her, he reached out to close his hand around her pale, slender forearm. "Now that I've found you again, nothing else matters to me."

She said haltingly, "It's very strange to me, but I feel the same way. And the odd yearning—that peculiar disquiet in me is no longer there when we are together."

"We belong together."

"I would be happy to remain this way for the rest of time, Bowie."

He was about to reply in kind when a harsh voice cut through the peace. "Do not move, Micronian! Stand slowly!"

Bowie found himself gaping at Karno and two others more or less just like him, and the big dark muzzles of their guns.

CHAPTER
TWELVE

When the Robotech Masters first appeared, Earth sent its only mecha factory off on a far, SDF-style orbit. It went to Code Red and manned battle stations. It issued heartening war bulletins.

No wonder the situation got so crazy. Southern Cross had forgotten the lessons of terrestrial wars, and nobody had warned us that we might see the enemy as Human beings.

Louie Nichols, *Tripping the Light Fantastic*

"MUSICA, MOVE AWAY FROM THE ALIEN AT once," commanded Darsis. More guards with their guns leveled appeared from among the massive vines.

"He is an enemy of our people," Karno stated. But Musica defied him, moving to stand between Bowie and the Guards, arms spread.

"You mustn't hurt him, Karno! I forbid it! He's done you no harm!"

She forbids? The insanity of it boggled Karno's brain.

Darsis frowned. "Anyone shielding an enemy of the state will be punished! Now, stand aside, Musica!"

The Guards were in a quandary, though; Musica was far too vital to the Robotech Masters and their hold over the population of the ships to simply shoot, and she knew it. It was a situation the Guards had never encountered before.

They were saved from the inconvenience of thinking by the revving of a van engine. Louie came hot-tailing at the

Guards, yelling for Bowie to make a break. Karno and his men got a few rounds into the van, but then had no choice but to hit the dirt or scatter.

They were up again right away, firing into the vehicle's stern, and it arced toward the ground leaking smoke into the distance. Louie managed to get out of the van and saw the Guards racing after him. He turned to go, but realized there was a beeping in his pocket.

He pulled forth one of his gadgets, studied it, smiled broadly, and raced off to make his escape.

Bowie, going for cover in the midst of a tangle of the colossal vine-roots, skidded to a stop. More guards emerged from it, hemming him in against those pursuing him.

Louie shook off his hunters and followed his gadget; it didn't take very long to find what he had detected. Some sixth sense comprehension of systemry and Robotechnology led him to a vaulted compartment in what had to be the center of the flagship. To his amazement, it was unguarded. What he found there left him speechless.

In the center of the vastness was a device the size of an upright shuttlecraft. Top and bottom were sawtoothed halves, as if a cylinder of taffy had been sawn apart and stretched. What hung between them was—

Whaaa-at? Louie asked himself, dumbfounded. It looked like a single braided mass of fibrous tissue, red, black, pink, and yellow like some textbook illustration of a muscle. But pieces hung from it, curled and kinked in the way of sprung wires peeling from a cable, or fibers of steel wool.

The whole circular chamber was lined with instruments stretching up and up out of sight. The central device itself was orbited by slow-moving amoeboid shapes of pure blue-white light.

What an amazing creation! The flagship's control nexus.

Louie still had the alien energy-burpgun he and Bowie had managed to steal. He worked it as if he had been using one all his life, preparing to empty it in one blast, without regard to his own survival.

Destroy this, and the Robotech Masters are finished. And

there wasn't even anybody around to put him in for a post-humous medal, oh well. . . .

He decided to start high and blast a vertical cut in the thing. No sooner had he opened fire than jagged lightning broke from one of the amoeboid shapes. The weapon was sudden giving out heavy voltage. He managed to let go before his heart was stopped, and it was levitated away high into the air.

From the central tissue mass, a hundred ghostly ribbons of force, or ectoplasmic lariats, were dropped. They wound around Louie and squeezed his breath from him, sending an awful surge of energy through his body. He was lit up like a Christmas tree ornament. One of the less fortunate martyred saints.

Word went out that the Living Protoculture had captured its assailant. The search for the other raiders intensified.

Dana didn't want to hear or see any more.

Latell had taken her past too many glassy spheres filled with bubbling fluid. In them, naked, wired-up clones wearing helmets floated, dead to the world. One of these clones was supposed to be the *actual* Latell the Stonecutter, or perhaps the embodiment of the triumvirate of Stonecutters, but then who was this talking to her?

This time, the guards who showed up didn't do much talking. The doors parted and three charged in shooting. The first few rounds shattered the container of Latell's "original body." The Latell she had been *talking* to gave a grievous moan as she pulled him behind the other containers and apparatus for cover.

The clone-fetus, slick with fluids, looked at Dana. Then its eyes rolled up into its head and it expired there among the shards of its container.

Something in her snapped, and several objects on which she could vent her rage were right close to hand. The guards weren't really much as soldiers; apparently all they had ever had to do was keep docile slaves in line and now and then round up some extraordinarily aberrant one. Invaders were all but unknown, and the upshot was that the guards' combat skills weren't nearly so well-honed as Dana's.

She came flying at them from behind a pillar of support equipment, shrieking a *ki-yi* that froze them. She took out the first with the sword edge of her right foot, and that only fed her hatred. The second, too close to get clear, tried to swing the butt-plate of his weapon into her face. She ducked, and then broke his neck.

She bent down to pick up the weapon he had dropped, but the third had fallen back against the hatch to spray energy bolts in her direction, forcing her to throw herself back. Latell managed to find her among the disintegrating containers and sputtering power lines, and together they crawled off through a side hatch as still more guards appeared and converged on them.

The guards cornered them in the next compartment, a sort of nursery for infants. *Why would the Masters need infants*, it occurred to her, *when they can grow clones to adulthood* in vitro?

Latell palmed a tiny device to her. "This is a maintenance sensor; it will lead you to the control center. Destroy the center!"

Latell tried to push her to cover, tried to block the way. He was a dysfunctioning slave of no importance; the guards shot him down.

There was no place to run away. Dana cradled his head in her lap. He achieved a thin smile. "Please do not feel badly, Sister. You are Freedom, and my life was not worth the living."

And so the clone Latell the Stonecutter died.

The firefight in the power-relay area was one of the more interesting fights of Angelo Dante's life, although it did threaten to fix things so he would never collect any of his retirement pay.

Still, he and Sean had good cover. They had taken out a lot of guards already, and there was still some chance they could get free. Angelo stood and sprayed shots at the enemy. If the ATACs were pinned down, so were the guards, who had learned better than to try to rush the Human marksmen across the yards of open space.

Then the sergeant realized that Sean wasn't firing. He was about to holler something suitably crude and insulting when he felt a tug at the sleeve of his stolen guard uniform.

Angelo whirled to see ten, eleven, perhaps a dozen of the runabouts in an arc behind him, all crowded with guards and officers who had drawn a bead on him and Sean.

"Don't think I'll forget your face, slimeball, 'cause *I won't!*" Angelo growled as the guard thrust him headlong onto the detention cell floor. Sean, who had been more resigned and reasonable, disembarked from the elevator with his hands behind his neck. The elevator doors closed.

Dana, sitting on a sleeping shelf with her knees drawn up, simply looked at the two new arrivals. Louie didn't even look. Bowie knelt by Angelo's side. "You okay, Sarge?"

Angelo nodded, springing up and shrugging Bowie off, stretching and flexing his ample muscles. "Yeah. Gang's all here, huh?"

Dana grunted. They were all there, stripped of weapons and disguises, dressed in their ATAC uniforms.

"And we failed our mission," Angelo went on, as bitter at himself as at any of them or at fate. "We lost!"

Now Dana *did* look up, to fix him with her stare.

"Only round one," she said.

Gazing down on the captive specimens through their Protoculture cap, the Robotech Masters were taken aback, in spite of the information and insights they had gained through Zor Prime.

"Most interesting," Shaizan said. "They show no fear of their captivity, only anger that they have failed, and an illogical unwillingness to face reality."

There was an unspoken consensus among them: there were terrible, unsuspected powers in the one-mindedness and emotions of the Micronians.

Powers upon which a universe could turn.

* * *

It didn't take long, in a little bowl-shaped, inescapable confinement some fifteen feet across at floor level, for the ATACs to get on each other's nerves.

A crack from Angelo about Zor's spying. A hurt objection from Dana that she had no way of knowing. A blithe comment from Sean that love was blind, followed by Dana kicking Sean's feet out from under him, then both of them ready to twist each other's bones loose, and the others diving in to break it up.

"Fascinating. The Earthlings have a pronounced tendency to turn upon one another in confinement," Shaizan remarked.

Dag said, "They are too primitive to comprehend that what we are doing will ensure *their* survival as well as our own." It did not need to be added, of course, that that survival would be as a slave species. The Masters considered their slaves greatly honored, Chosen.

"If the Invid obtain the Protoculture Matrix before we do," Bowkaz put to words what they all knew, "it will in all likelihood mean the eradication of the entire Human species."

"The last part of that statement is not an entirely unpleasant prospect," was Shaizan's rejoinder.

"As to the prisoners," Dag went on, "my suggestion is that the five of them should be reprocessed as new biogenetic material for our cloning vats straight away."

"No—all but the female," Dag corrected. "According to our measurements, her intellect and biogenetic traits are extremely contrary to Human norms. Dissection and analysis are in order."

"I say it might be more efficient and safe simply to destroy them all," Bowkaz said.

Jeddar, group leader of the Clonemasters—whose triumvirate floated nearby on its cap—took the extraordinary step of interjecting a comment. "Excuse me, my Masters, but we propose that you delay these actions until we've reprogrammed Zor Prime's memory, restoring full awareness to him."

Tinsta, the female of their triad, continued, "His experience on Earth has increased his bio-energy index above that of any other clone, even far above precious Zor clones."

"We believe it has something to do with his prolonged exposure to Human emotions. We think that these emotions maximize certain aspects of clone performance. But we cannot be certain until further—eh?"

A message was being broadcast over the ship's annunciator system. "Attention, all sectors. This is Clone Control. Quadrant four reports that Zor Prime is missing. Repeat, Zor Prime has left his assigned sector. All guard units begin search pattern sigma. Security leaders contact Clone Control at once."

Musica's attempts to drown her grief in her songs were unsuccessful. Even the accompaniment of her sisters on spinet and lute couldn't lift her spirits or erase the image of Bowie from her mind's eye.

At last she hit a dissonant note and turned to them. "I am sorry, sisters, but there come upon me now times when I wish we weren't always together—the Three-Who-Act-as-One. I find myself wondering what it was like *before* the time of the triumvirates, when each individual was able to act independently."

Allegra and Octavia showed their revulsion, crying out at her to be still, but she went on. "A time when we were capable of feeling pleasure, pain, happiness, even loneliness! I wonder what it is like to love."

She bent over her Cosmic Harp, face buried in her hands.

The words of three guards, making a sweep through the chamber, brought her up sharply. In answer to Allegra's question, they explained about the escape of Zor Prime and their search.

I know what I must do now, Musica realized.

Zor Prime wandered aimlessly through the various districts of the flagship's residential sector. He hadn't evaded the search by any conscious effort; he was too disoriented for that.

The ancient stone buildings seemed to fade in and out, to be replaced by scenes of Monument City, so that part of the time he thought dazedly that he was back on Earth. The sun seemed too bright and hot, too intense, overhead. Often he saw Dana coming toward him, beckoning, laughing, so desirable. . . .

A patrolling guard runabout failed to spot him because a veiled figure pulled him back into the darkness of an alley. Zor shook off his trance and saw Musica lower her veil and look up at him hopefully.

So many half images and confused memories assailed him that he lost balance and fell to his hands and knees on the gleaming terrazzo flooring. "Why is my mind so full of nightmares?"

"You are the clone of the original Zor," she said. "In a way, it might be said that you are the only *true* Robotech Master."

With her help, he found the strength to rise again. But just then a bright ray struck him from behind, and he fell once more. Standing behind him were guards, and the Clonemasters, on an antigrav platform.

"It was only a low-gain destabilizer," Jeddar told Musica. "We need the clone for a little while longer."

> *Dear Mom & Dad,*
> *Everything here remains quiet, as always, and I don't know*
> *why you two keep insisting there's bad war news. Take it from me.*
> *As I wrote you before, I'm in a rear-echelon unit that hardly ever*
> *sees any action at all. So I hope you'll excuse me for asking you*
> *both to kindly quit worrying. Especially with Pop in the condition*
> *he is in.*
> *I'm sorry I missed Christmas. There's always next year, after*
> *all. I think I might be able to pull a furlough soon, with things*
> *being so dull around here and all.*
> *Thanks for the fruitcake; it was great.*
>
> *Love,*
> *Your son,*
> *Angelo Dante*

THE ORDER OF THE DAY WAS EXECUTION, AND THE clones with the rifles weren't listening to any ATAC objections about the Geneva Convention. Dana and her squadmates had no room to try anything in the cell; they marched out with hands behind their heads, as per instructions.

Surrounded by guards, the troopers were marched through the detention center and into a side corridor. Without warning, the clones' exacting schedule was interrupted.

A driverless runabout with its engine shrilling came zooming at the lead guards. The triad was knocked high in the air with bone-breaking force, Dana just barely managing to pull back out of the way. In a shower of sparks and metal fragments, the runabout overturned and shrieked to a stop upside down. The first guards were crunched to the floor as the troopers jumped the other three, who seemed paralyzed by what had happened.

It was a short fight, Sean ramming an elbow back into

one rear guard's throat, Angelo crashing the heads of the other two together like cymbals. Even as the 15th was rearming itself from the selection of weapons lying around, Musica came running toward them. "Bowie!"

Louie was delighted to find that one of the guards was carrying the pulse-grenade that he himself had been carrying when he'd been captured. *Okay, Living Protoculture; let's just go another round, what d'ya say?*

In the Memory Management complex, Zor rested, strapped to a padded slab, at an acute angle, nearly standing upright. He was still unconscious, his head encased in a helmet like a metal medusa.

Technician clones were moving precisely, ensuring that no mistake would be made. Zor's original memories, as servant to the Masters, Bioroid warrior, battle lord of the fleet, must be restored to him and integrated with the memories of his time among the Humans. Then the totality of his memory would be comprehensible, and would be shifted to storage banks for further study. The lump of tissue that was the last Zor clone could be disposed of.

Jeddar watched the preparations with satisfaction. He would have been less happy had he seen what was transpiring on an upper tier of the chamber.

On a glass-walled observation deck, a big forearm locked around a guard clone's throat, and the guard was silently removed from active duty. Angelo resisted the temptation to dust off his palms.

Dana and the 15th looked down on the demons' workshop below. She saw what they were doing to Zor and almost gave out a yelp, but Louie shushed her, as he studied the instruments and machinery. He adjusted his tech goggles to detect energies on very subtle levels and looked the lab over like a sniper studying the landscape through a night-vision device.

"Screwy operation," Sean said wryly.

"But convenient," Louie countered. "See those gauges over there? When they hit the top, Zor's memories will all be back in his brain."

Louie indicated a bank of three stacked rectangles. The first was filled, all glowing blue; the second was filling, as if it were a resplendent blue thermostat marking a sudden, incredible heat wave.

The techs had to pry Zor's jaws apart and wedge a mouthpiece between them as the indicators rose. As the third stack filled, he began to convulse. Louie had to hold Dana back from hurling herself through the glassy pane of the observation deck to intervene.

At last a tech clone pronounced, "Full reinstatement of memory is now complete. Reintegration of memory will begin at once—" He was cut off by an intense barrage from above. The tier window and much of the complex's apparatus was shot to bits. Before anybody there could react, the ATACs had dropped to the main floor and had the clones covered.

"Don't anybody move," Dana warned. They could see from her eyes what would happen if they did.

Jeddar and his Clonemasters were more astonished than afraid. This was, after all, their first close encounter with Humans. Behind the raiders came Musica, and Karno was visibly shaken to see her, breathing her name.

In another second, Louie and Angelo freed Zor from his restraints and cranial wiring. The big sergeant got the unconscious clone over his shoulder with ease. As much as Angelo might have berated Zor, Dana noticed that now he glared around furiously at the creatures who had tortured him.

The troopers were so busy making sure that no one on the scene made any hostile moves that they missed the slight motion it took Jeddar to press a button on his wristband. A moment later, a door snapped open and three more guards leapt into the opening.

Everyone opened fire simultaneously, and those guards who were already in the lab took the opportunity to spring for cover, as did the Clonemasters, the ATACs, and Musica. The energy bolts crashed and flashed; the air began heating up at once. Shots set off eruptions of power from the complex's systemry.

"I believe you've gone mad, Musica!" Karno called to her over the din of the firefight. "What have these monsters done to you to make you a traitor to your own kind?"

Musica, flustered, didn't know how to explain except to say, "Zor is their friend; they're saving him!"

Then Bowie was towing her along. "We're getting out of here!"

Intense fire from the 15th had cleared the doorway; three guards lay dead or dying there. With practiced calm and precision, the five troopers fired as they moved. The remaining enemy had no choice but to keep their heads down, only able to risk the occasional shot.

There was another runabout outside the complex; in a moment, the escapees were roaring away, with Dana and Sean keeping up a high volume of fire to make sure no one followed or tried for a parting shot.

Released from the grip of the mind apparatus, Zor began to stir, then came around. Dana was overjoyed and stopped shooting long enough to gush about how happy she was, but Angelo, at the controls, growled, "Secure that hearts-and-flowers crap! We've still gotta find ourselves a way outta this joint, remember?"

At that moment three red Bioroids appeared, skimming along close to the ceiling of the high central passageway in which the runabout was traveling. Angelo managed to dodge their first bolts, nearly smearing the vehicle along the nearby wall, then made a desperate turn into a side way, losing the enemy mecha for the moment.

"We've got to get back to the Hovertanks!" Dana yelled over the wind of their passage.

"I'm workin' on it, ma'am."

She consulted the tiny sensor Latell had given her. "Take that next right!" Perhaps they could retrace their steps from the control center, which Musica had pointed out along the way.

They slewed and hairpin-turned and blasted along, coming around a corner only to run head-on into another triad of guards. Disinclined to stop, Angelo gritted his teeth and slammed into them, hurling two to either side, slamming the middle one to the floor.

But the impact made the runabout defy its controls. It hit a stanchion, bounced back the other way while Angelo fired retros desperately, then hit the floor surface and slowly upended. Its occupants were spilled out and it came to a final rest with a clang and crunch.

Dana shook her head, looking up. Directly before her was an open hatchway, and beyond—"Look! It's the central control area!" The housing in which the Living Protoculture was situated was closed, protecting it.

For the moment.

They heard Hovercraft approaching and scattered to find concealment in the center. In another few seconds, the three reds settled in for a landing, dismounting and scanning the area.

Seeing the Bioroids sparked something in Zor's still-disorganized memory. He turned to Musica, who crouched with him under a huge conduit. "Why did the Masters send me to Earth in the first place?" he whispered. Somehow he knew that she, Mistress of the music that was part of the Masters' power over their realm, could answer.

She looked at him with infinite sadness. "You were their eyes and ears. You were sent to Earth as a spy," she mouthed the words more than whispered them. "They planted a neuro-sensor in your brain. You weren't even aware of what you were doing, Zor!"

The entire center, the entire ship, began thrumming with a peculiar vibration, something that made their hair stand on end. The Bioroids cocked their heads, registering it.

"It's a battle alert," Musica mouthed to the ATACs. "Your forces must be attacking us!"

"Time to make our move," Dana said. "We take out this control center, whatever it costs, understood? Otherwise Emerson won't have a chance." With a little luck, Louie could figure out some way to put it out of commission. But first the reds had to go.

The 15th troopers fanned out, firing at the Bioroids, dodging from cover, heading for the Living Protoculture. They kept close to the systemry, shooting from its protection. The enemy mecha seemed reluctant to fire, enduring the minor consequences of the small arms fire rather than risk damaging the ship's core. One was angling for a clear shot at them; Louie reluctantly used his pulse grenade on it, but only staggered it instead of putting it out of the fight.

Only Zor and Musica remained behind, she stunned by what was happening, he immobilized by surfacing memories. Then Zor found himself remembering, remembering much. His gaze traveled to the 15th's commanding officer.

Dana...

He knew what he had to do. He crept away to one side, getting clear of the shooting.

At the same time, Musica was coming to a decision. *There isn't much time. The ship will be destroyed soon. I must get to the barrier control!*

She raced for the stairs that wound up around the housing that protected the Protoculture. Bowie, seeing her go, yelled her name and sprinted after.

Musica ran like a deer up the broad steps. But she was in the open, and a Bioroid risked a shot as she neared the top. At the same moment, a bolt from Angelo's weapon hit the red's discus gun; its discharge hit the housing near Musica, missing her, but dazing her and damaging the housing.

In a moment, Bowie was at her side. "Bowie, the barrier! It *must* be deactivated!"

He nodded, and sprang up the last few steps to the control panel she had been trying to reach. The 15th was pitching at the reds with everything they had, and the damage to the housing kept the reds from attempting another shot at Musica or Bowie.

At her direction, he pushed a button, pulled down on the gleaming lever that appeared in response to that. A world-shaking hooting rose above the first alarms and even the firefight. "Hurry!" she called to him. "We must go!"

The Bioroids were at a terrible disadvantage since it was forbidden by the unseen Masters to fire any shot that might endanger the ship's systemry. The ATACs had been quick to exploit this fact; five rifles were a lot of firepower if the users knew where to aim, and the troopers had had plenty of practice at hitting faceplates.

As Bowie helped Musica down from the steps, the last Bioroid tottered backward and came to rest leaning against the bulkhead. The fugitives raced into the passageway, but another trio of reds dropped from nowhere, blocking their way. The rifles were all but exhausted, and there was no hiding behind systemry now. The leader took dead aim with its discus handgun—

The gun and the arm blew apart in an eruption that almost knocked them flat on their backs. Jetting down the passageway behind them came a well-remembered red on its Hovercraft.

"Go get 'em, Zor!" Dana cheered.

Zor was still the greatest battle lord in the enemy fleet. He dodged the other reds' blasts deftly, firing with great accuracy all the while. He leapt his mecha from the Hovercraft, and let the saucer-platform crash into them, destroying his opponents in a collision that half-deafened the fugitives.

Zor's Bioroid landed with a deck-shaking impact. "Dana, you and the others go ahead; the Hovertanks are that way, through there. I'll stay here and delay any further pursuit." His voice was the voice of the Zor they had served with, not the eerie, indrawn-breath voice of the Masters' slave.

"Huh!" Angelo said, with something like approval.

"We'll be waiting for you," Dana said somberly.

There was no other option; the escapees dashed on. Zor turned to wait patiently. It didn't take long; three groups of Triumviroids raced into view on Hovercraft. Zor took aim and began firing.

Astoundingly, the tanks were just as the 15th had left them.

"But what good'll they do us?" Angelo asked, as the squad fired up their mecha. "There's no way we can reach Emerson on just tank thrusters!"

"Don't you think I know that?" Dana snapped. With their mecha in tank mode, the 15th followed her as she tried to retrace the route she had taken on her first evasive dash with Bowie and Louie.

At last she found what she was searching for, a sort of

cul-de-sac compartment piled high with salvaged components and disabled equipment. It was obvious that a lot of repair work was done there as well.

The tanks stopped, cannon trained on the only hatchway. The troopers rose to stand in their cockpit-turrets. Dana pointed to a rank of Hovercraft that had seen better days.

"Louie, you've got to find us the five best out of those, and make sure they'll get us to Emerson."

Easy for you to say! he thought. Was she crazy, or just ignorant? "Lieutenant, I—"

"I don't want to hear it! I'm not talking about winning a Formula X race; we'll only need them for a few minutes. If we're not back with the fleet by that time, it won't make any difference."

Aboard his flagship, Emerson had long since reached the conclusion his subordinates were warily expressing. The Earth forces were going at the Masters with hammer and tongs once more, but couldn't take the beating they were getting for much longer.

There was no sign of the 15th and no radio contact. Emerson ordered that the fleet prepare to withdraw, that the A-JACs prepare to return to their transports. When Lieutenant Crystal objected, he dressed her down brusquely, and reiterated his orders.

But the whole time, he thought, *Bowie. Dana.* And he knew the other names as well.

CHAPTER
FOURTEEN

Bowie, life in danger with you is
so much more than
Life without you would be
even if death strikes its chord

Musica, "End of the Old Songs"

WHILE LOUIE DID HIS WIZARD-OF-ROBOTECH number, Dana and the others, with Musica's help, discovered the controls that opened the shaft overhead. The ATACs redonned their armor, and Bowie made sure his canopy was tight; Musica had no other protection.

In Battloid mode, the 15th boarded the Hovercraft. Dana's *Valkyrie* reached out a huge finger to flick a Bioroid-scale switch. The shaft hatch opened, triggering the closing of emergency doors in the passageway leading to the cul-de-sac. The 15th rose amid a storm of junk and debris hurled upward by the escaping atmosphere.

It was the first and last time such an unlikely combination of Robotechnology took place. Weaving through volleys from their own forces, the ATACs started their survival run. There was still no sign of the red Bioroid, and it was too late to turn back.

* * *

Unstoppable, unbeatable, Zor not only sent his opponents reeling back, but actually fought his way forward towards the control center.

Knowing all the Triumviroids' weaknesses, he was also their superior in experience and speed and adaptability, master of virtuoso tactics they had never even had time to learn. He had left a trail of death and destruction through the flagship's passageways.

Now Zor stood before the Living Protoculture, which still hid within its armored cylinder. He knew, though, that it was too weak to defend itself, depleted and wounded by the battle raging through the ship. He felt that it sensed its impending destruction.

I betrayed my friends. Just as it happened so long ago, with the Invid! Am I damned, doomed to live this agony over and over? The red Bioroid raised its discus weapon and aimed at the cylinder. Fire and smoke rose around it.

And now my only way to redeem myself is by betraying my people. Everything I touch turns to ashes. So be it.

Dana, good-bye!

He triggered the weapon just as the cylinder slid open, and the Living Protoculture lashed out in a last desperate effort to save itself.

The explosion was bigger than anything ever seen from a mother ship before; an entire section of the stupendous vessel was simply vaporized, its edges pushed outward as the Main Control section detonated.

"You stupid alien," Dana said in a small voice, looking back at it. "You said you'd catch up."

"I'm truly sorry, Dana," Angelo fumbled, not used to soft words. "I—I know you were fond of him. And he liked you a lot, I could tell."

Sean was already in contact with Emerson's fleet. The 15th hadn't beaten the clock by much; they just about had enough time and fuel to catch the withdrawing strikeforce.

Louie also watched the explosion. He adjusted his tech

goggles, trying to see what information they might offer. He did a slight double take, changed magnification and spectrum bands, and looked again. "Lieutenant? I think you better check this out."

It was beginning to be visible to the naked eye against the glare of the explosion so close behind it—a form resolving itself into a red Bioroid on a Hovercraft.

"It's him!" Dana's heart had never been so full. At first it looked as if Zor was helping along a wounded red, but then they saw that he had his Battloid clasped to him.

"Whaddaya know," Angelo drawled. "He even brought along a change of clothes."

Zor, racing to overtake them, wondered about the ways of fate, and the Shapings of the Protoculture. The last effort of the living mass that served the Masters had only contained the inevitable explosion for scant seconds—enough time for him to retrieve his tank and find a Hovercraft and flee.

But he was still an alien in a strange land. He wondered if what waited ahead would be any better than what he left behind.

The Masters knew their flagship was doomed.

Invader assault ships, forward command ships, and the other smaller craft that were berthed in the Masters' flagship took aboard as many clones as they could in the little time they had left. But because the Masters were impatient to get to safety and unwilling to risk themselves or their possessions for the sake of unstable clones, many were left behind. And so they abandoned their faithful slaves.

In one evacuation ship, Allegra and Octavia clung to each other, Karno staring out the viewport furiously as explosion after explosion rocked the flagship.

Musica! the two sisters sent out the silent, plaintive cry.

In the cockpit of the *Re-Tread*, Musica gasped. But when Bowie asked what was wrong, she just shook her head and said it was nothing.

"The whole thing's gonna blow!" he yelled excitedly.

She turned in time to see blue, concentric rings leap out

from the flapship. Then a star grew from it, hurling forth a gaseous cloud.

Farewell, my sisters, she thought, as the 15th got ready to link up with Emerson's fleet.

While Emerson elected to withdraw to the ALUCE base with the main body of his command, damaged vessels and as many of the casualties as possible made a run for Earth. One such vessel was the one that happened to have picked up Dana and her companions.

In the tremendous confusion, it wasn't hard to smuggle Musica to a place of temporary safety, but that left the problem of Fokker Base, and debarkation. Fortunately, the rest of the 15th, having been separated from them, were on another ship, bound for ALUCE base with Emerson's main force, leaving fewer to keep the secret. Surprisingly, Angelo was loudest among those voices raised to protect the Mistress of the Cosmic Harp.

"We can't let the GMP get her! Remember what they did to Zor, all that testing and probing and scanning, like he was some kinda animal?" It was already a matter of barely spoken agreement that there would be no mention to Southern Cross Command of Zor's temporary defection, at least for the time being.

Dana was calmer. "Don't worry; anybody who messes with Musica is going to have to mess with us first."

"Blast him!" Leonard bellowed in Southern Cross Army HQ. "I question Emerson's commitment! I question his sanity!"

It was all for the benefit of UEG observers who were on the scene; Leonard knew his words would reach Moran and the rest of the council promptly. "The enemy fleet still has five fully operational mother ships, and yet he withdraws!"

But Leonard was upset for another reason. Now he could no longer fall back on Emerson's genius and leadership. There was no one to whom he could delegate authority; the defense of Earth, the responsibility and the culpability, fell squarely on him. He was unsure now; his attitude toward Emerson's absence in the field was very different.

Zor had passed out just after being brought aboard the transport and had suffered the injuries to justify it. Dana had no choice but to turn him over to a med team and hope he would keep the secret of what had happened in the flagship, as the 15th would keep it.

The ambulance with Zor in it had barely pulled away when Nova Satori showed up. "Welcome back, Dana. What —what did they say about Zor?"

They hadn't spoken to one another since Komodo's death. They felt uneasy in each other's company.

"He'll recover. Listen, Nova, I'm really busy right now, so if you don't mind . . ."

That kind of evasiveness from the 15th's CO set off alarm bells in Nova's head. *Now* what were these eight balls up to?

Musica held back panic, enclosed by armor that seemed ready to crush her, fearful of what life among Humans might hold. Oddly enough, it wasn't any of those, or the danger of exposure, that beset her the worst just then. Instead, it was a comparatively little thing, the sickly-sweet, rubbery smell of the ATAC helmet's breather mask; she was nauseous, not sure how long she could control herself. The 15th, long since oblivious to the smell, had forgotten how it sometimes affected boot trainees.

She did her best to be brave, but wasn't sure she was up to it.

"Looks like somebody else took a hit, too." Louie and Angelo, suit helmets doffed, were carrying the stretcher themselves. As they passed Nova, they both suddenly put on expressions more appropriate to a poker game than a homecoming.

Nothing they could say could keep Nova from getting to the stretcher, throwing back the blanket. Dana sighed, and took off the reclining trooper's helmet when Nova threatened to do it herself.

Sean Phillips smiled up at her. "Shrapnel, right in the big toe, can ya believe it? But I still qualify for a medal and recuperative leave, and it *does* smart, and—"

Nova upended the stretcher and walked away. Dana was yelling at the few 15th troopers around her—her core group —to get busy and off-load the Hovertanks, and she even gave Sean a swift kick. Then she barked at another, "You, too! Hurry along there, Private Doppler! Double time!"

Then they had disappeared back into the transport. Nova stalked away angrily, but stopped suddenly. "'Doppler'?"

Minutes later, GI personnel staff was confirming that the only Private Doppler was a 15th trooper who had died during the assault that had temporarily brought down the mother ship, weeks before.

Who could Dana be hiding, if that's what she's doing? The only possibility seemed too farfetched. Even Dana wouldn't be *that* crazy.

"Here: Lemme take a look at you." Dana felt only mild jealousy that Musica looked better in one of her outfits than Dana herself.

Musica turned 180 degrees self-consciously. Her green hair would fit in with current Earth fads; caught back as it was in a heavy clip, nearly reaching her waist, it was gorgeous. "But—these garments expose my legs."

"With legs like yours, Musica, I wouldn't let it bother you. See for yourself, in the mirror."

Musica did, pulling at the puffy sleeves of the pink blouse, the hem of the full skirt. "Why is it whenever *I* wear something like that it makes me look about ten years old?" Dana wondered aloud.

They decided to let Bowie enter at last and cast his vote. It took him a while to find words, and when he did all he could say was, "I'll write a song about it." Musica's face shone.

Angelo called from the hospital to tell them Zor was being released. The rest of the 15th was in one of the ships that had gone to ALUCE with Emerson, and had been seconded to the 10th ATAC squad, another Hovertank unit.

Since the 15th was badly under strength, it wasn't on alert or standby; Dana decided that a party was in order.

"Get Zor over to the Moon of Havana by eight, okay, Angie? We'll meet you there."

It was good to be alive.

In the mother ship to which the Masters had withdrawn when their own flagship was atomized, Allegra and Octavia were thrust into a detention area.

They were still in shock. Muse clones simply weren't treated this way!

But they saw that much had changed, and this wrath of the Masters was only part of it.

Deprived of their instruments and, in Musica's absence, a vital part of themselves, they trudged into the cheerless and impersonal holding area. The clones confined there were dispirited and lethargic.

The two Muses huddled together in a corner, fearful of what might come next. "It's all because of Musica," Allegra said bitterly. "She abandoned us and betrayed her own people! They can't understand that her sins aren't ours, so they've cast us away in here!"

"Allegra—"

But she cut Octavia off. "I feel—" Allegra made a vague, angry gesture, to express the rage for which she had no word.

"Musica is our sister; we three are one," Octavia said soothingly. But she was troubled. Didn't Allegra see that she was falling victim to the same malady that had claimed Musica? Apparently, the sickness called "emotion" had more than one symptom.

The party started with a toast to the ATACs who had been killed or wounded in the battle. Then, one to the members of the 15th who had been redeployed to ALUCE. After that, life, love, and happiness were the subjects. The ATAC troopers had no urge to toast victory or rehash the battle—it was time to forget the war for a while.

The manager gave the 15th a great table, a circular banquette. Soon Bowie was at the Moon of Havana's piano. Musica sat, absorbed in his playing. And the songs he played were new, like nothing she had ever heard or thought of before! And he was *making some of it up as he went along*! These Humans were truly astonishing.

Things were going fine until they realized Nova Satori was standing in front of their table. Dana couldn't think of anything to do but invite her to sit down.

Nova sat, and turned to Musica. "I don't believe we've met. I'm Lieutenant Nova Satori of the GMP. You are . . . ?"

Musica looked nervously to Dana for rescue. "Friend of Bowie's," Dana replied. "We haven't been able to get her to say 'boo' all night. Another musician—plays the ukulele or something like that, I think he said."

Nova was about to press Musica some more, when Dana interjected, "What d'you hear from Dennis, Nova?"

That shook Nova off the track. "I—he's part of the force that went to ALUCE with General Emerson. He, he got in touch on a back-channel and said he's all right."

Before Nova could go back to her interrogation, Bowie finished a number and the crowd's uproar drowned her out. Bowie was forced to do an encore. Musica floated on the sounds he made, but she couldn't help thinking, *If my sisters were here, we would play them music of great beauty, too!*

She was suddenly filled with emptiness. She hung her head, shaking it so that the green hair swayed. "Oh, sisters, forgive me!" She said it low, so the policewoman wouldn't hear.

"No, Musica," Zor, next to her, countered quietly. "Betrayal cannot be forgiven. I am beyond forgiveness and so are you."

His memories were merging, surfacing, becoming available to his conscious mind. He was becoming the original Zor, with all the regrets and despair. He was thinking, too, of that awful final moment, when he destroyed the flagship, and the deaths of uncounted defenseless clones—no, *people*!

Angelo didn't interfere, for the moment. He saw how living among Humans was both a joy and a torment to Musica, a lot like a kid's story he remembered, *The Little Mermaid*. Funny how that just popped up; he hadn't thought of it for decades.

Sean grabbed the shoulder of Zor's torso harness. "Hey, modulate, there, trooper!" But Zor wrenched himself loose and strode from the nightclub.

Musica, watching him go, began to slump into a faint. Sean and Louie were quick to catch her. As tactical withdrawals went, dropping off Musica at her nonexistent apartment was a little thin, but it was all Dana could come up with.

Nova watched the 15th leave, just barely having kept them from sticking her with the check. *Go ahead and play out your hand, Dana. You haven't got much left.*

CHAPTER
FIFTEEN

Hey, Billy!
You said you owed me one, and if I needed a favor, just ask.
Okay.
Things are a little tight right now, and living on deuce private's pay is tougher than I remembered. You and I know each other, so you'll forgive me if I call the debt in.
Things've gotten strange here, but when was it otherwise? By the way: that kid they gave my 15th squad to? She could've been worse.
Anyway, I'm gonna need some money and I'm gonna need some favors. We've got the Plague of Love around here.

Your old pal,
Sean Phillips

SNEAKING MUSICA BACK ONTO THE BASE AND THE barracks compound wasn't too hard. The ATACs were a little worried about Nova, but they forgot about that when they saw Bowie and Musica embrace.

It's a good thing we've got some vacant quarters available, Dana thought. She was thinking more and more these days of how well Sean adjusted to losing his commission and hoped she could be as upbeat once they busted her. Bowie and Musica's being together seemed, against all expectation, like something that justified that risk.

Then a commotion off to one side had the rest realizing that Zor had wandered off and Angelo had followed. "What d'ya *mean*, you shoulda stayed on the mother ship?"

Zor was leaning against a tree, eyes to the grass, arms folded. He answered in a low voice, "It was where I belonged."

"And you'd've been killed." Angelo's fists were on his

hips. He didn't look aside as the other ATACs and Musica came up.

"That's exactly my point. Besides, then I'd merit a hero's funeral, isn't that right? A golden opportunity for you to display those precious emotions of yours—weeping for the fallen comrade, and all that."

Angelo felt betrayed. He had doubted Zor from the beginning, had seen him turn traitor—then come back to his senses and fly right again. He had carried Zor over his own shoulder, saved Zor as Zor had saved him.

Zor was one of the 15th, and it wasn't something Angelo granted lightly. And now Zor was spurning that, making a fool of the sergeant.

But worse, infinitely worse, Zor was saying that Angelo *liked* grieving for dead buddies, got some kind of sick charge out of the most wrenching pain the sergeant knew. It insulted Angelo and, more, made a sham of the deaths of brave men and women.

One minute a red tide was rising up Angelo's neck and face; the next, Zor was flat on the ground with a split lip.

Dana knew words weren't going to do much good, so she got in Angelo's way and threw a straight right to the sergeant's sternum. It was like punching a bus tire, but it halted him—more through shock than pain.

"Get up. You ain't hurt. Yet," Angelo told Zor.

Zor rose, rubbing his jaw. "So I'm to be happy that I'm alive to go out and kill or be killed again tomorrow?"

Dana pushed Angelo away when he would have gone at Zor again. "Back off! That's an order!" She could hear Musica running off, sobbing, and Bowie going after her, but Dana had no time for that lesser crisis at the moment.

She turned to Zor. "You think it's going to make you feel better to get us to hate you? It won't! Quit punishing yourself and quit trying to get Angie to do it for you! Whatever's in your past is over with! And besides, you had no control over what you did; we all know that. Zor, it's time to let all of that go, and begin again."

He looked down at her as if seeing her for the first time:

just an uncivilized Micronian, scarcely more than a wild animal by the standards of the Robotech Masters. Where was she finding these words? What were the sources of this wisdom?

But his inner torment gave him the strength to resist her. "Begin what? Dana, *it will always be the same! This incarnation, like all the others. That is my punishment! I can't even trust my own mind and I'm tired. I'm so tired of it all!*"

He didn't even know why he had escaped the flagship's destruction at the last moment; some survival reflex had taken over. He had begun regretting it at once.

He brushed past them. When Angelo snarled some objection, he shot back, "Just leave me alone! It's my problem, and I'll deal with it."

"Bowie, I'm so sorry. I feel that this is all my fault." Musica said, tears rolling down her face.

"Sorry that we survived, Musica? Sorry that you and I are together?"

"Oh, no! But—why am I so unhappy? Why is there pain all around us?"

"Because our people are at war. But we can't let that keep us from loving each other!"

He took her in his arms. She was slightly taller, laying her head on his shoulder. "You and I will be different," he told her. "We'll be an island of peace in the middle of all this hatred and misery. We'll have each other."

"Her name is Musica. You'll find her at the barracks of the Fifteenth ATAC squad."

Nova couldn't believe what she was hearing; she looked at the phone handset as if it were an alien artifact. Around her, the bustle and buzz of Global Military Police HQ seemed to fade. "You mean the girl I saw at the Moon of Havana?"

"I suggest you apprehend her as soon as possible," the firm male voice said, "before she manages to—"

"Just hold on. Who *is* this?"

"Can't you guess, Nova?"

"*Zor?* Listen, what's this all ab—"

But he had hung up.

Dana, deciding it was time to make more concrete contingency plans, was about to knock at the door of her own quarters when she stopped, transfixed.

It was a sound so ethereal that at first she didn't recognize it as a Human voice. Then she knew Musica was singing, and that the Muse herself was an instrument as hypnotic and magnificent as the Cosmic Harp. The notes soared, evoking emotions both familiar and unknown.

> "come, let me show you
> our common bond
> it's the reason that we live
> Flower, let me hold you
> we depend upon
> Power that you give...."

She sang of the galaxies, of the depths, of the long story of the eons, and Dana found herself seeing stars swarm before her eyes. Musica's voice moved her with powerful tidal forces of feeling, giving her Visions.

She sensed a great epoch unfolding, something about Zor and a frightening but tragic alien race and—things just beyond the realm of her perception.

> "we should protect the seed
> or we could all fade away
> Flower of Life
> Flower of Life
> Flower..."

Outside, Zor turned to hear the siren song. Then he continued on his way to await Nova.

Dana saw worlds from other star systems. She saw wonders and horrors. It seemed that the voice coming from the other side of the door had split into three, harmonious and almost identical, flawlessly matched and perfect.

She saw something from her own dreams and visions: a triad of three-petaled flowers of a delicate coral color, drifting through the air, trailing long stamens. The flowers themselves grew in a Triumvirate. One drifted past, brushing her cheek. She looked down at it in amazement, where it rested on the corridor floor.

The song faded; the Flower disappeared. Even as Dana blinked herself back to full awareness, many of the things she had envisioned faded from her memory, and she was left with vague shadows of recollection.

She lunged into her quarters. Bowie was still on the bed, Musica by the window.

"What was that?" Dana burst out. "Musica, you sang something about—the Flower of Life, was that it?"

"Yes, Dana. That is right."

Dana turned to Bowie. "I'm *sure* that's the flower we found in the ruins of the SDF-1! The day we sneaked in there, remember? Those plants that moved by themselves?"

How could he forget? It was like some malign greenhouse, something that didn't belong on Earth, that belonged on no sane world. "And you think there's a connection?" He didn't sound excited about it, just alarmed.

"Could that be it, Musica?" Dana asked. "Could that be what the war is all about?"

"The Robotech Masters have not given it to me to know that, Dana, but for your sake, I hope there are no Flowers of Life here. They are often accompanied by great evil."

Louie Nichols burst into the room. "Read it and weep! Nova's downstairs with a bunch of GMP gorillas and she wants to see you, Dana."

"It'll be all right," Dana told the frightened Musica and the grim Bowie. "C'mon, Louie; let's go see what the Gimps want."

"Unauthorized person in the barracks?" Dana gave Nova her best wide-eyed look. "What makes you think there's one around here?"

"Zor told me."

The odds looked bad. The GMP apes were armed, and outnumbered the unarmed ATACs. *Maybe there'll just be time for Angie to finish what he started on Zor.*

Zor, for his part, stood studying the floor, ready to accept their loathing—anticipating it. Dana wondered if Zor's treachery was committed to make it easier for him to end his own life or perhaps, commit some even worse betrayal.

Dana turned back to Nova. "She saved our lives. When it comes right down to it, Musica saved the whole fleet."

"Tell it to the brass."

"Sure, Nova, while they're busy sticking electrodes in her ears and trying to light her up like an arcade game. Would it help to tell you she and Bowie love each other?"

Dana knew it wouldn't—not now, with all the GMP goons standing around as witnesses. But she wanted Nova to know just how much harm she was doing, every bit of it.

"I always thought, as Gimps went, you were the exception to the rule, Nova, but I see now: you fit in just fine! C'mon; let's go."

Dana turned to lead Nova and her squad upstairs. She had hoped she could hide Musica until Rolf Emerson could get back from ALUCE and intercede. All that was hopeless now. Maybe Dana could go outside the chain of command, appeal directly to the UEG council? Her career was over either way.

Zor was standing near the stairs. Dana gave him one brief, chilly glance. "You had the chance to do something good and kind for a change. It might have made up for a lot of the stuff that's torturing you so, did you ever think of *that*?"

Zor put on a sardonic look, but what she had said went through him like a dagger of ice.

Nova got her troops ready, and they went through the door of Dana's quarters in a SWAT-style rush, guns ready. The balcony door was open, the curtain wafting gently on the night breeze.

The Gimps searched the place just to be sure, but it was easy to see their hearts weren't in it; they hardly even busted anything up.

Dana stood looking out at the night and wondered where Bowie and Musica could possibly find refuge in such a world.

Bowie got them over a compound wall and across a road, yanking her into the bushes out of the sudden glare of a GMP patrol's headlights. They plunged deeper into the forest.

They ran through the darkness hand in hand; her feet were cut and bruised, branches and rocks seemed to lie in wait for her. But she didn't complain; Bowie had enough to worry about as it was.

Musica had lived her entire life in the confined structures of the Robotech Masters and she fought back the agoraphobia that beset her now. The darkness made that a little easier, but she wondered how she would cope when the sun came up again.

An abrupt glare turned the whole world black and harsh white. A sound like the end of the Universe, coming with a concussion that shook the ground, made her lose balance again. She was sure that the GMP had used some sort of ultimate Robotech weapon, that the final battle with the Masters had come, or that the Earthlings were willing to wipe out an entire region of their planet to make sure she was dead.

Bowie helped her up. "Just thunder and lightning," he said. "Harmless electric discharge." *Unless it hits us, or a tree near us*, he amended to himself, but there was no point in worrying her. They ran on.

A winged creature of some sort gave a hateful caw and took to the air on the next lightning strike. And then, astoundingly, droplets of freezing-cold water were falling on Musica from out of the sky. She knew about condensation in a cerebral way, but this was her first experience with it.

It seemed a planet that was infinitely cruel; it seemed she had followed Bowie Grant into hell. But her hand was in his, and she recalled how bleak and pointless life without him had been. She steeled herself and went on.

"Don't expect us to do your dirty work for you," Dana told Zor in the unit ready-room, as the torrential rain struck the windows. "If you want to be punished, go do it yourself."

She didn't know what to feel about him anymore. There was still, somewhere, the love she felt for him, the yearning to stand by him and to take away the pain. But he had shown that he was just too good at keeping anyone from doing that. Dana wasn't quite ready to let him have the victory of making her hate him, but she despaired, feeling that soon he would win.

"At least he remembered his duty, Lieutenant," Nova said as she entered, shaking rainwater off her cloak. Her Gimps were still beating the bushes for the two fugitives, but she knew it was in vain; this called for more extreme measures.

Zor took advantage of the distraction to wander out, as Dana and Nova faced off. Dana was mounting some good arguments on Musica's behalf, but Nova cut through it with the news that the ATAC commanding general had granted Nova temporary operational control of the 15th.

"At first light, you and your unit *will* begin search operations, apprehend Grant and the alien, and place them under close arrest, is that clear enough for you, Sterling? In the meantime, I will consult with the Judge Advocate General's office with regard to court-martial proceedings against you and your men."

Just when Musica had resigned herself to dying at Bowie's side in the endless forest, lights appeared ahead—an outlying army equipment storage facility. Bowie left her for a moment, disappeared into the rain, and came back mounted on a Hovercycle.

He pulled her on, and they jetted off through the driving rain, headlights coming alight behind them as jeeps took up a pursuit. It was a mad chase over benighted roads that even the cycle's headlights couldn't seem to light. Bowie's major advantage was that mud and slick road conditions didn't matter much to a surface-effect vehicle.

But Musica was unused to riding and couldn't help him by leaning correctly on the turns. They got a lead on the posse, staying ahead by one or two bends in the road, but just about the time he was assuring her that he was a past master at Hovercycle racing, he snagged a branch and almost rammed a tree.

As it was, they slewed through a screen of bushes, and he laid the sky-scooter down in a not-quite-controlled fall that sent them both tumbling.

It turned out to be a blessing in disguise, because the pursuing jeeps roared on by. Bowie crept over to where Musica lay and couldn't breathe until he saw that she was all right.

He got her under the shelter of a tree, the lightning having stopped. The rain was letting up a bit; he drew her to him, opening his jacket, trying to warm her.

"Bowie . . ." She sounded so exhausted. "Lying here like this, I can feel your heart beating against mine. It's such beautiful music; I wish we could stay like this forever."

He felt such fear for her, such apprehension about the future, the pain of the fall, and the cold and damp of the night. It astounded him how much of that suffering and unhappiness she took away with a kiss.

* * *

"Zand, I haven't the time for—"

"Yes you have, Mr. Chairman." Zand didn't move out of Moran's way. "I'll be brief."

Even with the flock of squawking flacks and bureaucrats trailing him, waiting for the chance to get the ear of the chairman of the UEG, Moran didn't brush Zand aside.

He saw by the look in Zand's strange, liquid-black eyes that the Robotech genius wouldn't stand for it. Moran made a casual-seeming gesture of the hand; in seconds, his security people had the followers fended back, and Moran, Zand, and Zand's aide were ushered into an empty conference room.

Zand saw no reason for preamble. "There's word that an alien woman has been smuggled back to Earth and that your people are looking for her so that you can use her as a peace envoy. Don't do that, Mr. Chairman."

Chairman Moran—white-haired, white-mustached, kind old Uncle Pat, as some commentators called him—frowned. "That's not for you to say."

Zand's vacuous-faced, unobtrusive aide had taken a seat off to one side. Now Zand shot him a look. Russo leapt to his feet. Suddenly, instead of a vacant-eyed hound, he was once more the senator, the kingmaker and wheeler-dealer he had been back in the days of the old UEDC, despite the persona that fooled younger people.

"'Lo, Patrick," he said. "You know what the boss, here, wants." It was as if he were still wearing pinky rings, and carrying a long Havana cigar. "Listen: You've gotta start following that party line, fella."

Zand concealed his own fascination with Russo's transformation. In the wake of the terrible attack of Dolza, at the end of the war with the Zentraedi (but before the attack of Khyron), Russo had simply been listed as missing and presumed dead.

It was Zand's good luck to discover him, babbling and insane, in a refugee center: the man who knew most of the secrets of the Earth's government, and had leverage against so many rulers and would-be rulers. Zand's Protoculture powers put Russo under his control with a mere pulse of thought.

Russo was still talking in that back-room-boys voice. "Paddy! Patto! We're not asking you *not* to make the offer, fella! We're just asking you, man to man, to hold off a while."

"We don't have a while—" Moran began.

"There's time," Russo said, a little more sternly. "Time for Doc Zand, here, to get a better deal! But if *you* wanna play hardball, *we* can play hardball."

Moran was looking at him, but not saying anything. Russo went on, "Those fingerprints are probably still on file in the vaults down in Rio, Pat; I think *they* survived the war. And what about that prosecutor? D'you think his skeleton is still there?"

Zand silently congratulated himself on having salvaged what was left of Russo's brain and the body it came in. The kingpin of prewar politics was a henchman devoutly to be grateful for.

"How wouldja like the opposition party to force a confidence vote?" Russo hinted darkly. Zand was pleased with the look on Moran's face.

"Not now. We could have peace, I think—"

Russo almost pounced at Moran. "You still can, Pat! We're not saying you can't! We're just saying: Give us until tomorrow. Is that so much to ask? The peace you make could be better than anything you ever imagined! My friend, if you want your place in the hist'ry books, this is the time to be brave!" Russo subsided just the right amount. "But you gotta play along."

Moran was lost in thought for a second; his opposition would certainly be able to call for a vote of confidence if Russo's secrets were made known. Now, of all times! *How did I get involved in such terrible things*, Moran wondered a little dazedly, *trying to do good?* "Very well, but only twenty-four hours."

He touched a timer function on his watch; the twenty-four hours began.

"You'll never regret it, Paddy," Russo said. Moran made a noncommittal sound and moved for the door.

With his hand on the knob, he swung around to Zand, indicating Russo. "Keep that thing away from me, is that understood?"

Zand snapped his fingers, but more importantly, sent out a mental signal. The thing that had been Senator Russo went blank-faced again and sat down in the nearest chair.

Moran gave a fatigued, grudging nod, and went off to stick his finger, his head, his body into the hole in the dike.

CHAPTER
SIXTEEN

Little Protoculture Leaf,
Waiting for our palates,
Where will you take us?
Flower of Life!
Treat us well!

Ancient song of the autotones of Optera

HOVERTANKS WERE NOT THE SORT OF TRANSPORTA-
tion appropriate to stalking fugitives in the wilds, so the 15th
took out two jeeps and got ready to go afield.

There was something like a picnic air to it; any break
from combat and combat alert was to be enjoyed, and nobody really thought Dana was going to hand Bowie and Musica over to the GMP, although no one was sure what she
would do. So they loaded up the jeeps with weapons, field
gear, rations, detection equipment, commo apparatus, and
the rest.

At Louie Nichols's tentative inquiry as to whether or not
she had any idea where Bowie might go, Dana hedged. But
she declared, "We play this one by the book. Isn't that what
we've always done?"

Well, no, it wasn't—her words didn't reassure them, but
her sly wink did. The ATACs were a lot happier—except for

Angelo—as they set off, just as the sun came above the horizon.

Above them, Zor watched their departure from the ready-room. At the command of the SCA brass, he was ordered not to accompany the hunters. He thought about the wording of the order, as the jeeps disappeared.

From her vantage point nearby, Nova Satori studied the route the 15th was taking, and revved her Hovercycle.

Protoculture was accessible to the Masters only through the Matrices and the power-supplying masses the Matrices produced. The germinal stage of the Flower of Life was contained in a balance something like that between fusion and gravity in the core of a star.

But eventually, the urge of the Flower of Life to bloom overcame any means of prevention ever devised, and that was happening now. Making matters far worse was the disaster of the loss of the flagship and its Protoculture mass.

The Robotech Masters' options had all been used up; they would have to strike, all-out, at once, or lose the means to strike at all.

"And that is my decision, approved by the council," Supreme Commander Leonard was saying. "We'll launch a final, no-quarter offensive against the alien fleet commencing at thirteen hundred hours today."

All preparations had been made in secret. No one pointed out any of the hundred strategic inadequacies in the plan; at Moon Base ALUCE, Emerson heard the news through a direct commo link to the command center, but made no comment.

"We will drive them from our skies forever or die trying," Leonard finished.

Long, slanting rays of sunlight wakened Musica. She shivered a bit, lying on Bowie's jacket with her own dew-covered one over her, but the day was already becoming warm.

She heard a melodious sound and opened her eyes. On a large open area of water nearby—a smallish lake, but much bigger than anything she had ever seen before—an egret swept in low for a landing. Smaller birds trilled to one another in a natural symphony that delighted and amazed her.

Bowie wasn't next to her. Rubbing her eyes drowsily, she looked around for him and saw the tree under which they had taken shelter the night before. A thrill ran through her as she remembered what had happened between them then, the most beautiful music of all.

The clouds were all gone, making way for a clear blue sky; moisture dripped from the leaves and the air was filled with the scent of renewal. *How could I have thought this planet so awful? It's beautiful, it's magic—oh, I have so much to learn!*

Then she spied him and heard him. Bowie was working on the Hovercycle with tools from its small kit. "Just about ready to go," he said when she called out to him, then he stopped, taking a longer look at her. "You're even more wonderful to look at in the morning than you are at night."

"So are you, Bowie."

In another few minutes they were on the cycle and racing down the road. Musica had never felt so free, so deliriously happy.

Bowie got his bearings, and turned his course for his objective. Soon, the mound that was the burial cairn of SDF-1 came into sight.

Veritechs were launched from Fokker Base while A-JACs were trundled into the transports for the assault. Hatches were run back from missile silos as ground armored and artillery units deployed to defensive positions against enemy counterattack.

"General Emerson, you are aware that the enemy is on the move with his entire fleet, preparing to attack Earth?"

Emerson looked at Leonard's sweating face on the screen. "Yes, sir." Was aware of it, had expected it, and had marshaled all the moon's forces to try to help cope with it.

"You will move at once with all units under your command and engage the enemy, blunting his attack and otherwise bringing your total force to bear against him," Leonard ordered. "You will under no circumstances break off contact or withdraw; you and your contingent are totally committed, do I make myself clear?"

A death warrant wasn't too hard to read. "Yes, sir."

When Leonard signed off, Emerson turned to Colonel Green. "Find Rochelle, please—oh, and Lieutenants Crystal and Brown—and meet me in my office. Pass the word to stand ready; we'll be launching in ten minutes."

Sean was at the wheel, Dana in the 90% seat, lost in thought.

Louie pulled up even with them so that Angelo could yell, "You can stop worrying about what you wanna do with them when you find 'em!"

He was holding a pair of compu-binoculars and he jerked a thumb toward the road behind. "We got a little tail with GMP plates on it. Hovercycle."

"Nova!"

Sean didn't seem disturbed. "Want to lose her? Fasten your seatbelt, ma'am." He tromped the accelerator, and Louie did the same.

At the base of the mound, Musica said, "Are you sure this is the right one? The one where you saw the Flowers of Life?"

There were two others. Under one rested the SDF-2, and under the other the remains of the battlecruiser of Khyron the Backstabber.

"This is the one, I'm certain," Bowie said. Somewhere deep within were the remains of Admiral Henry Gloval, enlisted-rating techs Kim Young, Sammie Porter, and Vanessa Leeds, and Bowie's aunt, Commander Claudia Grant—five names that rang in Earth and Southern Cross history.

"Bowie, this place frightens me." The mound was a high, Human-made butte scraped together from the surrounding countryside to cover the radioactive remains of Earth's one-time defender. The short half-life radiation was safer than it had been fifteen years before, but it still wasn't a place in which to linger long. Still, they had to do what must be done.

"Trust me," he said, taking her hand again. They entered the cave-tunnel he and Dana had found some weeks before.

A few yards in, they made their way over a rock and into an underground corridor. It was a prefab walkway that had been dropped in along with so many tons of rubble and building materials in the frantic effort to seal up the radiation.

It took several reassurances from Bowie to make her believe the bats, spiders, and other creatures rustling around her or scuttling overhead wouldn't hurt her.

The burial material that had been piled here so long ago had been originally slated for installation in a new government building. Ageless, round Buddha-like faces gazed out at the explorers from each pour-formed block. Mushrooms, moss, and fungus were in abundance. Water seeped from the ceiling and walls, to form brackish, vile-smelling pools.

Bowie felt his way along one wall, fingertips brushing through the slime, as Musica clung to his elbow. In time, they spied a light ahead and quickly went toward it.

It was an exit to the space in the center of the mound. Just as they were about to go through, a gust of golden dust, fine as fog, hit them.

"Wha—" Bowie's head reeled and he went to one knee.

"Bowie! What's wrong?" She knelt next to him.

He shook his head, clearing it. "Just dizzy for a second."

"The Flowers! It must be the Flowers of Life!" She looked out at the open space in the center of the mound. "Bowie, we've come too late!"

Something was strobing and gleaming up ahead; she ran toward it, leaving it for him to catch up. He tottered through the doorway and stood reeling as if he had taken a punch.

Above them glowed something that reminded him of a kid's diagram of an atom—a complex assemblage of ring orbits that glistened in rainbow colors. It was two hundred feet across, hanging unsupported near the ceiling of the place; it seemed to be playing notes like a delicate carillon.

But he only had a moment to gape; Musica gave a woeful cry. "It's just as I feared! We're too late!"

They were looking down into a vast circular pit like a transplanted rain forest, in a shallow soup of nutrient fluids. There the Flowers of Life flourished in their triads, some open to show their triple structure. Most of the buds were still closed in shape like a twisted, elongated teardrop, a shape that made Bowie think at once of the shape of the mother ships' cannon. Among them, too, blew the golden pollen.

As they watched, more of the buds burst open, spewing forth the golden smoke. But sporangial structures in the Flowers also cast forth seeds like miniature parasols, which drifted toward the ceiling, defying gravity and air currents. It was like a gentle rain of glowing dandelion seeds in reverse.

Bowie tried to remember his botany classes and make some sense of it. The Flowers looked like some kind of angiosperm, producing the golden pollen, and yet they cast forth spores, like gametophytes. He couldn't guess what their alien life cycle might be like, or how it fit in with this Protoculture business.

She pointed to the tiny, drifting parasols, which looked like seeds to Bowie, but which she insisted on calling spores. "The Invid will sense this, no matter where they are. They're probably on their way here even now."

"The Invid? Who're they?"

"The enemies of your people and mine!" That was true enough, though it didn't *tell* the truth, but it was all that she had been taught.

There was a rustling and a series of shallow little sounds, as if something alive was moving around somewhere in the mass of Flowers. Bowie strained to see what it was, or hear it again, but could detect nothing.

Musica went down closer to the vast growing place, sandal heels slapping. He followed, calling for her to be careful.

He had never been sure of exactly which part of the SDF-1 this open space corresponded to—hangar deck, or Macross City compartment?—but he was beginning to suspect he knew.

The plants were growing so thickly that their stems were compressed into a mass that seemed to move and twist of its own volition. He looked up and saw that, while the quickened spores drifted up seeking release through a chimney-like opening at the top of the mound, something seemed to be confining them to the cavern. Perhaps there was still hope.

He looked again to the shining, chiming energy rings, listening to their song. There was something, something he seemed to remember. . . .

He tried to get his bearings again, having been told since the time he was a kid just how the SDF-1's last battle had been fought, how it had crashed, and in what mechamorphosis configuration. And then it hit him.

"I, I know where we are, Musica. This is the power section, where the sealed Robotech engines were, the engines that not even Doctor Lang dared to open."

He gripped her excitedly, pointed to the shining orbits. "This is the Protoculture Matrix! The one that the Zentraedi came and attacked Earth to get in the first place!"

The one that Lang and Exedore and Gloval and the others thought had disappeared along with the spacefold equipment, after the castastrophic jump to Pluto's orbit; the last Protoculture Matrix created by Zor. The only one in existence.

He knew the history of that war better than almost anyone, because he had seen copies of excerpts from his aunt's diary that were still circulated in the family, even though the originals were classified. He knew that once, a truce had been declared between SDF-1 inhabitants and Zentraedi, the ship had been scoured for any sign of the Matrix, and none was found.

But he had already learned from Musica that the Protoculture had its own Shapings, its own destinies to weave. Surely, hiding in the enormous sealed engines and turning aside sensor emissions or fooling passive sensor equipment would be a small marvel compared to the other things it had done. And there, hanging above Bowie, singing to itself, was the collection of interlocked rings that was the manifestation, on this plane of existence, of the Protoculture Matrix.

And though he didn't realize it, he and Musica were being watched. The triumvirate of wraiths that guarded the mounds was attentive to what was transpiring, though the trooper and the Muse had no idea they were there. The hour of the wraiths' long-awaited liberation was close at hand.

Bowie gripped Musica's shoulders. "This is the Protoculture Matrix! We've found what they've been looking for, what they've been fighting over for twenty years!"

She moved to put her arms around him, to lay her head against his shoulder. "Yes, but we found it too late."

"It can't be! We've got to think of something!"

"Oh, Bowie . . . if you had any idea what the Invid are like, how horrid they are—"

Pebbles knocked loose from a ledge higher up in the cavern. Bowie looked up to find that the 15th had followed him and, after getting lost, somehow ended up there. "Dana, I'm warning you: We're not going back."

"We're not here to bring you back, numb-nub!" she grinned.

When his squadmates made their way down to him and he explained what he had found out, Bowie had the dubious fun of watching them all fish-mouth in shock. He was more than passingly interested in Dana's response, though; this wasn't just some new kink in the war, to her—it was a part of her heritage, a part of herself.

She breathed the golden clouds, looking out on the coral triads of the Flowers of Life. She felt a strangeness—not a dizziness or faintness, but something closer to the opposite: as if she were being galvanized on some subcellular level.

Nova stole forward through the gloom, on the path the ATACs had taken. She had her sidearm out and was alert to every sound; something behind her made her turn.

Zor pushed the pistol barrel aside gently but firmly, as if he were dealing with a child and a child's toy. His eyes glowed in the darkness. "You won't be needing that. Come."

He set off for the light of the cavern. "You, you followed me?" she said.

"Yes. Now it is you who must follow *me*."

Musica and the 15th heard a groan and looked up to see Zor, muscles tensed in agony, hands clenched in the long lavender hair, gazing madly at the drifting spores. Next to him stood Nova Satori.

Nova managed to pull herself together a bit. "I'm here to take Musica back to headquarters," she managed shakily, then cast another frightened look at Zor.

"No, you're not," Dana answered.

Nova plunged down the steps that connected her level with the one below. But when she was halfway there, Zor, remaining where he was, let out a tormented howl.

"This plant is responsible for my becoming the monster I am!" He gasped for breath, staggered for balance there at the brink of the ledge.

He was only dimly aware of them all staring up at him. The scent of the spores and the presence of the Matrix forced his memories to merge and open themselves to him with the same compulsion that made the Flower of Life blossom. He stared out into the resplendent rings of the Matrix, his creation.

"I stole the secret of Protoculture from the Invid, and betrayed them. I was betrayed in turn, and my contemporaries became the Robotech Masters." He went down on all fours at the very lip of the drop.

"But I broke free of their will at last! I thwarted them! And they've brought me back as a clone, again and again, hoping I would give them my great secret. *But they won't have it!*"

"I don't know about that," Bowie yelled back in the echoing chamber, "but this is all something the Invid want"—sweeping his hand at the Flowers of Life—"and *they're on their way!*"

That seemed to jolt Zor back to a measure of reality. Nova continued her descent of the steps. She couldn't understand how she had ever felt drawn to Zor, felt such attraction to him; some alien trick perhaps? The thought made her all the angrier.

"We can sort all of that out later. Musica is still my prisoner, and I'm taking her back with me." Nova came to the bottom step.

Dana stepped to block her way. "Sorry, Nova. No."

CHAPTER
SEVENTEEN

*And the mountains in reply
Echoing their joyous strain*

Prewar Earth hymn

THE ROBOTECH MASTERS HAD DEPLOYED THEIR AS-
sault ships and command ships and lesser warcraft. Blue and
red Bioroids were set to fight, mindlessly, in a *Götterdäm-
merung*.

Emerson's fleet was coming at flank speed, to hurl itself
on the invaders' rear. In an order that had his staff gulping,
Emerson directed that his *Tristar* flagship lead the attack.
The equipment that had let him work his singularity ploy
was fused and useless; this battle would be toe-to-toe.

As Emerson's battle-weary elements threw themselves
into a last, almost spasmodic attack, the Masters' advance
faltered. Virtually everything in the Southern Cross capable
of getting off the ground rose from Fokker and a dozen
other bases, braced for the Twilight of the Robotech Gods.

Marie Crystal and Dennis Brown led their A-JACs forth,
and the Triumviroids thronged to meet them. The Earth

mecha did their best to use the tactics that were successful against the invaders for the 15th. Dreadnoughts lit the eternal night with cannon salvoes. Missiles left their ribbon-trails.

Nova ignored Zor's attempted intercession. "I'll expect you all to remember your oaths of service," she said, sweeping her eyes across the 15th. She gave Bowie Grant a particularly fixing stare; he was the key to it all. If she could get him to see past his deluded attraction to the clone woman, the whole affair would be resolved peacefully. If not . . .

"I'm not part of the military anymore," Bowie said stubbornly, squeezing Musica's hand.

"General Emerson is," Nova invoked the name. "And *he's* fighting with everything he's got to save this planet."

"*I don't care!*" Bowie burst out. "*Musica's my friend—not my prisoner or my enemy, and not yours either, do you hear me? Why can't you leave us alone?*"

Nova saw that all the ATACs quietly agreed—even the normally duty-bound Dante.

"Is love so difficult for you to understand, Nova?" Dana asked angrily. "Why d'you always have to be so cold-blooded?"

The question rocked Nova a little, almost as if Dana had struck her. She had felt like an outsider all her life, the more so when she had joined GMP. The bewildering attraction she had felt for Zor, and then the sudden absence of it; the slow warming to Dennis Brown; the pity she held for Captain Komodo, because she knew how it felt to be rebuffed— those were things she didn't dare inspect too closely.

She drew her sidearm, holding it close to her hip and leveling it at them.

"It's my duty, that's why," she told Dana. "And for me, Earth comes first. And the Human race. I'm taking Musica back, whether some of you get hurt or not."

It was all too melodramatic, Dana thought, even as she got set to play out her role. Bowie had stepped into the line of fire, shielding Musica, and Musica was already making timid but determined insistence that he move aside, to avoid bloodshed.

The rest of the 15th reacted to the appearance of the pistol with predators' reflexes, shifting weight, edging this way and that slightly, barely seeming to move their feet. They turned their bodies side-on to Nova to minimize their target silhouettes, bracing to take her.

"What happened to all that *talk* back at GMP head-quarters, Nova?" Bowie challenged, holding Musica back. "Honor. Freedom. Defending Human ideals and our way of life. You said you could be a friend to anyone who valued those things."

"Well, *this* is my life." He put his arm around Musica's waist. "D'you really have it in you to be a friend?"

"I—" Nova had forgotten those talks, an attempt to win over a friend in the enemy camp of the 15th. It had started out as a turning operation, at Colonel Fredericks's direction. But it ended up with her actually feeling something for the maverick trooper private, if only an unspoken sympathy for his confusion, his alienation. And then he was also Claudia Grant's nephew.

Nova had the flash of memory again, not clear but *strong.*

It was Christmas in rebuilt Macross City, the Christmas that would see Khyron's sneak attack. Little Nova Satori was out with her older sister and her sister's friends, caroling, as the snow drifted down. They happened upon a tall, regal black lady, beautiful as a Snow Queen, who looked very sad.

But when she spoke to them, Nova's sister recognized the lady's voice, as all the older girls did. Back on the SDF-1, hers had been the PA voice that so often restored hope in the midst of war; told the people where to go and what to do; gave the world calm; transmitted courage.

She was Commander Claudia Grant. The chorus of little girls gathered close in a ring around her and sang, the best they ever sang. There was no question about what carol it would be:

"An-gels we have heard on high!
Sweetly singing o'er the plain!"

They all wanted to *be* Commander Grant; Commander Grant wanted them to be more. She'd hugged them all to her and wept.

"—I'm a friend. . . ." Nova managed, not sure what she was saying. Her training and the pistol gave her command of the situation: She knew what moves to make and procedures to follow, even what tone of *voice* she ought to be using at this point to ensure that Phillips and the others didn't try any of their absurd heroics.

She had singlehandedly managed situations against even greater odds, against truly ruthless and evil people, and that last part was the glaring incongruity. She was disarmed of her greatest weapon: the conviction that she was totally in the right. And all her other resources, powerful though they were, began to fail her.

When Zor's big hand closed over the weapon and took it from her, Nova barely registered it through the sudden numbness she felt. "You won't need this," he said in an almost conversational tone. She could have had the pistol back at once, by using an infighting trick; she didn't.

Nova shook herself loose of the paralysis, the realization that she couldn't fire at these people, that her oath conflicted with the ideals it was supposed to uphold.

She looked to Zor. "But—isn't she one of the clones? Zor, they did such terrible things to you—"

Zor was shaking his head, the lavender curls swaying. "She is a Muse, the very soul of harmony. She is vital to the Robotech Masters, however. Look!"

Nova and the others followed Zor's pointing finger. They were watching the great mass of the Flowers of Life, hearing the tonalities from the Matrix that were so like the Muse's songs. "From the Protoculture all life flows. Once the clones have been quickened, it is the playing of Musica and her sisters that keeps them docile and obedient. That tells them, in effect, who they are."

"And now, she's learning to play the songs of Human-kind," Louie Nichols said quietly, the words forming a core of argument there at the very center of Nova's decision. There was too much happening for her to consider the fact that it was an amazingly profound thing for such a mechie—as she had always thought of him and his ilk—to put forth.

And if Fredericks and Leonard and the UEG got their hands on Musica? They would pull her every which way like a wishbone—cruelty was one of their first resorts. Musica embodied the hope of peace, but Nova dreaded to think what her songs would sound like once she had been put into the United Earth Government's mill.

"We have to move quickly," Nova said. "I commoed for a flying squad of GMP officers; it'll be here any time now."

"We've gotta get out of here!" Dana snapped. Emerson was in battle, and there were few others she could trust. But the world was wide, much of it unpopulated, and a Hover-tank squad mounted plenty of firepower. They would have to lay low, try to get to someone sane. Perhaps they would have to contact the Robotech Masters as well, and force some kind of ceasefire. Then a truce; then peace.

She threw aside her oath in that moment; the other party —the UEG and, by extension, the Army of the Southern Cross—hadn't kept its end of the bargain. She sensed that her ATACs stood with her, as did Nova and Musica.

Peace renegades! It sounds so weird, she thought.

"Your officers won't make any moves without instructions from you," Zor, who knew from experience, reminded Nova. "We must move calculatedly, but very quickly now."

He showed no emotion as Dana clapped her hands and began organizing the escape, somehow drawing Nova into her little band as if the GMP lieutenant had always been an ally. That instinctive talent for commanding loyalty and co-operation must be something Dana had inherited from both her warrior-woman Zentraedi mother and her ace-of-aces Human father, Zor reflected in passing.

Suddenly there was that sound again, the one Bowie had heard before, as if something was moving among the mass of Flowers. They all heard it, as they heard a sudden, high, playful sound, like a cross between a small dog's yip and the tones that came from the Matrix.

"Polly!"

Dana was on one knee, beckoning to him, and Bowie groaned. "I should've known." Nova and the others stood trying to fathom their latest marvel.

The little creature looked a low-slung white dog or mop-head, some kind of crypto-Lhasa apso with a sheepdog fore-lock, until one noticed the knob-ended horns and feet something like untoasted muffins. He showed a miniature red swatch of tongue and yipped again, running to her.

"You *know* this thing?" Angelo demanded, scratching his head.

Bowie answered for Dana. "All her life. Her godfathers introduced her to him. Only—*I* never believed in Polly till now, never saw him. I, uh, always thought he was imaginary."

Dana was nuzzling and laughing, hugging the little beast. A *Pollinator*, her three unlikely, self-appointed godfathers, the former Zentraedi spies Konda, Bron, and Rico had called him. Three-year-old Dana had given him his short-ened name right then and there.

She had quickly learned that Polly was a magical beast who came and went as he willed; no walls or locks could hold him. He showed up very rarely and went his way when he wished, simply vanishing while she was looking the other way. In her whole life, she had seen him perhaps seven or eight times. He never changed, or seemed to grow older.

"A Pollinator, yes," Zor said, looking down. "And now you know what he pollinates." *She's been tied to all this since she was a child—perhaps before her birth. Dana, Dana: who are you?*

Dana couldn't picture Polly buzzing around like a bee there in the Flower mass, but obviously *something* had been at work. She let the little creature lick her cheek again, then stood up with him in her arms, petting him.

"What're you all staring at? Let's go!"

Zor looked to the Flowers of Life that would no doubt be detected by the Invid. He still couldn't recall everything, but one thing, he knew:

The Masters' power must be broken. The original Zor was not altogether responsible for what had happened once he beguiled the Invid Regis. Perhaps I am not either, though I am him and he is me.

But it lies within my power to do what must be done. Let this be the lifetime when at last I accomplish it!

The fighting raged around the five great surviving mother ships of the Masters' fleet. The Humans were proving to be enemies even more terrible than the teeming Invid.

But that was not the worst news. Optical relays showed an invader in the realm of their Protoculture masses, a thing to be feared more than any Invid or Battloid.

It was small and white, yipping and chasing its own bedraggled tail among the storage canisters. A Pollinator.

The Masters knew better than to waste time attacking it. Try to stab the wind; shoot a bullet at the sun.

The Masters accepted the devastating news with the same emotionless reserve they had always displayed. To say it was stoicism would have been inaccurate. It would have implied they had some other mode of behavior.

The dissipation of Protoculture made itself felt not only in the declining performance of the Masters' Robotechnology, but in the failure of judgment, dispiritedness, and lack of coordination of the clones themselves. Never had the Masters' own—the primary—Protoculture cap been so weakened.

Even now, whole masses of Protoculture were transforming, all through the fleet, into the Flowers of Life, just as was happening below.

Their unspoken conference was short. Shaizan gave the order. "Transfer all functioning clones and all Protoculture reserves to Our flagship. Set automatic controls on an appropriate number of combat vessels to land them on the Earth's surface, and fuel them for a one-way voyage. Process as many clones as is feasible to serve as mindblank assault troops."

The Scientist bowed his head, swallowing his objection. The clones were mere plasm, subject to the dictates of the Masters. Who dared declare things otherwise?

Even if it meant genocide...

Allegra and Octavia had not so much adjusted to their reduced status as gone into a sort of lasting shock that insulated them from it. Even though they were Muses, Musica and her Cosmic Harp were the key to their triad's power and effect. Without her they were all but useless to the Masters. Since being interned, they had seen the horror of reduced Protoculture and the *dissonance* of Musica's absence all around; they had become desensitized to it.

But a new flurry of activity roused them a little. The most ambulatory of the malfunctioning clones were being injected by guards, shunted along in a torpid line, at the end of which was a door. None who were passed through that door returned.

Antipain serum, the words came quietly among the despondent prisoners near them; Allegra looked to Octavia. They both knew what that meant: clones who would be all but immune to normal sensation once the drug took effect—who would be aggressive, terrible antagonists. Their minds would be blanked to anything but fighting, until they were blasted apart or until the drug burned up their physiology completely.

"Mindblanked assault troops," a voice said. Octavia turned to see who it was, and gasped.

In the advance stages of Protoculture deprivation, the clone had become a crone, witchlike, nodding out the last moments of her life.

She gazed, glassy-eyed, at the other clones being injected. "Sacrifices on the altar of war. That is the Robotech way."

* * *

Resistance from the mother ships seemed to be failing, but Marie Crystal kept herself from any hope or distraction, dodging through enemy fire and preparing for another run. At Emerson's order, she began to consolidate elements of the various shattered TASC units.

But we better get some help soon, she thought, *or that's all he wrote.*

"General, you *have* to commit all your reserves *now*," Emerson's image said to Leonard.

The supreme commander kept his face neutral. "Current tactical trends preclude that at this time."

So much easier than saying "screw you," Emerson thought, as his flagship shook to a Bioroid assault and the guns pounded.

"There'll be no other chance!" he roared at Leonard. "Move now, you fool!"

Leonard's wattles shook with his anger. "You dare give *me* orders? Carry out your mission!"

He had barely broken the connection, and was picturing Emerson's imprisonment for insubordination under fire, when an aide leaned close to say, "Enemy assault ship descending for landing, sir, about five miles outside the city limits."

Leonard turned back to raise Emerson again. There must be no more penetration of Earth's defensive forces, whatever it took.

Predictably, Emerson claimed that the order was unworkable, was simply contradictory to reality. Leonard let him go on, and then hit him with a blow he had been saving until the battle was over.

"Carry on! Oh, and it may interest you to know that your ward, Private Grant, has deserted in the company of an enemy agent. The GMP is hunting him even now."

Emerson wanted to cry out in grief, to insist that it had to be a mistake or that Bowie had been brainwashed. But he saw Leonard was enjoying it too much to be pursuaded of anything Emerson might claim.

Emerson broke the commo connection and began redeploying his remaining forces for a direct assault on the only remaining mother ship.

On Earth, Leonard exulted that he had managed to give Emerson such agonizing news when the man couldn't even spare a moment for regret or memory or worry.

But he didn't have long to enjoy it. An appalling new enemy teemed from the assault ships that were slipping through, to wreak havoc in Monument City.

Assault ship hatches dropped open, even as Leonard watched from his tower, and the mindblanked assault troop clones charged forth like insane demons.

CHAPTER
EIGHTEEN

It's ironic that the SDF-3 expedition was on its way to find the Robotech Masters to strike a diplomatic accord, at exactly the time the Masters were on their way to Earth. Ships passing in the night, in truth.

There are those who lament the fact because they believe the second war could have been averted. I do not share this view. Do Humans, mining for precious gems, make deals with the monkeys whose jungle they invade?

The Masters were arrogant in a way that, in Humans, would certainly be diagnosed as psychotic. They were as single-minded as the mindblanked clone troops they were forced to use in their final offensive.

Major Alice Harper Argus (Ret.), *Fulcrum: Commentaries on the Second Robotech War*

"**D**OESN'T EVEN FAZE 'EM," AN INFANTRYMAN gritted over his tac net. He put another burst into the alien, and this time the raving, long-haired wildman in offworld uniform went down.

But not for long. The thing got up again, hollow-eyed, skin stretched tight across its face, leering like a skeleton. It raced at him with unnatural speed and dexterity, firing some kind of hand weapon. The grunt flicked over from teflon-coated slugs to energy and held the trigger down, until the zombie was burning chunks of debris.

But all at once another zombie reared up, grinning, to bear him over and grapple hand to hand, not skilled but as unrelenting as a mad dog. They pressed rifles against one another. Only the infantryman's armor kept him from having his throat bitten out.

Everywhere it was the same. Only a few Southern Cross

units had been deployed here to Newton, to guard against a landing at the outmost perimeter of Monument City. The grunts were badly outnumbered by the Living Dead. What had happened among the defenseless civilians, the soldiers could not bring themselves to think about.

The zombies kept coming even after their weapons were exhausted, trying to grapple hand to hand, wanting only to kill before they themselves died from the supercharged overdoses they had been given. In time, the Human survivors rallied near the town's central plaza. They formed a tiny square of fifteen men and women, one rank standing and one kneeling.

Like something from a nineteenth-century imperialist's fantasy, the square fired and fired on all fronts as the damned rushed in at them. Time and again the tremendous firepower of modern infantry weapons cleared the area, and each time more mindblanked assault clones stormed forth, some still firing but most not, their weapons exhausted.

At times it was hand to hand; body armor gave the infantry a powerful edge. But each time they drove back their foes, a new wave came to crash against them.

The square shrank to a triangle, eight desperate men and women. And then, high above, cross hairs fixed on them.

It was regrettable that two assault ships' cargoes of mindblanked clones had been mistakenly disembarked in the target population center. But such things were unavoidable, given the haste of the operation and the unreliability of some of the crew clones.

Still, the demonstration of Robotech Master power had to be made as ordered, even at the cost of a few expendable null sets.

From a third assault ship, a beam sprang down and the entire middle of Newton disappeared in a thermonuclear inferno. Friend, foe, civilian—all vanished instantly, as blast and shockwaves spread holocaust.

Leonard heard the news without showing any response, cold as a Robotech Master. The technical officers clamoring at him with their assorted explanations of how the alien ray worked, some claiming it was a new development, others disputing it, were of no importance, and he waved them aside.

Two towns had been utterly destroyed, but that was of no importance to him; Leonard knew as well as anyone that Monument City might very well be next, and it had no defense. There was no time to consolidate forces in the UEG capitol, but he gave the command that it be done nevertheless.

An aide tapped his shoulder tentatively, *"We're receiving a communication from the Aliens!"* The face of Shaizan appeared on the primary display screen before him, Bowkaz and Dag standing behind and to either side.

They knew his name. "Commander Leonard, we are now capable of destroying your species with very little effort. You will therefore surrender and evacuate your planet immediately."

Leonard looked at the screen blankly. Evacuate? He had once read a war college projection that if spacecraft production were to continue at full speed and the birth rate were suddenly to drop to zero, such a thing might be possible in another ten years or so. As it was, the aggregate space forces of Terra *before* the current battle wouldn't have had a hope in hell of carrying out such a mission.

But where was the Human race supposed to go? A few frail Lunar and Martian colonies, and several orbital constructs were the only alternatives, unless the Masters meant to help, which they manifestly did not.

That left an instant for Leonard to marvel at how the Masters overestimated the Human race in assuming *homo sapiens* could pull off such a miracle. But again, it was more likely that the Masters simply didn't care; maybe "evacuation" only meant, to them, the escape and preservation of the power structure—the government.

Thoughts and evaluations boiled in Leonard's mind then: perhaps it *would* be possible to take the very most essential personnel—himself chief among them, of course—and thus avoid total annihilation.

As he was studying the Masters' sword-sharp faces he

heard Shaizan say, "Within thirty-eight of your hours. Else, we shall have no option but to slay you one and all."

Leonard's fists shook the desk with a crash, as he stood. "Now you listen: this world has been ours, from the time our species stood up straight to use its hands and its brains! Through every disaster and our own wars and the ones you and your kind waged on us! *This world is ours!*"

He was shaking his bunched fists in the air before him, speaking an unprepared speech for once. Then he realized, with surprise, that a few of the men and women around him were nodding their heads in agreement. He had come to think of himself as a man who could never have the heartfelt support of those around him.

He was thinking along new lines when Bowkaz, speaking up, dashed his hopes. "Leonard, this is an ultimatum—a fact of life—not a suggestion or a mere threat. The Invid, our bitter enemies, have already detected the presence of Protoculture on your planet."

"They will be here soon," Dag said. "And, it seems, there will be more war. You can leave or you can be crushed between; there is no third way. Go, and leave this matter to us."

Leonard resisted the urge to duck offscreen to consult with his advisers and image-makers, or break the connection. But pride made him stand there, as the Masters knew by now that it would, protecting to the last his Lone Warrior, his Gunfighter-Patton-Caesar persona.

But the self-preserving side of his mind was making very, very fast calculations. If only a portion of the Human race were to survive, it was his duty to rule them.

"Impossible," he told Shaizan, hoping the word didn't sound too tremulous. "More time!" Leonard added. He grabbed a figure from the air, "At least seven days!" There was something Biblical about it, but nothing workable.

Shaizan raised his arm, but Leonard couldn't see that he, like his triad mates, was touching the Protoculture cap.

"Forty-eight of your hours, and no more," Shaizan decreed. He cut off Leonard's objections. "And after that, *no life on Earth.*"

The screen de-rezzed, then went clear. Leonard turned to his nearest subordinate, saved from an agonizing decision because the Masters had insisted on the impossible. "Reconsolidate all units in the area of Monument City and prepare for an all-out assault."

There were only a few tentative hesitations; all of them jumped-to when he bellowed, "Do it now! On the double!"

They were compliant because no other attitude was tolerated in Leonard's inner circle, and so there was no contradiction. They scurried.

Leonard reflected, *We whipped the Zentraedi and we can whip these Robotech Masters! And the Invid, whatever in hell they are!*

Men and women prepared as best they could: Some children were shielded or remanded to shelters by their elders, but many found a weapon and got ready to be part of the final battle.

There was a brief calm in the wake of the beams, something to savor even though it wasn't meant to be savored. Soon, the sky split apart again.

The holding action fought by the *Tristar*, Emerson's flagship, was the sort of thing children's stories and patriotic poetry are made of. Emerson himself would have given anything not to be there, or at least not to be the last living crewmember among the dead.

But that was how it had happened. An enemy blast took out virtually all the bridge systemry and killed the senior gunnery commander who had been standing between him and the nearest explosion. But he had taken shrapnel and the command chair under him was stained with his blood. His head had been rocked against his headrest at an angle where the padding was of little help, dazing him.

Emerson felt infinitely tired and regretful—regretful that he had never spoken his heart to Bowie; that he had lost the battle; that he had made such a mess of his marriage. More than anything, he was regretful that so many lives had been or were about to be sped into the blackness.

Smoke roiled from the control panels in a bridge that

would soon be a crypt. Emerson's head lolled back and he had only an instant to recall something he had read in Captain Lisa Hayes-Hunter's war-journal, *Recollections*.

It was getting harder to think, but he pulled the quote together by an act of will. *Why are we here? Where do we come from? What happens to us when we die?* Questions so universal, they must be structured in the RNA codons and anticodons themselves, it seemed to Emerson.

He had no answers, but expected to shortly. He was pretty sure those answers would be as surprising to the Robotech Masters as they would be to dead Terran generals.

Then he was blinking up at Lieutenant Crystal and Lieutenant Brown. Emerson couldn't imagine how they could have landed their craft on the critically damaged *Tristar*. He couldn't decide if they were real or not. But the agony he felt as they dragged him over to an ejection module convinced him it was all real, and even revived him a bit.

Dennis Brown didn't quite know what to say to Marie; the whole Emerson rescue had been so improvised, and they had only gotten to know one another as unit commanders. Sitting crowded into the little alloy-armored ball with the injured general made things different, somehow awkward. But there had been no time to get back to their mecha, and anyway both craft were so badly damaged that the ejection capsule was the better bet.

"Looks like we made it," he ventured, as the *Tristar* began to blow to pieces behind them, jolting the metal sphere along on its shockwave.

She considered that. "Yes," Marie hedged.

But then they saw that they had been premature; the maw of an enemy cruiser, one of the last still functioning, came at them like the open mouth of a shark, like something out of a nightmare.

They were swallowed up.

At some point, Dana looked down and the Pollinator was no longer frisking along behind; she was used to those sudden disappearances, but wondered if she would ever see him again.

The 15th and its friends and allies, having made it to the top of the mound that buried the SDF-1 and every vital secret of Protoculture, looked down at a circus of light and sound. The GMP appeared to have gotten there first, with troop carriers, giant robots, and crew-served weapons. There was an energy cordon farther out, and a lot of activity at the foot of the mound. In the distance, cities burned and smoke went up in mile-wide clouds where the enemy had struck. For some reason the GMP troops, following Colonel Fredericks's orders to recapture the aliens at all costs, were forgotten or couldn't be reached by Southern Cross brass desperate for reinforcements.

As Zor thought about the madness of it all, Dana thought about Zor and how very badly she needed to understand him and understand herself. As the eight who stood there dealt with their wildly varying thoughts and memories and impulses, another shadow crossed the land.

They all looked up, as did the Gimps below, to see, hovering above, a cinnamon-red, whiskbroom-shaped Robotech Master assault ship.

Karno and his triad mates were gazing into an enormous lens. "There rests the last Protoculture Matrix," Karno said in his single-sideband voice. "But who are those, atop the mound?"

Theirs was the ship and the mission for which all the rest were providing a distraction. The last thing they had expected was to find the mound surrounded by combat units.

It was all very confusing. There was no sign of the three frightful Protoculture wraiths, no least indication of any counteraction, and that was enough to make anyone knowledgeable in the ways of Protoculture cautious.

But *this*? As the focus zoomed in, Karno saw his onetime fiancée, Musica, the latest of the Zor clones, and six Earth primitives ranged about at the brink of a cliff.

"Zor is with them," Darsis observed with a dispassion worthy of the Elders themselves.

"Even Musica," pronounced Karno, forcing himself to

match that proper tone, willing to die before admitting the hot, hateful feelings coursing through him.

Dana looked at Zor in surprise, as he stepped to the brink and addressed the empty air. "If you attack, we will destroy all that is here. Flowers. Protoculture. Muse. All.

"Go to your Robotech Masters! Tell them this war must end. You in the depths of your ignorance, you and your Masters: it is time for you to learn how to learn."

Zor was intent on the ship, but Nova looked at him wonderingly, and had misgivings. What if, somehow, he wasn't bluffing?

The godlike voice from the assault ship gave the Humans a start, but Musica and Zor were braced for it. "We will be back," it said, as flames rose from alien strikes all around, all the way to the horizon and beyond. The assault ship lifted away, for space and the flagship.

Nothing Nova had ever been taught quite served in analyzing what had come to pass. She, too, set aside her oath of allegiance as Dana had, silently but finally. "Zor, the Flowers—the Masters . . . you remember now!"

He made the barest of smiles. "Yes, but only in fragments." He turned the smile on Dana. "It's all beginning to coalesce in my mind now, and Musica is the key!"

Dana's back went stiff. *And that's all, huh? Musica?* Ignoring everything Dana had . . . *Ah, hell!*

Zor started giving orders, and Nova for one seemed to be ready—*willing*—to take them. Zor outlined his plan to have Angelo, Sean, and Louie infiltrate the GMP perimeter and come back with the 15th's Hovertanks tandem-towed.

Dana walked over to the ventlike opening in the mound, watching the minute parasol spores bump against some invisible barrier and float back down, to rise and bounce again. She couldn't sort out for herself the reason why there was such immense fascination in it for her. She resolved that, if they lived, she would make Zor explain.

Zor looked up at Earth's sky, while Bowie hugged Musica to him. Some people were fleeing Monument City, terrified of another onslaught of the destructive rays or the arrival of the Bioroids.

Last of a long line of one selfsame entity, heir to brilliant mastery of the Shaping forces of the Universe and to every misdeed of his predecessors, Zor Prime sniffed the breeze.

And now the war ends, he promised himself, promised all Creation.

> *This sudden shifting of focus, from Matrix to Muse—and Zor Prime—is bewildering only to those who haven't familiarized themselves with the subtler powers of Protoculture.*
>
> *From a distance, we can see it, of course, and feel smug in our overview. If the players on stage that day were mystified and even illogical, who can fairly blame them? The Shaping of the Protoculture had the world in its teeth and was shaking it.*
>
> S. J. Fischer, *Legion of Light: A History of the Army of the Southern Cross*

THE CAPTIVES COULD SEE THAT IT WAS A VERY HIGH space. The multicolored invader lightstructure, as faceted as a stained glass chandelier and as big as a Hovertank, was hanging unsupported very high above them.

It looks like—radioactive diamond; a crystallized thought—I dunno, Emerson thought woozily, as Brown and Marie tried surreptitiously to hold him upright on the couch.

"Well?" Dag repeated. "Will you make your species see reason, and surrender?"

Emerson took a breath and looked again at the three strange beings who floated before him on their Protoculture cap's small standing platforms. Would Leonard have gone insane right on the spot? It was intriguing to consider, but not very helpful.

"'Surrender'?" Emerson repeated the word tiredly, feeling the wounds on his face and neck, and in his side. "Haven't you arrogant ghouls learned *anything* about the

Human race yet? Your Zentraedi came after us, and now you come after us—*sss*—"

Emerson hissed in pain, going a little faint but coming around almost at once. Lieutenant Crystal wedged up against him, propping him up so that Emerson hadn't teetered. Good soldier!

"—after us," Emerson resumed, stiffening his spine. "But you don't seem to realize: *It doesn't make us weaker; it makes us stronger!*"

Dag looked down on him. "A great pity; our information led us to hope that you are seeking the same peaceful settlement as we—that our goal was the same."

Emerson shook off his fatigue and pain. How old *were* these apparitions, these seeming Grim Reapers before him? *How many Protoculture-grown Dorian Gray portraits in the old closet?* he speculated, then pulled himself together. It was no time for whimsy.

"Nice try," Emerson shot back, "but you know as well as I do that you opened fire on us first. You never *tried* to negotiate."

"Regrettable," Dag parried, "but we respect you as we do other intelligent beings who have the same Human form as we, the same biogenetic structure—even a kindred intellect."

"That so?" Marie glowered up at the Master from beneath her long black brows. "Then why haven't you called off your Bioroids?"

"You're liars, the whole pack of you," Emerson told the Masters.

Shaizan's eyes opened wide with his surprise and displeasure. "Truly, you are stupid creatures!"

Emerson smiled mirthlessly. "Map reference point Romeo Tango 466-292; that's where you intend to make your initial landing, right? *That's* how stupid we are. And you're going to see more mecha and more fighting-mad Human beings than you could've dreamed of in your worst nightmares!"

It was only a wild guess on his part, based on repeated alien activity there, and those last transmissions from Leonard's staff before commo was knocked out on *Tristar*. The gambit was worth a try, Emerson had decided. Earth's defenses were nearly finished, but perhaps the Masters didn't know that, and Emerson's words would throw them off balance for a bit.

And, terrible as the aliens' new beam weapon was, they would not use it on the mounds, that much was obvious; they didn't want to destroy the mounds, didn't *dare* to, or they would have done so long ago. It was tragic irony that, now that the Human race finally knew something about the Masters' original, bewildering demand, the Masters had upped the ante. Emerson saw, just as Leonard had, that there was no way to evacuate the Earth, and no place to go even if such a thing were possible.

"And we know about the Protoculture," Marie was saying, even though the intelligence report on the 15th's discoveries inside the flagship, and analysis of the Masters' transmission to Leonard, had been very sketchy.

"We know that if you don't get it, you die," Brown added.

That gave the Masters pause again, and the captives had the impression the invaders were in silent conference once more. After a moment, Bowkaz said, "Tell us just how much you people of know of us, of our history."

"We know about your weak points," Emerson answered. "The Earth is ours, and nobody's taking it away from us or making us leave it! But if you'll agree to a ceasefire, then perhaps we can help each other. We can stop this war."

"The Invid are coming, do you not understand what that means?" Shaizan demanded. "You will all be wiped out!"

"We cannot allow your stubbornness or the fate of one tiny world to endanger the establishment of our Robotech Universe," Dag said.

"Your small-mindedness merely illustrates how primitive you are," Bowkaz added.

Emerson laughed madly, so that Marie and Brown feared for a moment that he had snapped. Then the general met the Masters' glares with one of his own. "Then, so be it."

An area of mottling on the mushroomlike cap grew

bright, and Bowkaz put his palm to it. The cap spoke so that the Humans could hear as well, "I am receiving information on Zor Prime.

"Zor and the Human military unit in which he served are now at the site of the buried Protoculture Matrix. Musica is with him, but she is no longer connected to the Cosmic Harp; she has given her loyalty to Zor and and Humans."

"Bowie!" Emerson murmured. "I knew you were no deserter, son."

Shaizan turned back to Emerson. "Our reprieve is withdrawn! Your Earth has just run out of time!"

Sean and the others had simply slipped back to their concealed jeeps, put on combat gear, then made their way back through the GMP lines as if they were a recon unit going to the rear to make a report. Passwords given to them by Nova made it easy. No one thought to question them with the Masters' attacks and the chaotic situation in Southern Cross HQ.

The return trip was in some ways even easier, the piloted mecha lifting the unpiloted ones over the GMP perimeter. The Gimps were hesitant to shoot at friendly forces without specific orders, until it was too late.

Now the 15th stood around their Hovertanks, watching smoke rise from the blasted Monument City, which had taken scattered beam hits but not the sort of all-out, fused-earth attack that had claimed Newton.

"Bowie, I'm so ashamed," Musica said, tears wetting her cheeks, as they saw the ragged lines of survivors making their way from the city.

"It's not your fault," Bowie told her, holding her to comfort her.

She looked up at him, trying to smile. "The harmony is strong, between you and me. I feel your joys and sorrows; they are my own." Being close to him was so wonderful, a divine gift of happiness that shored her up in the horror that was around them.

Off to one side, Dana asked Nova quietly, "Do you think Zor knows what's going to happen next? That he sees the future?" It was no time to voice a more personal question to herself, *And, have I?* All her dreams and Visions crowded so close about her.

Nova considered that. "What are you saying?" The results of her interrogations and observations were inconclusive but—if Zor *did* have some sort of precog powers, perhaps the Human race could turn them to good use.

Dana was looking at Zor, who stood alone, watching the pyre that was Monument City. "He doesn't want to help Musica," Dana faced the truth. "He wants revenge, and he wants to die more than he wants to live, I think." Her voice caught a little; she still loved him.

Zor studied the destruction and suffering before him, standing near the *Three-In-One*; Dana had supposed he named his tank that because of its three configurations, but understood now that it was some deeper memory that had moved him to do so. Zor was repeating the silent vow as if it were a mantra, *This time they'll pay! This time I'll stop them!*

That was when he heard the crackle of Shaizan's voice over the cockpit speaker of Sean's Hovertank, the *Bad News*. "Zor! Traitor! Are you there?" Sean nearly jumped out of the tank like an ejecting pilot.

Zor was in the cockpit of his *Three-In-One* in an instant, hands on the control yoke grips. "I hear you."

Somehow, the Masters had contrived to send their image over the tank's display screen. "You are aware that the Protoculture Matrix is undergoing degradation, as the Flowers bloom." It wasn't a question. "And by now, the Sensor Nebula has surely alerted the Invid."

Zor looked at his onetime Masters. The words made bits of memory and realization fall into place. "I—yes. But I also know that *I* control the key to this planet's survival. I dictate the terms."

"We are of the opinion that you are mistaken," Shaizan replied. "Watch closely, and you will see."

The other ATACs were watching on their own screens, with Musica looking over Bowie's shoulder and Nova over Dana's. They saw Rolf Emerson, teeth locked in pain, with Marie and Brown trying to comfort him.

"Emerson," Bowie said numbly, while Sean whispered Marie's name like a hopeless prayer, and Dana heard Nova breathe, "Dennis."

Then the Masters were onscreen again. "These three men will be released when you return Musica and remove your troops from this area."

Men? Sean Phillips found a second to think, wondering if they had gotten a good look at Marie. *I suppose everybody in armor looks the same to them but—maybe these vampires aren't as smart as everybody keeps tellin' me they are. Anyway, if that's what it's like to be immortal, they can keep it!*

"Do you find this acceptable?" Shaizan continued. "We trust that we need not mention the alternative."

Zor fought down his fury long enough to ask, "What are your conditions?"

"You will be picked up, and we will exchange prisoners onboard our mother ship." The Masters disappeared from the screen.

Zor lowered himself from his tank wearily and had barely begun, "I do not wish for the rest of you to be invol—" Bowie hit him with a shoulder block, driving the bigger Zor up against the armored side of *Three-In-One*, trying to choke the life out of him.

"They're not getting Musica! I'll kill you!"

Zor grimaced, trying to twist free, but didn't strike out at him. "Then stay here and do nothing, and watch your good friend be killed! The techniques of the Masters can be more cruel than anything you can conceive of!"

Dana was dashing to intervene, but somehow Musica got there first. "Stop it, Bowie!" He had no choice but to risk harming her or back off. He let go his grip on Zor.

"I will not permit you all to suffer because of me," she told Nova and the 15th. "I will go back."

Before Bowie could object, Dana said, "She's right. Saddle up, Fifteenth! C'mon, what're you all gaping at?"

Nova was the one among them most distanced from Emerson's predicament. The fate of a few Human beings, even a flag-rank officer and two TASC fliers, was insignificant against the survival of the Human race and its homeworld; everyone who took the Southern Cross oath under-stood that. Shaping strategy and policy on the basis of hostages and emotional responses led to disaster; it had been one of the major contributing factors to the Global Civil War.

Marie thought about her pistol again, but realized that events had gone too far for that, and that she must see things through along with Dana's ATACs. Protoculture seemed to have some barely hinted-at power to shape events, and she could only hope that the benign side of that mystical force was working now, because Fate had the bit in its teeth.

"There's no telling what'll happen," Dana was telling her men. "We'll have to play it by ear. But this thing isn't about Southern Cross or the UEG anymore. I don't think even the mound, here, is as important now. This thing is between us and the Robotech Masters."

In the wake of her experiences on the flagship and her exposure to the spores, pollen, and Flowers below, and to Musica's song, something in her was coming fully to life—was flexing its powers like a butterfly emerging from its cocoon and pumping out its wings.

Dana didn't know exactly how, but she knew the words were true. "Maybe this was always meant to be, right from the start."

The contact broken, the Masters easily reached an unspoken consensus: Musica was critical to their plans, and there was no longer any need for the others—not even Zor. Furthermore, there were disturbing things about the halfbreed lieutenant, Sterling; some genetic throw of the dice had embued her with insights and an affinity for the Protoculture that made her dangerous. It was best that she and her unit be terminated as soon as possible; the Masters could tolerate no rival in the matter of the Protoculture.

The units encircling the mounds simply held their fire as a flotilla of a dozen assault ships came low to pick up the Hovertanks. Hopelessly outgunned, the GMP troops breathed a universal sigh of relief when the invader craft lifted away.

In due course the 15th came forth to form a spearhead on the huge hangar deck: Dana's *Valkyrie*, Angelo's *Trojan Horse*, Bowie's replacement tank, the *Re-Tread*, which had taken the place of his *Diddy-Wa-Diddy*, abandoned on an earlier sortie aboard a mother ship. Sean's *Bad News* and Louie Nichols's *Livewire* completed the roster.

There were ranks of clone guards with rifles aimed at them, rabbits policing the wolves. But the ATACs only watched and waited, the tanks' headlights and downswept hoods making them appear to be glowering.

When Dana had looked the place over, she switched her mike to an external speaker and announced, "First of all, we want to see Chief of Staff Emerson."

There was some conferring among the invaders. Finally they opened ranks and the Hovertanks fell in to follow a guard runabout, moving into the vaulted passageways of the residential district, so much like those of the Masters' original flagship.

Guards stood on ledges all along the way. Dana wondered if they realized they were scarcely more than so many pop-up targets before the armor and firepower of the Hovertanks. They didn't seem worried, and that worried her.

But while she didn't have words to explain it, *something* told her that what she was doing was right, that against all logic, what she was doing was what she *should* be doing. Again she felt connected to something much greater than herself, and breathed a quick prayer that it wasn't some kind of self-delusion. It was nothing but faith, really, but if she had understood her Academy philosophy courses, what cognitive process wasn't?

The guard runabout stopped at a bulkhead hatchway as big as a hangar door, and the tanks settled in behind it, idling.

"From this point, Musica and two others may continue, but no more. The exchange will be made at once."

Dana stood in her cockpit-turret, taking up her tanker's carbine and slinging it over her armored pauldron. Her winged helmet, with its crest of bright metal, and her flashing armor seemed to daunt the guards a little. "That's you and me, Bowie." She couldn't figure out why the Masters weren't luring Zor in, too.

"Right." Behind Bowie, Musica rose to her feet, to show that she was ready.

Valkyrie and *Re-Tread* were escorted among more of those stone-faced corridors Dana remembered so well, and through more technological-looking passageways as well. At last the runabout leading them stopped, and the tanks settled to a halt. At Dana's signal, Bowie and Musica dismounted to join her, both ATACs carrying their carbines. They were led to a triskelion hatch that rotated open.

Emerson looked up with a resigned smile. "It's you." Dana knew some of it was for her, but most of the general's warmth was for Bowie.

"Rolf," Bowie said simply.

"General Emerson!" Dana strode over to him, carbine still at sling-arms, as Dennis Brown and Marie Crystal helped him to his feet. "You're wounded."

She could see there wasn't much she could do with her combat med kit that Brown and Crystal hadn't already done with theirs. "It's nothing serious," the general told her, a lie and they both knew it. "I'm glad you're here, Dana."

Then he turned to Bowie, who stood rooted. "Good to see you, soldier."

Bowie inclined his head to his guardian. "Pleasure to be here, General." But his eyes danced behind his helmet visor, and Dana took an instant from her scheming and calculating to be glad. Whatever had gone wrong between the two had somehow been made right again.

Dana was figuring the best order of march, meaning to use Musica as insurance—something Musica had already agreed to—when there was a muffled cry. Dana whipped around, the carbine slung down off her shoulder butt first and the muzzle coming up, to see Musica being borne back, wrenched from Bowie's grasp, and carried through two firing ranks of clone guards. The guards had appeared from nowhere, their backs to what she had assumed was a solid wall —she had fallen for an old trick. The ranks closed, and the guards assumed firing stances.

* * *

"Dana!"

Sean had never quite heard that tone in Angelo's voice before, but there wasn't much time to stop and reflect on it. Sean himself had been preoccupied, worrying about Marie.

But Dana had left her mike open, and there was no mistaking the sound of a firefight or the lieutenant's yell for reinforcements.

"I'll come with you!" Angelo roared, as the tanks' thrusters blared. Nova, riding with him, was all for that, thinking of Dennis Brown.

Sean automatically reverted to a command voice, even though the big sergeant now outranked him.

"You know your orders! Hold this position! And you, too, Louie; you've got to secure the escape route!" Sean fired up *Bad News* and bashed through the hatch before him while Angelo was still making strangled objections.

It wasn't too hard to find the way; Dana and Louie each had a transponder in their armor's torso-instrumentation pack. Then, Dana's vanished from the display screen.

But Bowie's still functioned, even though Sean couldn't raise him or the lieutenant over the radio. Sean had clones ducking low every which way, indifferent to their puny small arms fire, laying out an occasional burst just to keep them discouraged.

The race to get there seemed to take forever. Dana's signal was dead and she might be, too; and Marie was in there, along with the others. . . .

He bashed through a final hatch like an iron fist through rice paper, holding fire because he didn't know where friend or foe might be. Energy bolts began coming his way at once.

Still he held fire, trying to get his bearings. It was a singular piece of discipline; as someone in an earlier war had remarked, you would shoot your own mother if she happened to charge across your field of fire in battle.

Bad News settled in for a low hover, as a triad of guards concentrated their fire on it. Sean would wonder later if the clones had any real idea of warfare, would feel as though he had simply executed them. But in the heat of the moment, seeing there were no friendlies near, he laid out a single bolt from the cannon and was on the move even while the immolated bodies were turning to ash.

He was too zoned-up for combat to feel sorry for them; there was only one thing he cared about, and the voice Sean heard then sent waves of relief and joy pushing through him, remarkable in their intensity.

"You took your time getting here!" Marie scolded from behind a fluted column, snapping off judicious shots with a fallen guard's rifle.

"But my heart was with you all the while. Believe me, my little pigeon!"

The romance had started, for him, as just one more conquest. *When did she come to mean everything to me?* Sean couldn't help wondering, even while trying to keep his mind on business.

Maybe it was because Marie Crystal wasn't dazzled by him, having more than enough medals and decorations of her own; or maybe it was bound up in that spooky destiny stuff Dana kept yammering about and Sean refused to accept. Most likely, if he and Marie lived to be together again and spent their whole lives that way, they would *still* never figure it out, he decided.

He thought all that in a tiny slice of time, pivoting the *Bad News* and laying out heavy suppressive fire, blowing beautiful friezes to cinders and fountaining tiles from the deck to keep the enemy's head down.

The clones didn't seem to care about their own lives. Some stood right up into the fire and shrapnel; their small arms counterfire was radiant dotted lines running at every angle across the compartment.

Emerson! Shoulderer of sorrow!
Champion of the light! Although—
It wasn't given him to know that
Until his work was done

Mingtao, *Protoculture: Journey Beyond Mecha*

ROLF EMERSON LOOKED UP, CLUTCHING HIS wounded arm to him, to see Bowie and Musica sheltering in the lee of a column not far away, and a guard clone angling to get a clear shot at them from behind.

Dispassion and logic were no part of it; Emerson was sprinting headlong through the gauntlet of weapon blasts before rationale had any chance to come to bear. The space between his cover and Bowie's column was fairly safe; the shots were well directed by then. Emerson launched himself through the air just as the clone pressed his cheek against the stock of his rifle for maximum accuracy, down on one knee.

There was a split-second image of Musica's face, frightened, worried for *him,* Emerson could see.

So beautiful, it occurred to the general as the charge hit his back. *Perhaps she's the better part of us all; we must listen to her.*

The bolt hit him squarely in the back, vaporizing flesh and singeing bone, setting his tunic afire. The next thing he knew, he was in Bowie's arms and the clone rifleman had been mowed down by Dana's fire.

Sean was walking his tank's secondary-battery fire back and forth in the compartment; most of the enemy withdrew and the rest died. In moments, the violent echoes gave way to silence.

Bowie threw his helmet aside, kneeling to gather Emerson into his embrace, smelling the charred flesh. "Rolf. Father . . ."

Emerson found his hand, gripped the cold alloy. "I heard your music. The night before they sent me to take over ALUCE base, I stood under the barracks window and listened to you play. It was beautiful, Bowie; you have a gift."

"I wasn't—I haven't—" Bowie wanted to talk about love and found only apologies on his lips, and knew there was no more time.

Emerson's hand squeezed the metal-sheathed fingers. "You and Musica . . . it's such a *good* thing, Bowie. You must both teach it. Son."

Emerson was still alive for another few seconds, though he would never speak again. He looked up over Bowie's shoulder to see Dana with her helmet faceplate open. Her armor was seared where an enemy bolt had burned out her transponder, but failed to wound her.

She might have even more to teach than Bowie or Musica, it occurred to him. Dana gave him a nod, knowing words wouldn't serve. Then she slipped away out of sight, rifle held at high port.

Emerson saw with some surprise that the world wasn't going dark, the way traditional lore said it would. Instead, the range of his vision and perception went out and out, encompassing things wonderful and terrible, things defying all description—a terrible beauty beside which mortal life seemed a lesser matter.

There was a celebration of light around him, and he threw himself forth willingly. The Universe embraced him, opening all secrets, answering every question.

* * *

In his protected sanctum, Dr. Zand, monitoring the battle through technical relays and paths of information of his own, suddenly straightened as if he were about to suffer a stroke. But he relaxed again in a moment, breathing raggedly.

He grasped the front of Russo's tunic. "Emerson is dead! The Moment comes! Gather my special equipment!" He sent the smaller man on his way with a shove.

As Russo slunk away, Zand began unbuttoning his uniform jacket. Nevermore would he wear false colors! It was time to garb himself in more fitting vestments.

Today a new Universe begins!

Nova was wearing a spare suit of ATAC armor, a thing with long horns that had originally belonged to Cutter, who had died in that first assault on the mother ship. She looked a little like a metallic steer, gazing back in the direction from which the two tanks—formerly three—had come on their rescue mission.

"I don't see Zor anywhere," she leaned down to tell Angelo Dante. "He's sneaked off somewhere."

In another part of the mother ship, Zor stepped his red Bioroid forth, stalking the passageways, willing to die so long as he could work his revenge. For a moment the image of Dana's face was before him, for no reason he could name, but he thrust it aside and went on again, the ultimate intellect, bereft of any thought but revenge.

"Sarge, these passageways all look the same to me!" Louie called over the tac net. "How'll we ever find them?" Some new interference was jamming all long-range commo and even blotting out Bowie's transponder.

"We keep lookin'," Angelo said. Damn Phillips anyway, for not marking his trail!

Just then figures came dashing and dodging from a side passageway up ahead, fire ranging all around them from behind. "It's Lieutenant Crystal and Lieutenant Brown!" Louie yelled.

Bowie and Musica came close after, ducking for cover at either side of the passageway, as the two TASC pilots did. Intense fire from the guards splashed from the bulkheads. The guards' counterattack was so sudden and determined that the Humans had been forced to leave Emerson's body behind.

Sean's holding action back in the "senate" chamber wasn't keeping all the guards pinned down. More showed up, from the the other direction, with a clear line of fire. But before they could cut down their prey, a sustained burst from a Hovertank's secondary batteries felled them all in a squall of blazing rapid-fire bolts.

Bowie and the others turned and, stunned, saw Dana drift her *Valkyrie* to a stop, its quad-barrels sending up shimmering heat waves.

Bowie was momentarily confused. Hadn't *Re-Tread* and Dana's tank been parked in the *other* direction? He hadn't seen her slip away while Emerson lay dying, to make an almost suicidal dash for her mecha.

Now she jumped up in her cockpit and fired with her carbine, afraid that the heavy guns might hit friend as well as foe. A last guard pitched from a ledge just above her friends' heads. Then she whirled and fired into a guard runabout that was bearing down on her from the opposite side; the runabout's windshield melted and the little vehicle rolled, throwing guards every which way, and plowed to a stop.

Sean fought his way free and caught up, as Angelo, Nova, and Louie came to a stop with blaring retros. While Dennis Brown and Bowie supported Sean in holding back the guards who had chased them from the "senate," Marie Crystal jumped into the runabout and got it started up.

Musica, Bowie, and Brown piled in. Marie gunned away, convoyed by the four Hovertanks. It was only then that Dana realized Zor was missing.

The decision had been made to strike, the Humans' determination to fight notwithstanding.

"We must consolidate our strength," Dag declared. "Eliminate all clones functioning beneath an efficiency factor of eighty percent." The other four mother ships and most of the combat vessels were almost useless for combat now, depleted as they were; the flagship was the only remaining hope.

Jeddar started to object. He knew that the Master didn't mean simply denying the clones Protoculture, but also to eject them from the flagship.

"They may not *submit* to elimination, m'lord," Jeddar pointed out.

"Then confine them for the moment!" Shaizan lashed out. "And get ready to dispose of them. Begin the assault on the buried Matrix below!"

Even the fanatic loyalty of the guard clones failed before the massed firepower of the tanks; in time the running fire-fight became an unchallenged withdrawal. Dana couldn't believe the Masters didn't have more of their Triumviroids around—but why weren't they using them?

The ATACs had lost their bearings, and even Musica couldn't tell where they were. They burned through hatches, and came at last to a hangar deck where whiskbroom-shaped assault ships were ranked side by side.

There was only time for brief kissing and hugging—passionate between Sean and Marie, more reserved but plainly heartfelt between Nova and Dennis—before the question of how to get out alive took center stage.

Marie and Dennis weren't sure if they could fly an assault ship; planetary approaches in an unfamiliar spacecraft were a lot different from joyrides in a guard runabout.

"See what you can do," Dana said, revving *Valkyrie*. "I'm going back for Zor."

Angelo felt like tearing out his hair. "Lieutenant, this just ain't fair! It ain't *army*!"

"I'm not working for the army anymore, Angie," she threw back, the tank pivoting on its thrusters. "If I'm not back in twenty minutes, go on without me."

She was scarcely gone when Bowie and Musica went to stand before the sergeant hand in hand. "I'm going back, too," Bowie announced. "Musica says her people are in terrible danger."

"I can sense it," she explained. "My sisters and I are linked—are one."

Bowie touched her shoulder gently. "It's all right; we'll find them." Perhaps this was part of the teaching that Rolf Emerson had said he and Musica must do; in any case, Bowie knew he couldn't abandon Musica's people.

Suddenly, Nova stepped forward, letting go of Dennis's hand. "I'll go with you. Dana's right: we're not working for the army anymore, and it's time for the dying to stop."

Then Brown joined her, and Marie; Angelo Dante surrendered to the inevitable. The flying officers outranked him, but that meant nothing since this was a Hovertank operation. "Sean, you 'n' Lieutenant Crystal stand pat here with *Bad News* and hold this position! See if you can figure out how to fly these things. Rest of ya, do me a favor and try not to screw up."

The Southern Cross had rallied everything it had, mobilizing reserves and arming any willing civilian, no questions asked. Cops, students, robots, convicts, bureaucrats, homemakers, kid gangs—the Human race readied its remaining resources for a last-ditch stand.

What regular forces there were would go out and meet the approaching flagship head-on; the rest would wait, to fight it out on home soil if that was what it came to.

Supreme Commander Leonard heard details of the hasty preparations, then dismissed his staff for a moment to see to a matter of personal readiness. Opening his desk drawer, he checked to make sure that the charge in his pistol was full.

He burned again with his loathing of the aliens. Leonard tucked the gun into his tunic and closed the drawer. He had no intention of letting those monsters take him alive.

It smashed its way through a stone partition and came face to face with three red Bioroids. Perhaps they recognized Zor's mecha as that of their onetime battle lord, or perhaps not; it made no difference.

Even if they had been operating at peak efficiency, the Triumviroids would have found Zor a formidable opponent. But they were depleted—scarcely any kind of match for him at all.

He dropped them with fast, accurate shots from the thick, discus-shaped handgun his Bioroid carried, its muzzle bigger than a howitzer's. But as he stepped into the compartment, three more reds dropped from above, springing their ambush.

Zor proved how experience counted; his Bioroid held up a great slab of stone to shield itself from the ambushers' fire, then blazed away in response, leaping high. He dropped one, two, three, holed through at the point where their operating clones sat curled in the control spheres.

Zor broke into yet another compartment only to see a high ledge lined with Triumviroids, dozens of them, waiting for him. Here and there were armed guardsmen, looking like insects among the mecha.

"Take me to the Masters!" he commanded. "I mean you no harm; my business is only with them."

He saw Karno, standing to one side, drop his arm in signal. Zor's Bioroid's external sound pickup caught the shouted order, "Fire!"

Zor's red ducked aside, as the blasts volleyed in all directions, ricocheted from bulkheads or penetrated them, lanced through the deck and overhead. A secondary explosion from a weakened power routing system knocked the mecha sideways.

He was momentarily in the cover of the hatchway frame, rolling and about to surge to his feet again, his red's armor striking rooster tails of sparks from the deckplates.

Karno reached out to pull a long lever nearby. "We knew you would come."

There were carefully planned explosions, and the overhead gave way; tons of metal and conduits and organic-looking Protoculture systemry landed on him like a cave-in, pinning him. At the same time, the bulkhead collapsed, tearing aside, leaving him exposed to his enemies' fire.

Karno looked down on Zor, not with the dispassion of a cloned slave, but rather with the cold hatred he had felt since losing Musica. Emotions were seeping throughout the servants of the Masters, unstoppable and often unrecognized.

"You're a fool, Zor," Karno snarled, "if you believe you have the power to stand against us! Now that this lunatic quest of yours has failed, I am instructed to offer you one final chance to repent, and rejoin us." The tone of his voice made it clear that Karno offered reconciliation unwillingly. He would much rather give the order to fire again.

Zor's red managed to lever itself up. But despite all its immense strength, it still couldn't fight its way clear of the pinning wreckage.

Zor looked into the muzzles that had been brought to bear on him, his red's gleaming black visor panning slowly, and said, putting weight behind each word, "Never. I won't stop until I end the Masters' tyranny or they end *me*."

Karno nodded, not unhappy with that pronouncement. "It shall be as you wish it." He raised his hand again to give the signal to resume firing, and the fetal clones curled in each Triumviroid's control sphere sent out commands of readiness, preparing to shoot Zor's mecha to incandescent bits.

"And so passes the very last of Zor." Karno hissed out the words, looking like a handsome young demigod turned angel of death, signal arm ready to fall.

But like a wash of pure light, an enormous bolt from a Gladiator's main battery came through another gap in the bulkheads, sending one Triumviroid leaping off the firing ledge in a volcanic blast. The Gladiator, standing in the smoking breach, traversed its great gun to blast another enemy, and then another, like clay pipes in a shooting gallery.

The lack of Musica's harmonics and the decline in Protoculture energy had the clone operators at a level of functioning that was near failure. Instead of firing back, they awaited orders, or turned and collided with each other, or merely stood waiting to die—except for the one or two who shot, inaccurately. Karno was enough of a realist to flee through a side hatchway, seething with the need to slay, to avenge himself—reverting to a level as primitive as that of any primate, without realizing it, because his intellect fed him justifications.

CHAPTER
TWENTY-ONE

When I was a little kid, after my parents left in SDF-3, I had three godfathers for a while. Maybe you heard about them, the ex-Zentraedi spies—Konda and Bron and Rico.

They knew I was half Zentraedi and that I had no close family after my folks went, so—they appointed themselves.

What I'm getting at is, they were kinder to me than anyone ever was. They had loved three female techs who were killed in the SDF-1, and I suppose to some extent I was the Zentraedi-Human kid they never had.

And when I was—I don't know, six or so, I guess—they got very ill. I found out later that the doctors said it was something that came from being reduced to our size in the Protoculture chambers. What I didn't know was that there was a possible cure, but it would only work on a full-size Zentraedi. But they stayed Human-size, so they could look after me.

They died within weeks of each other. So what I'm saying is, don't ever ask me if I'm ashamed of being half alien, or ask why I'm willing to grant Zor the benefit of the doubt. A lot of people think courage is something you can only prove on the battlefield, and love is something noisy and—what's the word I'm looking for? Demonstrative.

But aliens taught me differently.

Dana Sterling, in a remark recorded by Nova Satori

DANA FIRED AGAIN, THEN SAW THAT THE TRIUMVIR-oids were making no meaningful resistance, and ceased fire; her war wasn't with mind-enthralled, blameless clones anymore.

She operated controls and imaged with her winged, crested helmet. *Valkyrie* pivoted end for end, changing, rearing up, and in an instant she was an armored Goliath, holding a rifle the size of a field piece.

Something about the mechamorphosis made some of the reds react, it seemed; they were in motion again. She laid out a few rounds to keep their heads down, but suddenly they moved with more purpose. Dana leapt to crouch by Zor's red Bioroid, partly shielding it with her own Battloid, pouring out covering fire.

"Zor, stay down!" She shot from the hip, and a red that had been about to nail Zor went down in a subsidence of ripped armor and glowing components. But others stirred, raising their discus pistols shakily.

More reds were being brought back under control, getting ready to take up the attack once more. *Valkyrie* swung its weapon back and forth, Dana was well aware that so many Triumviroids, even hindered as they were, would shortly prevail unless she did something. She fired with one hand, trying to drag Zor free with the other. A red tromped over to a point on the ledge behind her, ready to shoot directly down.

Zor's red's arm pulled free and swung its weapon; fierce artificial lightning crashed, and the red above toppled from the ledge, even while others staggered to move into positions of advantage.

"Thank you for saving my life, Dana," Zor said, a little numbly. "But I must go on alone."

Dana dismissed the matter of who had saved whom from what in the time since she had first seen him. Each had spared the other in combat; did that count as a higher form of rescue?

Anyway, there would be better times to sort all that out; the problem was living to see them. "No way, trooper!" She was helping his mecha to its feet, pulling wreckage off it, supporting it. "It's my fight, too."

It is, in some ways I can explain, and others that—I just can't, yet.

Then he was up, and the red Bioroid and the blue-and-white Battloid were pounding along the passageway shoulder to shoulder, so that the deck alloy gonged. "Be warned: I mean to confront the Robotech Masters and destroy them," he said.

"Long as you don't destroy *yourself* at the same time. Or me," she cautioned. He heard her concern for him in her tone; and in the midst of his killing wrath, he felt a calm, clear sanity flowing from her to himself.

But a hatchway loomed up before them just then. "Look sharp, now," she said.

They took it ATAC style, poised to either side with their backs against it, like infantry in house-to-house fighting, or SWAT cops going in. Another red's shots fireballed through the hatchway past them.

Zor waited for the right moment, went through the hatchway firing, bent low, and rammed his foe shoulder-on. Dana followed, waiting for a clear shot.

"*There* are my people! Oh no, no . . ."

Musica was nearly collapsed against a crystal concavity of a viewport taller than herself, seemingly close to a faint. Bowie, Angelo, and the others halted in some confusion, not sure what she meant and thoroughly spooked by the abandoned residential district around them.

The Humans had been forced to leave their tanks behind, to pass through the tight confines of the Human-scale areas. They were armed and armored, though.

The other troopers set up security and fingered their rifles, as Bowie caught Musica just before she slumped. She was again wearing the ceremonial vestments of her office— the blue tights and torso-wrapping, the cold alloy ring around her neck with its arrowheadlike emblem.

She had found the clothes in an empty guard command center and, for some reason, insisted on changing into them while the ATACs searched nearby. But there had been no sign of her sisters and her people.

Bowie couldn't help worrying about the ceremonial clothing. The Masters had brought it with them from their other flagship and held it ready. Zor had been compelled to turn traitor; must Bowie fear such a thing from Musica?

Now, though, the riddle of the missing clones was answered, and the answers made a horrifying sense. "They *are* outside the ship!" Musica added in a small, forlorn voice.

She had sensed it, but the enormity of such a thing, the sheer incomprehensibility of it, had kept her from considering it seriously.

The troopers gathered around Musica and saw what was going on. There were many ships, drifting close by because the Masters' new flagship hadn't finished its waste disposal yet; every viewport and dome in the inert combat vessels out there was crammed with motionless, seemingly sleeping clones.

Louie Nichols looked out at it all and thought, as his stomach turned, of an animal gnawing its own leg off to escape a trap's iron teeth. What the Masters had done was infinitely worse. *God, it's all stripped away! Compassion . . . mercy.*

The pure intellect and the rational organization of society —this is where they point. Dana was right. He teetered a little, then caught his balance, and looked around to see if anyone else had noticed. But they were all transfixed.

Nova Satori looked out at the sight, rocked with surprise at herself because, until this awful moment, she had never really been able to bring herself to think of the aliens as Human beings. She had never thought of them as creatures with souls, all Zor's appeal and powers of persuasion aside. But she gazed upon genocide and knew she had been blinding *herself.* It hadn't taken so very much ordi-psych indoctrination or so very many pep talks from Supreme Commander Leonard and Colonel Fredericks to set her attitudes in concrete.

Now, though, those were wiped away. There were people out there who needed rescue.

There were other castaways, set adrift in spacesuits and smaller craft. *Now why didn't those Masters just space 'em?* a practical side of Angelo wondered. *Why leave 'em safe and sound, as it were?* Maybe the Masters meant to come back and reclaim their slaves, if the Masters won.

But the ATACs intended to see to it that the Masters didn't win. "Are they alive?" Bowie asked, gripping Musica by the shoulders.

"Yes, but doomed. Cut off from the Protoculture and the Masters' will."

And from the music of the Cosmic Harp, she admitted to herself. The Cosmic Harp was nowhere to be found; perhaps it had been destroyed in the first flagship. She was cut off from it forever, a pain as sharp as any physical wound.

"A rescue mission would be just about impossible," Louie said in his best mechie, noncommittal voice. But within, he was plotting his own personal vector along new grids, and changing parallax. There were more spacecraft in the mother ship. *Maybe, sometimes, trying the impossible is the whole point.* "Maybe we can—"

Musica cut him off. "Allegra! Octavia! My sisters are nearby!" Her eyes rolled up so that only the whites showed, and Bowie had to bear her up.

He held her close, so that he breathed her sweet breath, almost tasted it. "Are they alive?"

Blue-haired Allegra, sundered from the harmonies upon which she and her Muse sisters had lived as upon food, drink, and the air they breathed, found a troubling and yet comforting new orchestration in ministering to those around her who were suffering. She hadn't known she knew how to do it, and yet the harmonies assured her, *conducted* her through every movement.

Now she was cooling the brow of a feverish stonemason clone with a damp cloth, feeling Octavia's gaze upon her.

Allegra, kneeling there by the stone bench that had been made a sickbed, said, "His bio-index has fallen too low, and his own reserves are gone. I'm afraid there is no hope for him." The clone was pale white, sweat slick along his face and neck, long hair damp and clinging, and yet his skin was cold.

But Octavia told Allegra, "There is always hope!" and wondered where the certainty, the rightness of the words that made them a new harmony, had come from. All the old certainties had been burnt away, but in the ashes she was finding bright, warming determination that had yet to find its form.

Allegra looked at her dubiously. "I wish Musica would come." They sensed that she was near, ever the centerpiece and the wellspring of their power.

"Without the eternal Song of Musica's Harp," the stone-mason clone who rested under Octavia's dove-gentle hand said, "I have no will left to live."

How much harder do you think it is for me? she thought.

"You must not say that!" Octavia found that her voice had become harsh, a commanding note a Clonemaster might use, or even a Robotech Master. "We must learn to live on our own."

The words and the very wisdom of them had come unbidden. Suddenly there was a current of awareness in the big holding chamber, which lifted the clones' lassitude and fed power back to her. Some shackle she had never felt, even though it had confined her life and her art, had been broken. But the rightness of what she had said was a clarity that she couldn't deny or stifle, a pureness of a profound inner music she had never heard before.

A tech clone stood up next to his pallet, nearby. Weaving as he stood, he got out, "We know nothing of the Dead Life, the Life of the One. We only know the triumvirates, and now the triumvirates are no more."

Octavia didn't realize she was moving, as she stood up and gathered her half-shawl, the words flowing to her as notes from some new, unsuspected song. "Then it's time for us all to learn a new way to live. Musica is willing to stand on her own two feet and survive."

Whence come these thoughts? she belabored herself, brain roiling. Perhaps some had been transferred to her by the link with Musica, and there was the breakdown of the Masters' power, the depletion of the Protoculture, and the silence of the Cosmic Harp. The suspect sources were many.

But the central melody of it, Octavia somehow knew, came from within: a music long subsumed by the narrow, repetitive themes the Masters had forced the Muses to play.

"We still may be rescued, or save *ourselves*," Allegra added. Octavia was shocked at first, but then felt more sisterly to her than she ever had.

But Allegra's patient hiked himself up on his elbows, feverish, to say as if in some fortune-telling trance, "Even if we *are* rescued, who among us could live a life so forlorn? A life where the triumvirates are broken apart? We are *parts*, we are not *whole!*"

Octavia didn't know how to answer that, exactly; she hadn't the right words in her vocabulary, or the right notes in her music.

And yet, bringing all her will to bear, she knew in a revelation as bright as a mountain sunrise that he was wrong.

From Earth rose every remnant of its military striking power. Nothing that could conceivably reach the approaching Masters was left behind; men and women readied for battle and took strength from a source greater than the Protoculture.

They were willing to die for their families and children and planet, if that be the price, so long as the Masters died as well. And if the Masters meant to end life on the planet, then *all*, invader and defender, would die alike.

The beings who had ruled galaxies, and meant to rule all the Universe, wouldn't have understood that sense of fatalism no matter how it was phrased.

Again, that terrible Human advantage had come into play. The Masters proceeded, as they always had, upon logical conclusions; the creatures Earth had bred rose up, in a manner that swept those calculations away, to stand and fight.

Just then a minor sub-subentity, an artificial intelligence construct of the Protoculture cap, reported to the Masters that there was no rational explanation as to why these creatures had not either totally destroyed themselves, or become a slave culture (a stagnant one, the subentity would have pointed out, if the Masters had created it to be more candid) like the Robotech Masters' clones. The concept of a third alternative had simply never been considered before.

Zor, Zor . . . you sent your dimensional fortress to no random world! Earth was a deliberate choice for the centerpiece of this great War, wasn't it? Some least-constrained part of the Masters' unified consciousness whispered the insight, a death-dry croak that sent panic all through them and made the cap pulse like an alarm beacon.

Then they had it back under control again, and themselves as well. "The Micronian fleet is advancing, m'lords," Jeddar said, head bowed low, frightened by his own boldness in interrupting them but frightened even more by the long barracuda shapes of the Terran warships.

Then Shaizan, Dag, and Bowkaz were alert once more, eyes so bright that it seemed rays of divine wrath might shoot forth. The Masters had shaken off or put down every misgiving. If there was some small voice within their communal mind that persisted in faint, tormented murmurs of mortality, it was altogether drowned out in their drumming mental din of conquest.

Or at least, *almost* altogether; none of the three would dare admit he heard it.

Shaizan sent out the command, "Let half of our remaining attack forces go forth to engage this enemy fleet. The remainder will descend to the planet and retrieve the Protoculture Matrix."

The other mother ships were all but useless, as were the combat craft and clones and mecha remaining to them. But the Protoculture cap told them the resources still available to the Masters in their flagship would more than suffice.

As long as the Matrix was recovered, any and all losses suffered would be negligible. But if the mission failed, such sacrifices would be immaterial: the Robotech Masters themselves would have no hope of survival.

Shaizan touched the Protoculture cap again, so that the Masters were gazing down on a scene of the three mounds near Monument City. Sensors indicated that the aura of protection generated by the guardian wraiths below was weakening. As the energy of the last Matrix began to fail, the powers of the wraiths diminished. There was yet a tiny, unique window of opportunity. The Protoculture cap had already gotten a precise fix on the Matrix's location, like seeking out like, across the negligible distance between planet and space.

Shaizan had activated another mechanism. Like magic, a circular gap appeared in the deck behind them, and from it rose a glassy sphere a yard in diameter. They turned to regard it.

Within it was the last major Protoculture mass left to them, not a Matrix that could perpetuate itself and spawn other Matrices, but still a power source of vast potency. It was a tangled collection of vegetable-looking matter, glowing and flickering, sending out concentric waves of faint blue light in a nimbus. It was far different from the huge mass Louie Nichols had seen and by which he had been captured; this one was uncontaminated and unbloated.

It was contained in a clear canister only a little larger than and the same shape as an earthly hurricane lantern, with flat metal discs of systemry at either end. The container and the globe around it rested on a stem of metal that was grown around with leaved creepers of a Flower of Life stem.

Ranged around the compartment were other such vessels, the Flowers within them now blooming—the masses useless, their remaining power shunted into the single remaining viable one.

Its power, too, would soon show signs of atrophy, but it would serve. The three looked on it silently, thinking greedy thoughts of the vast energies waiting for them on Earth, exulting in the contemplation of the absolute tyranny they could establish.

"Our victory is within reach," Shaizan said aloud, and the words had a death-knell echo in the chamber.

"I shall *never* allow that victory!" a new voice cried, a ringing challenge. The Masters whirled, shocked.

CHAPTER
TWENTY-TWO

Lazlo, my dear friend,

Comes now a parting of the ways; you know our quandary. Max and Miriya Sterling will not consent to bringing their child, Dana, along on the SDF-3 expedition for fear that the Shaping endangers her, and for mistrust of me, I suspect. It may even be that Jean and Vince Grant leave their little boy behind for kindred reasons.

Of course, you will be monitoring Dana's progress and seeing to her welfare and education; that is a given. But I warn you to do nothing, nothing, to harm her. The scales of the Protoculture, we know, often take a long time to come back into balance, but ill is always paid for ill, and good for good, despite your ponderings.

Parents are a fearsome breed anyway; how much more so, Earth's greatest Robotech ace and the battle queen of the Zentraedi?

While we may look to the Shaping for certain protection, do not make the mistake of forgetting that there are Powers far and above anything we see in the Protoculture.

Your colleague,
Emil Lang

"**S**O, ZOR PRIME, YOU HAVE FINALLY COME," Shaizan managed to say. "We have been expecting you, and you have not disappointed us."

And they had expected him, but not quite like this. How had he survived the Triumviroids? He was armored, though unhelmeted, and had a Southern Cross assault rifle leveled at them. Dana was backing him up, the stock of her tanker's carbine clamped against her hip, muzzle swinging a bit to keep them all covered.

Still, the Masters were little dismayed. In the final analysis wasn't Zor one of them? The Protoculture's intoxicating effect on them, the rush of its sheer power, made them sure that if they offered to share it with the clone, he would be theirs. The halfbreed enemy female was of no real importance.

"So—you know why I'm here?" Zor asked, eyes narrowed.

Shaizan nodded serenely. "But of course. Your purpose has always remained the same—through *every incarnation*."

"You are the embodiment of the original Zor," Bowkaz added, "creator of the first Protoculture Matrix, the Master responsible for our race's ascendency."

The words had Dana reeling; she had good reason to know some of the Masters' works. "You mean . . . Zor also developed the Zentraedi people?"

Dag studied her. "Zor was the prime force behind *all* the advancements of our race." He sensed that Zor Prime hadn't yet recalled all the things the Masters and their Elders had done to the original Zor. If he had, Dag thought, the clone would have entered firing.

Dana studied Zor Prime, reincarnation of the man who had created her mother's race—he who was therefore, at least in part, her own creator as well. She looked back to the Protoculture mass, and wondered if it was the key to everything: the war, peace, and her own origins and destiny.

"But his most important discovery—the one from which our lifeblood flows—is the Protoculture that makes possible eternal life," Shaizan was saying.

Zor, though, was shaking his head angrily, eyes squeezed to mere slits, breathing hard. "No! I was never a Master, never one of you! And the Protoculture hasn't brought life; it has brought only death!"

He brought the assault rifle level with his waist and fired, the weapon burping brief meteoric bursts that blew open a half dozen of the canisters of degraded Protoculture mass along the wall. It showered the deck with nutrient fluids and the raveled, dripping Flowers of Life, their soaked petals and spores, their intertangled roots and blossoms.

"I will end this here and now!" he screamed, turning the barrel on his onetime Masters.

In spite of their calm greeting, the Masters hadn't thought

to confront Zor at this moment, in this situation. It was suddenly clear that he was too overwrought to listen to reason or blandishment. The accursed Human emotions had thrown the Masters' calculations awry yet again.

Shaizan stepped from the Protoculture cap to stand protectively near the resplendent globe that held the remaining mass. Zor must be kept at bay, until the help that had already been silently summoned could arrive. "Surely you are not prepared to destroy your most precious creation, the embodiment of all your hopes and dreams. Without it, your own species and the civilization you founded will die."

Shaizan himself felt a strange ripple coursing through him. He felt as if he needed biostabilization and longed for contact with the Protoculture cap, but there was no time for that in this crisis. He could see that both Dag and Bowkaz were experiencing the weird perturbations, too.

"My civilization is *already* dead!" Zor hissed, and opened fire again, bolts chopping at the spilled, saturated Flowers, sending up steam and burning blossoms and bits of glowing deckplate.

Zor felt as if he were made of pure rage. Strange, that beings as emotionless as the Masters should find it so easy to use emotions to their own ends—to torment him and manipulate him so with guilt and sorrow—to batter down his resolve. They made it so hard to think clearly, and unclear thought could only work to their benefit.

Then, all at once, the scent of the Flowers came to him. The aroma summoned up a memory as clear and substantial as diamond, though it was a memory inherited from a Zor who had died long ago. He recalled how he had plumbed the mysteries of Protoculture, and why, and the tragedies of that great undertaking. He recalled, too, that he had never intended his discoveries to be used for the ends to which the Masters had put them. He saw that the civilization—if that was the word for it—around him was *their* perversion, their responsibility, not his.

And he saw, in an almost preternatural calmness, that it didn't lie within his power to *change* the Masters' civilization, only to *stop* it.

Zor brought his weapon around and blasted the base of the sphere. The glassy material shattered, in big fragments and infinitesimal ones, like the end of some Cosmic Egg. Shaizan bent aside, shielding himself with his hands.

A secondary explosion in the systemry under the Masters' last protoculture mass shot the hurricane-lantern canister into the air, as if a child had launched a tin can with a firecracker.

Trailing wires and dendrites, it turned slowly end for end. Unused to physical action, Bowkaz still sprang from his standing place at the cap to catch it before it shattered against the deck.

But Zor was pivoting, livid with anger. Perhaps he would have fired at *anybody* who came into his sights then—even Dana. Certainly, he shot Bowkaz, the impact of the blasts sending the Master back, setting his monkish robes on fire, his Flower of Life–shaped collar flopping, to fall to the deck.

But while Zor was distracted, firing at the Master, Dana was in motion, slinging her carbine over her shoulder and leaping high. It wasn't so different from football or volleyball, but it was the best save she had ever made. She had always been athletic, but a desperation to save what might be her own personal salvation and the key to the war made her faster and stronger than she had ever been before.

And yet, even while she hurled herself up for the catch, gauntleted hands closing in, she could hear the one called Dag actually screeching, "Do not touch the terminals!"

She had no choice; Dana caught it as best she could, and as her hands closed over the discs of systemry at either end of the canister, there was a bright discharge. She wailed, a long, sustained sound, as an absolute-zero shock of energy pulsed through her, and time seemed to slow.

She could see every detail of the vegetable mass in the canister. It was really very beautiful. Unhurriedly—though she could sense, somehow, that it was happening very quickly—the little twisted buds that reminded her of the mother ships' cannon began to open.

Sheets of crackling energy raged and swept through the compartment, throwing out harsh shadows one moment, then making her and Zor and the Masters all transparent as X rays the next. Bowkaz had barely begun to fall, but his fall was stopping, making him seem to her to hang in midair, contorted with pain from Zor Prime's shot.

The canister and its Protoculture mass glowed like a star. Shaizan, watching, registered *Impossible!* The Masters, in concert with their Protoculture cap, might have been able to work something like that effect, but no unaided entity—not Elder, Master, clone, Zentraedi, or Human—could so evoke the power of the Universe's most potent force.

But Dana heard. Somehow, as if from far away, she heard Shaizan's thought-speech, *The Flowers have blossomed!*

Far below, Flowers began opening faster and faster, as the three enigmatic entities set to guard and watch over the matrix by Zor sensed what had happened in the mother ship. The three wraiths began to gather themselves, depleted as they were, for their final task.

Zor felt himself engulfed in a quicksand of time dilation; he began to mouth a cry that echoed Dana's, a cry that seemed to stretch to Forever. And still the canister poured its full energies into Dana Sterling, who hung in a split-instant's graceful pose, high in the air with the Masters' last Protoculture mass radiant between her hands. . . .

With no sense of transition, she found herself awakening on a green field lush with the pink Flowers of Life. She still wore her armor; she looked around at hills and vales, not sure that they were of Earth, though she saw wind-blasted crags and what seemed to be rusting Zentraedi wrecks in the distance. She had barely begun to wonder how she had come to be there when she realized she wasn't alone.

"Huh?"

There were dark, cloaked figures standing back at a slight remove—female, she thought, feeling a bit drifty, though she couldn't quite be certain. Each of the dark figures held one of the three-stemmed Flowers of Life, the three-that-were-one.

But there was someone else, kneeling right before her, a

compact, blond young woman in gauzy pink robes, clutching a bouquet of the Flowers, wearing a necklace something like Musica's. The woman had a roundish hairdo and an upturned, freckled nose; she was calm, and yet there was a sense of life and gusto to her that made her very winsome.

Dana gave her head a slight shake and realized that she was looking at herself. And she realized that she, like this image of her, held a Flower of Life.

She levered herself up and saw that there were more of the dark figures, standing silently—making no move as yet —clutching their Flowers, forming a ring around Dana and her doppelgänger. Dana realized that she wasn't armed, but somehow the fact didn't bother her, and she felt only peace and a yearning to have her questions answered.

Then the kneeling image of herself suddenly shifted, separating out to either side so that there were three, smiling their mysterious smiles at her.

The triumvirate! She sat bolt upright, recalling what had happened—grasping the canister—and looking at the Flower in her hand.

The discharges released the Zentraedi side of my mind! I'm seeing those other sides of me that would have come to life if I were part of a triad!

She suddenly felt terribly alone. She had never known her family, never known much about her mother's race, had grown up cut off from most of the knowledge of self that people around her so took for granted.

And here was not just one other Dana, but three. A chance for a closeness and unity, a companionship, beyond anything Humans knew. No surprise, it occurred to her, that it was the first thing her expanded powers of mind had summoned up from the vast reservoir of the Protoculture.

But even as she was about to embrace her sibling-clones, something held her back. The image came to mind of Musica, and of the sad scenes in the mother ships of the Masters. She remembered the antiseptic cruelty of triumvirate life and the obscene murder of the clone Latell.

She still couldn't understand or see clearly who those shrouded entities were, gathered around her, but perceived that they were listening closely, were attentive to her response. Dana felt that some crucial judgment was hanging in the air.

But it didn't take a lot of soul-searching. She had seen all the sorrows of the submerged personalities of the triumvirates. She looked to her potential otherselves again. Their stares were somehow malign now, and hungry—as if they wanted to devour her, to subsume her in themselves and bury forever the personality that had grown up, for good or ill, as Dana Sterling.

Dana hurled the Flower to the ground; it shattered and disappeared like a de-rezzing computer image. "I am *not* a part of your triumvirate! I am an *individual Human being!*"

The triplicate visions moaned in concert—hollow sounds like the faraway wails of tortured children. They seemed to turn to smoke, becoming vacant-eyed ghosts that were rent in the wind like spindrift, their Flowers dissolving as well.

The dark listeners evaporated, too, with thin, pipe-organ howls like mourning specters, resigned to their eternal fate. They faded, now part of a reality that would never come to be.

Dana was on her feet. The green had vanished, and she ground herself in a bleak and blasted setting, lifeless as any lunar crater but still recognizably an Earthscape.

She threw the words out angrily. "I reject the horrors of your civilization!" She wasn't sure if she was talking to the Masters, or the Protoculture, or her own Zentraedi heritage. "I reject your values and your beliefs!"

Who is there to hear? she wondered, and yet she knew she wasn't going unheard. "I'm an individual, a free Human being of the planet Earth!"

It came to her that she was standing in a place of scattered Human bones, a skull nearly beneath her feet. There was no stirring of air, no hint of life, anywhere across a limitless plain covered with ash and roofed over by low clouds that might have come from some planetary cremation.

Is this it? Is this the future of both civilizations? Suddenly she was running, calling for help in a bleak landscape that even denied her echoes.

Her foot turned on a shattered skeleton, and she fell headlong. But as she fell, the ash smothering her, clogging her throat and nostrils, she heard somebody calling her name.

She shook her head to clear it, but when she looked up, she was in some strange, kinder place. There was the blue and green of growing things, but not any that she could identify. The smell of life and the clarity of the air made her gasp, though.

"Dana, wait for me! I'm coming!"

There were low crystal domes of the Flowers of Life before her, and a starlit sky with no constellation she could recognize. Somewhere there was ethereal music that reminded her of the Cosmic Harp's, and a little girl was dashing toward her.

"I—I'm not going anywhere," Dana said dazedly.

She was ten or so, Dana guessed, a black-haired, sprite-like thing with huge dark eyes, wearing a short, flowing garment of gold and white. Her tiny waist was encircled by a broad belt, her wrists and throat banded by the same red-brown leathery stuff. She wore a garland of woven Flowers of Life in her hair, and carried another.

"Who *are* you?" Dana got out.

The child stopped before her. "Your sister, Dana! The other daughter of Max and Miriya Sterling! I was born a long, long way from Earth, and I've come to warn you. Oh, Mother and Father will be so glad to know I've *finally* made contact with you!"

"I'm glad, too," Dana said haltingly, praying it wasn't just some hallucination. "But what are you supposed to warn me about?"

"The spores, Dana."

This, even while the little girl pressed the Flower of Life into Dana's armor-clad hands. "I've come to bring you these Flowers and to warn you about the spores."

"Please—" Dana couldn't bear it, was afraid the thought of the Flowers and the Protoculture and the rest of it would shake her loose from this Vision or contact or whatever it was. "Let's not talk about that. Tell me about *you*! What's your name?"

The little girl was giggling. But then she turned and raced away in the direction from which she had come. Dana was left to yell, "Hey! Please come back! I want to know more!"

Two more shadow-figures had appeared, a man and a woman, graceful beings whose figures were indistinct in the way of this strange half world. A cape billowed around the woman, and there was something familiar about the way the man had his arm around her, two presences Dana had felt before.

The child went running toward them, and they opened their arms to her. As the three apparitions looked to her, Dana heard voices she knew, speaking without speech.

The spores, Dana! Beware the spores, and the Invid!

"The—the what?" She felt dizzy. Her own memories and old tapes of Max and Miriya Sterling told her that she was truly hearing her parents' voices—or rather, their thoughts.

Beware the Invid! They will come in search of the spores!

She had a million things to ask them and to tell them, but the contact seemed to be growing weaker, for when the mind-message came again, it was faint.

Time grows short. So much has happened since our last contact with Earth, so many astounding things! Your powers are awake now, and they are growing! Use them cautiously; we of the Sentinels are only beginning to understand the true nature of Protoculture.

The Sentinels? Dana wondered at the sound of the words.

And then she heard was her sister's voice. *We love you, Dana! We love you very much!*

We love you very, very much, daughter, her parents added, as the voices faded.

"Oh, I—I love you, too! And I miss you so!"

Then the shadow figures were gone, and she was left to hope they had heard her, as the pink petals of the Flower of Life drifted around her.

CHAPTER
TWENTY-THREE

> *I lie down at night with my children safely asleep and my dear
> wife beside me and send up a—one hopes, modest—prayer to the
> One. And the prayer is thanks.*
>
> *But, oh! Those days! How I would love to have lived them,
> even if it were only to be slain on the first!*

> Isaac Mandelbrot, *Movers and Shakers: The Heritage of
> the Second Robotech War*

ZOR CROUCHED NEAR DANA'S BODY, GLARING UP AT
the images of the two surviving Robotech Masters.

He still held his weapon, but it would do him little good;
Shaizan and Bowkaz had struck in the moment Zor turned
aside to shoot down the android shock troopers they had
summoned. That had been the work of mere seconds, but in
that time, as Zor stood straddling the unconscious Dana, the
Masters had recovered the last Protoculture mass and made
their escape, protected by the powers of the cap.

But they had sent back their mind-projected simulacra to
deliver their death warrant. Zor heard Dana begin to stir,
but felt little relief; his hatred of the Masters was too all-
consuming for him to feel any gentler emotion.

Dana raised her head groggily, hearing the one called
Shaizan saying, "All those who stand against us shall perish!
Soon we will have the Matrix, and be all-powerful once
more. Therefore, surrender to us and be spared, Zor."

She saw the two Masters, but realized that she could see *through* them, as though they were made of stained glass.

Zor threw his head back and spat, "Your perversion of the Protoculture only proves how little you truly know about it. Do you think such things can go unpunished? No! And I'll never rest until there has been vengeance."

Dana had hauled herself to her feet, mind still whirling with the things she had seen and heard in her trance. But she drew a deep breath and said, "I'll be right behind you, Zor."

That seemed to bring him out of his seizure of blind rage. He turned and put his hand on her shoulder. "Thank you. Thank you many times over, Dana. For showing me kindness and . . . for caring for me. For helping me become whole again, and free myself."

He smiled, but it was bittersweet, as he shouldered his weapon. "I only wish you were safely out of here."

He indicated the compartment's hatch. "That's one barrier we could never burn through with hand weapons, and the Masters have sealed us in—given the ship's systemry an order through their Protoculture cap. We're trapped."

"Are you sure? It's worth a try, anyhow." She crossed to it. "Maybe we can short-circuit it, or something."

He was about to tell her that the Protoculture didn't work that way, that there was no hope of countermanding the Masters' instruction to it, when the hatch opened to her touch at the controls.

Zor Prime looked at her, open-mouthed. *"By the Protoculture!"* he whispered. *"Who are you?"*

She shrugged. "I'm only beginning to find out. In a lot of ways, we're the same. Now, how do we find those two and stop them?"

He had the rifle off his shoulder again. "Rest assured: we will find them."

"Musica's come!" Octavia rose from her ministrations to a dying clone, and Allegra did the same. Already, in the Muses' minds, there were the unheard harmonies of their triumvirate.

Musica appeared a moment later, leading the ATACs and

Nova Satori and Dennis Brown. The Muses were reunited in a three-cornered embrace. "I'm so happy you both are still alive!" Musica said. "Many of our people have been set adrift in space."

Bowie had come up behind her. "We've got to get out of here. The guards are headed this way!"

The Muses turned to their people, the three voices raised in urgent singsong, beseeching them to get up, to follow, and escape.

The phlegmatic clones didn't seem to hear, at first, but in moments the 15th troopers were tugging them upright. Dante's voice came in a roaring counterpoint, getting more of the clones moving the way only an experienced NCO could; he was perfectly happy frightening and intimidating people, if it was for their own good.

Nova, too, helped roust the Masters' slaves. She no longer looked on them as the enemy or soulless biological units; she had changed, just as the others had changed in this last stage of the Second Robotech War. Coming across the tiny infant clone that Dana had seen on the 15th's last foray aboard a Master ship, she saw no one else was looking after it and so gathered it up in her arms, calling on the adults to follow her lead.

In seconds, scores of clones who had been resigned to death were up and active. Hope, and the example of Musica and her sisters, filled the emptiness that had afflicted the clones when the Masters discarded them.

The patchwork Terran attack fleet moved in, deploying its combat forces, and opened fire. A-JACs, VTs, and other combat craft raked the mother ships with energy weapons and all the ordnance they could carry. Triumviroids swept out to meet them, fighting with a furious disregard for their own survival.

The Human battlecruisers let loose their volleys; missiles and cannon blasts lit the scene. Warheads blossomed in hideous orange-red eruptions. The Robotech Masters' Flower bud–shaped guns answered, filling that volume of the void with their eerie green electric-arc effects and white-hot volleys.

With power so low, though, the Masters couldn't afford to generate their snowflakelike defensive fields, and so the battle was a slugging match. The four remaining mother ships, drained of their Protoculture reserves, were sitting ducks for the Human gunners. Pass after pass by the mecha and broadsides from the heavier craft inflicted heavy damage on the mightiest machines of the Masters' Robotechnology. But what the Humans didn't realize was that they were wasting valuable time and effort on targets of no importance—on targets that contained only a few barely functioning zombies.

The Masters' flagship was far more effective, taking a heavy toll on its attackers and sustaining little damage. The Southern Cross forces, unaware that they had been outflanked, decided to concentrate on eliminating the other mother ships first. They would deal with the flagship once the rest of the invasion fleet had been destroyed.

One mother ship flared, and minutes later, another, their power systems rupturing and yielding up their remaining energy in explosions that expanded them and rent them apart.

Another mother ship, drifting, began the long crash-plunge into the Earth's atmosphere. Mecha and heavy craft raced after, trying desperately to shoot it to bits. The impact of an object that large could work more damage than any other blow the Masters had yet struck; Humanity had learned that with the SDF-1's crash, so long ago.

It was then that the first reports came through of the massive, renewed attack on Earth itself.

The Triumviroids dropped in waves on Monument City, Fokker Base, and a half-dozen other strategic objectives in the region of the mounds. Southern Cross mecha and defense forces barely had time to brace themselves before the countryside became a ghastly killing ground.

Reds whirled and swooped on their Hovercraft, strafing and spreading death and destruction. Outnumbered, the Humans fought grimly to make every death count, but still the uneven score mounted in the enemy's favor. All the volunteers and final reserves went into action. The death toll mounted and mounted.

Triumviroids met their end, too, in staggering numbers; it mattered little to the Masters if their mecha-slaves were wiped out to the last one. The Matrix was the only important thing now. Neither side gave quarter or asked it.

In his office high up in the Southern Cross headquarters, Supreme Commander Leonard looked down on the flaming graveyard that was Monument City.

Colonel Seward implored again, "Sir, the defense forces are simply outgunned and outnumbered! Monument City's doomed! We have no choice but to evacuate!"

Seward knew there was at that moment another flight of assault ships coming in at the city from the north. It might already be too late. For some reason, the enemy hadn't seemed to have understood that the slim white towers were the nerve center of the Terran military. But with the enormous volume of communications traffic now being channeled directly there, and the obvious disposition of surviving forces to protect it, even the aliens would realize it was a prize target.

Seward fidgeted, wanting to run. Good career moves might justify a certain recklessness, but all the threat-evaluation computers agreed that staying in the HQ was suicide. And Seward had no desire for a posthumous medal, no matter how high.

But Leonard didn't seem to see things that way. He stood, bulky and stolid as a stone, his back to the staff officer, watching as the city burned.

Even as Seward was begging for Leonard to see reason, alien sights were ranging on the white towers. Slim, gleaming pillars suggesting Crusaders' pennons and medieval ramparts, the HQ structures were an easy target to spot. Targetting computer gunlock was established almost instantly.

"Go if you want," Leonard said brusquely. "I'm staying here until this battle is over."

It wasn't an act of bravery or loyalty. He knew he had made a terrible blunder, answering the alien feint with the bulk of his forces. His hatred of all things unearthly, the loathing born in the terrible injuries he had taken in combat against the Zentraedi, had blinded him to everything but the chance for revenge.

He seemed bigger than life to the people around him, but the damage done him—to his body and thus to his spirit, his mind—that day of Dolza's holocaust attack, almost eighteen years before, was beyond any healing.

From the moment when Leonard had overridden Emerson's wait-and-see policy, when the Masters first showed up, things had gone from bad to worse. Leonard had long since admitted to himself that Rolf Emerson was the better strategist and tactician by far, the better general even in terms of commanding his troops' loyalty. But—*dammit!* The man had no true appreciation of the danger of these aliens, of *all* aliens!

Seward saw further argument was useless, and started for the door. His rationalization was that he was carrying Leonard's last dispatch, but in fact he was deserting his doomed post. The Southern Cross was finished.

Leonard let him go, waiting to die. Better that way, rather than to live, being known as the man who had lost Earth to obscene monsters from another star.

Leonard didn't have long to wait; the first salvoes hit while Seward was still in the doorway, a massive strike that lit the sky and shook the ground. The proud white towers of the Southern Cross were blackened, as concrete went to powder and structural alloys melted at the peripheries. At the centers of the hits, there was complete destruction. For Leonard, it was the end of an inner agony that had lasted some seventeen years; for the Human race, his death came too late.

The 15th had picked up more of the refugee clones, hundreds of them, until Angelo Dante began wishing somebody a little more suited to the mass escape was in charge—say, somebody who could part the Red Sea, for instance.

But there wasn't; even Lieutenant Satori was less qualified than he to lead a combat operation like this. *Just a big, dumb career sergeant waiting around for his pension*, he thought, *who happened to get his turn in the barrel at the wrong time. Just bad luck; drive on, ATACs!*

Going back for the tanks was out of the question. The 15th had to move onward, as fast as possible, and give their trust to luck.

"This hatch leads to an assault ship docking area," the clone who was guiding him said, crouched on the ladderway under an oblong metal slab. "I think it is the one you wanted."

Dante was hunkered down next to him, studying the hatch. Spread out behind him on the ladderway and the drawbridge-like catwalks leading to it were the murmuring, frightened clones marked by the Masters for mass extermination. Nova and the rest of the 15th were spread out through the crowd, trying desperately to keep the people from panicking.

People, Dante sighed to himself. Hell, no denying it: that was the way the ATACs had come to think of them. And ATAC-15's line of work was *not* letting innocent people be slaughtered.

Angelo gripped his rifle and awkwardly changed places with the clone, then eased the hatch up for a look. The place was empty, as far as he could see; more to the point, there were three or four of the whiskbroom-shaped assault ships waiting there, parked in a row. The hatchway was in a passageway leading to the hangar deck, which was at a slightly lower level.

He couldn't believe the ships hadn't been committed to the battle, but he didn't have time to question the gift from above. What he didn't realize was that the combat craft ferried in from the other, abandoned mother ships were so many that the Masters couldn't man them all with the functioning clones and mecha left to them. *Not much choice; this's the only chance we're gonna get.*

He couldn't see Sean Phillips around anywhere, though. Maybe this *wasn't* the right hangar. Nevertheless, it would have to do.

Angelo knelt in firing position by the open hatch, waiting for the snipers to smoke him. But when that didn't happen, he turned to face the anxious clone looking up at him.

"Get 'em all up here now, and start boarding 'em. Tell 'em to hurry, but keep the noise down."

The word was passed. The first of the refugees began pouring up out of the hatch and making their way, at Angelo's direction, down the passageway, gathering in it and awaiting the run for the ships.

He looked this way and that constantly, swinging his rifle's muzzle, even though he knew an ambush at this point would probably be the end of it. And it would save the army at least one pension, god*dam*mit all!

But as he tried to help people up through the hatch with one hand and guard at all points at the same time, help arrived. Louie Nichols came up, dark-goggled and very matter-of-fact, taking up a kneeling firing stance at the other side of the hatch. Bowie, having sealed the lower hatches behind them, was next, covering another field of fire, with Musica and her sister Muses flocking after. Angelo began to feel better.

Still the clones poured in, filling the area between the deck-level hatch and the much bigger one through which they would have to race for the assault ships. Nova Satori emerged, still clutching the baby, but with her pistol in the hand that held it, the other hand free to grip the ladder-well railing. Dennis was right behind, with one of the short two-hand weapons.

Hundreds came up; Angelo was sweating not just for the time when he could kick the hatch shut and seal it with a few shots, and get the hell out of the mother ship, but for the moment when he could turn his problems over to some brass hat. Anybody who wanted responsibility for this many lives had to be some sorta egomaniacal helmet case.

He was just thinking that when he heard the mewing of alien small arms, in the direction of the large hatch at the end of the passageway.

There wasn't much room for a stealthy approach in the bleating press of the frightened mob, but Angelo went bulling through them, holding his weapon high in the hope that it wouldn't be jostled and torn from his grip. Forging his way to the front of the crowd, he noticed that Louie and the others were doing their best to follow, but lacked his size and sheer strength.

The bodies of three clone refugees, two males and a female, lay dead on the deck.

There were huge containers and crates at that end, and ledges near the hatch. Now clone guard riflemen stood all along those, as the lights came up. "Stay where you are!" a clone voice was saying, in that trembling single-sideband quaver of the true Masters' slave.

Angelo heard somebody say, "Huh?" beside him, and realized that Louie Nichols was there, somehow, swinging the sights of his rifle to cover the left, leaving the right to Angelo, just like a drill.

"Make no move, or you will be shot." The lights brightened. A triad of clones marched in lockstep from behind one pile of cottage-sized crates, and Angelo couldn't even tell which one was talking—or maybe they *all* were—when they right-faced and glared at the escapees. "Everyone in this room, go back or be exterminated."

"Karno," Bowie heard Musica say. And Allegra added, "We're trapped here."

The Muses looked at their selected mates: Karno, Darsis, and Sookol, as alike as they could be without being one person. Musica said, "Karno, how can you *do* this? We all have a right to live!"

Darsis spat, "How *dare* you speak of rights, you who have betrayed the triumvirate? Traitors to our society and our way of life! All of you will return to your appointed places immediately, or be shot down where you stand!"

The crowd let out a concerted moan at that, but they didn't withdraw. They were creatures who knew logic—at least—thoroughly, and they saw that there was no survival in that direction, either. The ATACs and Nova were moved by something less subject to rational analysis, but they all stood shoulder to shoulder.

TWENTY-FOUR

Alpha! Tact'l! Armored! Corps!
Yo' ain't goin' home no more!
Yo' want comforts, yo' want millions?
Shoulda stayed wit' the civilians!

ATAC marching cadence

"**N**O ONE WILL BE LEAVING HERE," NOVA PROnounced the words slowly and carefully. Bowie noticed how open the words were to several different interpretations.

Nova patted the small bundle of the clone infant. She had tucked her sidearm in its holster, turning her hip away from the clones' sight, but was ready to grab it out if things came to that. Dennis was edging her way.

She was also drawing the guards' attention. She had noted that Louie Nichols was holding a shock grenade behind his back, fiddling with it by feel while he watched Karno and the rest, readying to toss it. Nova readied herself to dive for cover, taking into account the fact that no harm must come to the baby if she could help it.

"These are not your slaves!" Musica cried. "These are individuals, whose freedom of choice has made them free of your society. Now, stand away!"

"Then you will die, you who disrupt our lives!" With that,

Karno brought up his weapon, as did Sookol and Darsis, and opened fire. At that moment, the young man who had acted as guide for Angelo threw himself in front of Musica. He took the first five rounds of the firefight, all at once and all in one tight group.

The ATACs were standing straddle-legged, firing back at almost point-blank range, in the same second—all except for Louie, who slid the shock grenade the guards' way and hollered, "Get back!"

Refugee clones in the first rank fell like scythed wheat, but the ATACs' fire cut into the enemy guardsmens' ranks at once, and all the clones' accuracy was lost. Enemy shots rebounded from the troopers' armor, and the tankers laid down a suppressing fire that had the guardsmen ducking for cover.

The detonation of the shock grenade was like a freeze-frame of the guards' postures, lasting only a fraction of a second. Its blast sent them somersaulting and flying, while the refugees and the Humans scuttled for cover, and the ambushers struggled to regain the offensive.

Musica, crouched behind one structural frame, cradled to her the youth who had guided Angelo and taken the rounds meant for her. "Why did you . . . ?"

"You are the soul of us all. You are the hope of us all." The eyes rolled up in his head, showing only white, and the breath rattled from him.

She laid his head down gently, then rose and stepped back into the passageway, into the fairway of the firefight, the various beams and bolts and streams of discs bickering back and forth. "Karno! Stop this at once!"

Bowie, pinned down, couldn't reach her, but screamed at her to get to cover. Karno, crouched to fire from cover, bawled, "Musica, the Micronians have cast a spell over you!"

"That's not true! I've freely chosen a new way of life— ahh!"

There was no telling if the beam that seared her arm was from friend or foe. She went on through locked teeth, "The truth is... we are all free beings. With free will. *And you know that!*"

"You speak lies!" he shrieked. "You're bewitched!"

"Got any brilliant inspirations?" Louie asked Angelo, as they squatted in the lee of a huge packing crate.

"We *could* send 'em candy and flowers an' say we won't never do it no more," Angelo allowed, then snapped off another round. "Or, pray for a miracle—"

Just as he was saying that, the bulkhead was punched inward, one of the more curious coincidences of the war. It was as if one of those ancient beer-car openers was broaching a cold one, only the opener was a stiff-fingered shot by a Battloid.

The Battloid, having following their transponders, peeled back the bulkhead like wrapping paper and stood into the gap. Smoke curled around it and the guard clones shrank back in hysteria, forgetting their attack. A voice amplified to Olympian volume rang, "So for *this* you stood me up at our rendezvous?"

"Meant to drop ya a note, Phillips," Dante admitted. "But I got real distracted."

"No excuses!"

Where he might have used the towering mecha's weapons to wipe out every enemy there, Sean instead chose to chastise them. He had seen enough war, seen enough slaughter and, more to the point, sensed that a few more incidental enemy KIAs wouldn't influence the outcome of things. He had no heightened senses or Protoculture powers, just simple Human intuition that the outcome of the war—the very core of it—had nothing to do with scoring a few more clone body counts.

The colossal Battloid brushed a flock of guards into a wall; most of the others broke and ran, dropping their weapons. Among those downed was the Guard Triumvirate.

Angelo led the refugees the other way, toward the assault ships. But Karno reared up and spied Octavia, who had been promised to Sookol so long ago by the Masters. She looked so like Musica.

Karno dragged himself up and dug out his sidearm, to

shoot her as she dashed by. She screamed and fell, Bowie and Musica turning back to help her.

Sean turned his Battloid and brought up the Cyclopean foot. Even as Bowie and Musica were carrying Octavia to cover, Karno screamed. The last thing the clone ever saw was the bottom of the foot of the Battloid-configuration Hovertank *Bad News*, 15th squad, Alpha Tactical Armored Corps.

Bowie knelt in the lee of the alloy container while Musica sought to comfort her sister.

Octavia's hand caressed her cheek. "It's all right, Musica —I know my spirit and my songs will live in you!"

"We're still . . . as one," Musica struggled.

"Yes, I know, though greater things are in you now, such greater things! But to the end of space and time—we three are one . . . always. . . ."

And she was dead. Bowie tugged at Musica's arm because a sudden rush by counterattacking guards might put Musica in jeopardy before Sean's Battloid could make them see reason and drive them back.

The counterattack was repulsed, not much of a job for a mecha that had the firepower of an old-time armored troop. Sean's *Bad News* burrowed through a bulkhead like a big, glittering badger, and opened the way for the refugees, who went spilling into the assault ship hangar deck. "There; that oughta do it; everybody into the troop carriers!"

As planned, the battle on and just over the planet's surface and the decoys that were the surviving mother ships had led most of the Earth forces away from the flagship. Those that were left were of no importance. The Robotech Masters' last functioning mother ship closed in to execute the final portion of its mission.

Three segmented metal appendages, like huge blind worms, extruded themselves from the underside of the flagship and met, their completed instrumentality throwing out a light as bright as a solar prominence. A beam sprang down to penetrate one of the mounds below, and the second, and the third, with zigzagging sensor bolts.

Inside the Masters' ship, engines of raw power were brought into play. The distortions and occlusions of the Protoculture wraiths could not stand before that raw power, and the Masters saw at last where their target lay.

The three wraiths looked upward. Their hour was nearly sped; there was no resisting the focused might of the mother ship.

At the touch of the Masters' might, the mound covering the SDF-1 shuddered, then began to split open, as the Flowers of Life stirred, and the spores bobbed upward. Rock ground against rock, and tremendous volumes of soil were shifted with ease. The mound itself was split in half and pulled apart by the invaders' awesome instrumentality. As the gap widened, trees, boulders, and dirt from the mound's flat top rained down onto the wreckage below. In the place of the relatively small opening that had been above the Matrix garden, there appeared a rift that exposed the entire wreckage of the SDF-1.

The guardian Protoculture wraiths released the hold they had maintained on the spores for so long; the spores began drifting up toward the sunlight and the winds of Earth.

The Masters, studying their operations with satisfaction, watched the mound split open and willed their great ship to speed to it, for the extraction of the Matrix. There was time to save enough of it to provide them with sufficient new Protoculture to rebuild their galactic empire.

They were no longer on their floating cap, since its systemry had to be merged with that of the ship itself for this crucial function. Instead they stood on a circular antigrav platform, nearly at floor level. Without Bowkaz, it was less crowded than they were used to. Shaizan held the canister with the last mass once more, waiting for the moment when its total power must be brought to bear.

"Soon even the Invid will not dare stand against us," Shaizan declared. He turned to issue another order to the Scientist triumvirate, whose members stood nearby, supervising the mission, gathered around a big control module in the middle of the chamber.

But the opening of a hatch behind them made Shaizan and Dag whirl. Zor Prime entered, with the clone guard they had posted held in an armlock, his rifle aimed at them with his free hand. Dana followed, holding her carbine.

"Masters, heed me: the moment of retribution has come. Now you pay for all the evil you've done!" Zor Prime thundered.

Shaizan seemed almost sad. "Will you never understand, Zor? It is much too late." He gestured to the screens, which showed the opened mound, and Monument City in flames. "In moments, we will have the Matrix back, at last. You cannot stop us."

Dana snarled, "We're *not* going to let you snakes have that Matrix. It's too powerful!"

The Masters were mystified as to how Zor and the female had escaped; it was, perhaps, some effect from the sundering of their Triumvirate, Dag and Shaizan concluded.

Dana brought the carbine up and aimed it at the Scientist clones, clicking off the safety. "Stop the machines."

Dovak, the triumvirate leader of the Scientists, protested, "Impossible! They cannot be stopped now; they've been given final instructions!"

Dana decided to find out, with a few well-placed bursts into the controls—perhaps even into the clones, if they didn't see reason. But just then, Zor shoved her aside. Energy bolts blazed through the spot where she had stood, splashing molten droplets and sparks from the bulkhead.

The Masters' antigrav platform was rising, and from an energy nozzle on its underside, a stream of shots raged at the interlopers. Zor had dived for cover, hurling the guard against the bulkhead and the clone dropped, stunned. Rolling, Zor fired back, and Dag clutched his midsection, slumping, crying out in pain and hysterical fear of death.

Dana fired, too, but her shots at the weapon nozzle and the platform's underside didn't appear to be doing much good. Then she hit a hornlike projection, and the platform rocked, smoking and crackling with powerful discharges, and fell back to the deck.

The platform came straight at them, and Dana and Zor threw themselves to either side. Somehow, Shaizan, still cradling the canister to him, gained control at the last moment and managed to leap free, before the platform went on to plow into the Scientist clones and their control module. They screamed, transfixed with horror, as the platform crashed down on them and their control module ruptured, spilling out furious energy surges.

By the time Zor and Dana got back to their feet, Shaizan was already at another hatch, clinging to the Protoculture mass. Zor screamed, "Master, you can't escape me!" but the tripartite hatch closed behind Shaizan.

As they were rushing to catch up, Dana heard some monitoring system shrilling in alarm. A voice simulacrum wailed, "Warning! Warning! Guidance systems off-line! Power systems failing! Crash alert! Impact in three point five five units!"

Dana looked at the display maps, and saw the projected point of impact: it looked to her like Monument City. She wasn't aware that the city had already been shot to ruins by the Triumviroids.

"We've got to stop it, or it'll kill everyone in the city! Zor, there's got to be a manual control system!"

He shook his head slowly. "We must get Shaizan to release his hold over the systemry first."

He started for the hatch with Dana sprinting along behind. "Then we have to capture the last one alive!"

In fear of his life, Shaizan ran as he hadn't run in an age. Fright gave him more strength that he had ever thought possible, and the pumping of adrenaline in his system felt savage, bewilderingly primitive, after a long sedentary life.

But he was the quarry of young people in top condition; they soon caught up with him, in an ejection capsule access deck not far from the bridge. Zor saw Shaizan ahead and stopped to take up a firing stance. "Stop, I command you!"

"Zor, *don't*!" But before Dana could strike down the rifle

barrel, Zor fired. Shaizan dropped in a swirl of robes; somehow, the canister remained intact.

Zor went to look down at the old man. Somehow, death had taken away the constant anger of the Master's visage, and he was nothing but a frail, infinitely tired-looking creature with a smoking hole in him, head pillowed on a collar resembling the Flower of Life. How could these creatures have lived so long and thrived on the Protoculture without understanding its Shapings—without foreseeing this day?

"It's over now," Zor said, more to himself than to Dana.

"What d'you mean, 'all over'?" Dana barked. "This ship's gonna demolish the city!"

"The Masters brought their own punishment down on themselves, by their misuse of the Protoculture," he told her, putting a hand on each of her armored shoulders. "And I was the instrument of that punishment, ordained by the Shaping."

"But what about *my* people? It's not fair to punish them for something they didn't do—*mmmmm . . .*"

He leaned forward to put his lips to hers. Their mouths locked, they kissed for what might have been seconds or centuries. When they parted a bit, he smiled at her tenderly, and she was astounded to see from his eyes that—

He—he loves me!

Zor had her back in his arms, was lifting her off the deck. "Do not worry about your people, Dana. I will allow no harm to come to them."

She felt like relaxing, just letting him carry her where he would; like going limp and simply trusting him. But some inner, independent part of her made her start to object. Just then, she realized that he was setting her down into the cocoon padding of an ejection capsule.

"Good-bye, Dana."

At first she had thought he was going to join her inside— that they would cast aside the armor of war and never wear it again. And she had been working up the self-discipline to make sure everything really *was* all right before she took her own armor off, though the temptation was great.

But instead, he drew back, and she was so astounded that

she sat frozen while the hatch of the little superhard alloy sphere closed and secured. All at once she was staring at him through a viewport. His smile was wistful, as he made some adjustment to the locking mechanism, and it gave a loud click. He smiled at her again, fondly but mournfully.

"*Zor!*" She was pounding at the viewport and trying to work the locking controls, but it did no good. He disappeared from view. She was still struggling to get free, crying, shouting his name, when the capsule gave a lurch, moved by the transfer servos, preparing for ejection.

CHAPTER
TWENTY-FIVE

They give you clothes, they're free with guns,
And trainin', food and lodgin',
But tell me: what career moves
Can come from bullet dodgin'?

Bowie Grant, "Nervous in the Service"

"**S**ARGE, WE'RE PICKING UP SOME KINDA EJECTION capsule launch from the mother ship," Louie Nichols reported, sitting beside Angelo at the controls of the liberated assault ship.

Behind them, refugee clones were crowded in tightly, frightened, but used to the discipline of the Masters and so obediently quiet. Angelo, sweating over the controls, snapped, "So what? Maybe it's somebody makin' their own getaway. It sure ain't a raidin' party or a Bioroid."

That was true, and it was unlikely that there were many combat forces left in the mother ship, or that they would do the Masters much good even if they could get to the Earth's surface. For some reason, the Bioroid-pilot clones and other fighters of the Masters' invasion force had, according to the transmissions the escapees were monitoring, suddenly become almost totally ineffective. The attacking enemies' ability to fight, their very *will* to fight, seemed to have simply vanished, and Earth's ragtag defenders were counterattacking everywhere, a complete rout.

Something occurred to Angelo. "Get on the military freqs and find somebody who's in charge," he told Louie. "Tell 'em we got an airlift of refugees comin' down, and to hold their fire. Tell 'em...tell 'em these people here ain't the enemy."

Louie threw him a strange smile. "Hear, hear, Angie."

He felt Bowie, who stood behind him, clap him on the back, and felt Musica's light touch at his shoulder. Then Angelo pronounced a few choice army obscenities, the ship having wandered off course. He was no fly-boy and even the coaching of experienced clone pilots didn't make it much easier to herd the alien craft along.

"Everybody keep still and lemme drive," Angelo Dante growled.

Within the mother ship, Zor's red Bioroid stomped back toward the command center, its discus pistol clutched in its gargantuan metal fist. Below the ship, the mounds hove into view.

I cannot undo the damage I've done. Across a hundred reincarnations; across a hundred million light-years. And yet: I'll make what restitution I can.

The Invid would not have Earth.

Below, the Protoculture wraiths sensed Zor Prime's coming, all in accordance with the Shaping that had given the original Zor his vision and set the course of the Robotech Wars, so long ago and far away.

The wraiths summoned up the strength that was left to them, for their final deed. The rainbow-rings of the Matrix were dimmer now, but still dazzling, still playing their haunting song. As the wraiths tapped its power, the Matrix flared brighter.

Dana's efforts to contact Zor with the capsule's little commo unit had drawn no response. Now she blinked at the bright sunlight, as the hatch opened and the fragrant air of Earth drifted in.

The capsule had landed at the crest of a low foothill across the plain, just within view of the SDF-1's gravesite. She already knew from the capsule's crude monitoring equipment that the mother ship had followed her down through the atmosphere, headed for the mounds.

Dana drew herself out of the capsule and saw the five-mile length of the Masters' last starship come in to hover over the resting place of the SDF-1. "Zor. Don't—please!"

There is no other way.

Zor's red raised its discus pistol. The destruction of the mother ship directly over the mounds would ensure that the Flowers of Life and their spores would be completely obliterated, and spare the Human race the slaughter and ruin of an Invid invasion.

Some spores had already drifted free of the mound, though instruments weren't clear as to why that hadn't happened before; there were completely unique and unprecedented Protoculture aberrations down there, and no time to analyze them. But that didn't matter now. The radius of the blast would get all of them.

Now!

The red fired its pistol at carefully selected targets; it was easy for him to find the vulnerable points in the systemry the original Zor had conceived. In moments the entire ship was a daisy chain of ever increasing explosions, ripping open its hull, gathering toward that final, utter detonation.

He thought he would be swallowed up by grief in those last moments, to see only the ghosts of the victims, and the shadows of the suffering he had caused. Unexpectedly, though, Zor Prime's last thoughts were of the thing that had made this last incarnation so different from the rest, and let him free himself.

Dana, I love you!

Dana shrieked at the exploding ship, knowing it would do no good, until the explosions reached a crescendo. "Stop! Zor, there must be a better way—"

Then she threw herself to shelter behind the grounded, armored capsule and wept, face buried in her arms.

In the mounds, the wraiths gathered all their remaining energy, and contained the explosive force of the mother ship.

Zor's calculations were entirely correct, insofar as they went. The self-destruction should have vaporized the mounds and wiped out the curse that was the blooming Flowers, the drifting spores.

But the Shaping of the Robotech Wars had been set long before. Earth was to be saved from destroying itself in a Global Civil War and, at the same time, serve as the focal point that would let a tremendous wrong be righted. The time for the righting of that wrong had not yet come to pass, though the stage was now set.

And so the wraiths dampened the blast of the exploding starship. The Matrix flared like a nova, sang a single piercing note, and released all its power upward. The wraiths used it to muffle the blast in an unimaginable contest of warring forces, and won.

Still, the mother ship was blown to fragments and, even as Zor Prime soared to a higher plane of existence, freed at last of the cycle of crime and guilt in which he had been caught since his first terrible transgression, the fragments began to fall.

Even a small piece of the mother ship was enormous, and not all of the explosive force had been contained. Housings and armor and structural members pelted the plain and the mounds, raising huge puffs of dust, opening the mound even further; the explosive force caught the rising spores and sent them high and wide, to ride the winds of the world. Ripping down into the garden that had been the last Matrix, the blasts freed a hundred thousand times as many more, and sent them wafting, lifting petals and even whole plants, gusting them forth.

The winds that came from the Protoculture detonation behaved unlike normal air currents. It was as if they had been given a purpose, dispersing the spores, *sowing* them,

taking many into upper airstreams that would bear them far
—would seed the face of the planet with them.

The wraiths looked upon their work and upon the Earth
that the Shaping had made their home for so long. They had
been given life, of a sort, by the Protoculture, taking power
from the masses within the wreckage of SDF-1, SDF-2, and
Khyron's downed battlecruiser.

But now their part in the Shaping was over, and the Matrix's last energy was used up; it was gone forever. They
began their return to nothingness, making sure that the re-
sidual Protoculture around them underwent conversion to
the Flowers of Life.

Dana watched the drifting pink petals, the swirling
spores. *The Invid* are *coming!* Her parents' warning was
right, and nothing could stop this species that even the Masters held in dread.

Three shadows loomed up out of the mounds, growing,
but becoming more and more tenuous as they did. Dana, her
senses expanded by her exposure to the Matrix and even
more so by the jolt from the canister containing the Masters'
last mass, knew that the phantasms would do her no harm.

She was so preoccupied, thinking about her family, about
the Masters' words and Zor's, that she didn't hear the
stealthy footsteps behind her, covered as they were by the
moan of the winds. The projectile took her at the base of the
skull, where her armor offered no protection. She went
down.

"You *saw* them!" an eerie voice said. It sounded Human
but had some of the sepulchral emotionlessness of a Robotech Master's. "Without instruments or sensors, you *saw* the
Guardians of the Mounds!"

She lay on her side, dazed, unable to move though she
was fully conscious. She realized she had been shot with
some kind of paralyzing agent. A moment later, two peculiar
men came into view.

One she recognized, and the sight of him almost stopped
her heart. Zand, heir to Dr. Lang's secrets. He was wearing
gleaming angelic robes, shiny metallic stuff, cut somewhat in
the fashion of the Robotech Masters' monkish ones, and his

collar was shaped like the Flower of Life. That alone told
Dana what was happening, and the danger she was in.

Zand had gone completely insane and saw her as his pass-
port to divine powers.

Along with Zand was a stout, vacant-faced little man with
a pencil mustache, so different from the pictures in the history books that Dana didn't recognize him until Zand turned
to say, "Russo! Bring the equipment." The scientist tossed
aside the tranquilizer gun indifferently.

Russo scuttled away. Dana knew there was no aircraft or
surface vehicle around; she had seen none on landing. Had
they simply been sitting out here, *waiting*? She couldn't figure out how Zand had foreseen that she would be where she
was. Perhaps his powers were *already* greater than hers.

Russo returned with devices like nothing either Earth's
Robotechnology or the Masters' had ever produced. It
seemed to be all crystal nimbuses and rainbow whorls, humming faintly like the Matrix.

Zand smiled like a fiend. "Much more compact than anything you'll have seen even in the mother ships, I'll bet.
Those were crude toys compared to this."

He was assembling it in some fashion she couldn't quite
follow. "I've had plenty of time to study the Matrix, you see.
Years!" The apparatus seemed to shift and fold, as if it were
moving among dimensions. Its aura had a fractal look to it.

Zand laughed a bit. "The Masters and the Human race,
destroying each other over a mere *Matrix*! When the *real*
crux of the matter is *you*, Dana—and your Destiny, which is
to yield up your powers to me!"

He reached out to touch something like a node of pure
light against her forehead. It clung there, and she felt an
utter cold, even through the numbness. "Your powers will
grow. They will see *beyond* the Protoculture! They will be
matchless! But," his mouth flattened grimly, "they'll do all
that as *mine*, once I've taken them from you."

He looked around. "Where is the Protoculture cell?"

When Russo gave him a blank look, Zand lashed out and
sent him sprawling. Russo crawled and flopped away, whim-

pering like a whipped hound, to return with a prism perhaps a foot long, slender and glowing.

Dana fought against her paralysis, but couldn't shake it or defy it. Zand had planned it well. He had foreseen this day with powers of his own. As he took the Protoculture cell and prepared to shift Dana's gifts to himself, she had a moment to wonder: what, then, of her Vision, the Phoenix?

Her own life, she knew, was over. Zand was about to take something that was so much her essence that she would die like a withered husk without it.

He had mated the prism with the rest of his strange device. "So much Protoculture in one place," he smiled. "It took a long time to gather, even for *me*, diverting military supplies. But it's the power I need to draw your powers from you to me."

The device shone brighter, Russo was groveling, crouched with his face in the sand. Zand's strange voice was exalted. "First the power of the Protoculture fills me, then the powers of Dana Sterling!" The light was unbearable.

Zand seemed to swell and grow. Dana feared what the Universe was in for, with Zand striding across it like a god.

Just then she heard a bark.

Polly! In her paralysis, she couldn't even say it.

The Pollinator came traipsing up and sat down, head canted to one side, tongue lolling, to consider Zand. He barely registered the XT creature, though, because something was terribly wrong with him.

His enlarged form was vibrating. Soon he was contorting, convulsing, his device flashing like a lighthouse in an earthquake. Russo had thrown himself flat, covering his head with his hands, wailing.

Dana had a sense that the last of the wraiths was vanishing away. And with them, the last of the Matrix, as well as the last of the Protoculture in the area, was being *transformed*.

Zand voiced a howl of agony and fright so ghastly that she was to remember it all her days. The light engulfed him. Still the Pollinator sat and watched. The Protoculture in the Matrix had been changed to the Flowers of Life....

Perhaps it was the discharge of so much Protoculture. In any case, Dana felt the world slipping away, and saw the old Vision once again, the Phoenix. Only, this time she saw Zor, too. It was given to her, in that trance, to know why the Robotech Wars had come to be, and what the ultimate outcome was—just what the Phoenix was.

Just as the blinding light faded, Dana found that she could move a little. Either Zand had underestimated the dosage or her expanded powers were helping. Dana, Polly, and the whining Russo gazed on what had appeared in Zand's place.

In a way, he got his wish, was Dana's first coherent thought.

There had never been, nor ever would be again, one to match it, the biggest Flower of Life that ever was. It stood rooted in the sand, spreading its petals, a coral-colored tripartite beauty. Of Zand there was no sign except, perhaps, in the shape and detail of the central blossom; it might only be her imagination, or it might be that she saw his face there.

Of his fantastic device, nothing remained.

She found she had the strength to rise, but came only to her knees, swaying. She heard a cry and looked up to see Russo, shrieking and screaming, running off down the hill like a crazed ape. He was headed directly out into the wastelands; she let him go.

Dana dragged one foot to her, until she was on one knee, the spores drifting about her. The odd thought struck her that perhaps Zand's fate was some lesson from the Protoculture, some chastening, to balance the power she had been granted.

She found herself humming, then realized it was a seventeenth-century hymn her father had loved and her Zentraedi mother had approved of as holding much and proper wisdom; so Rolf Emerson had told her, when Emerson taught it to Bowie and Dana. As a little girl she had taught it to Konda, Bron, and Rico, and they had insisted that what was in the words and the tune was nothing less than universal truth:

Lead kindly, Light,
Amid the encircling gloom
Lead Thou me on,
The night is dark and I am far from home
Lead Thou me on,
Keep Thou my feet
I do not ask to see the distant scene
One step enough for me

TWENTY-SIX

Now our slaves, the Robotech Masters, are passed away
Now all our Protoculture balefires burn low
Now the Shapings turn; we surrender the stage to Invid and Human
Our cold light leaves the Universe
We see at the last that
Those who remain behind know no fear of the darkness
And we ourselves learn
What it is to weep

Death song of the Robotech Elders

DANA GATHERED POLLY UNDER ONE ARM AND walked tiredly back to the escape capsule. Russo, already a mile away, was barely visible as a mad figure capering and lurching into the wastes. The Pollinator licked her face.

A thin whine of engines caught her attention, and she looked up to see an assault ship coming in at her, flying unsteadily, seemingly about to go into a nosedive.

She threw herself flat, expecting the worst, but somehow the vessel righted itself enough for a jouncing set-down right near her. She remembered that she was unarmed, but she had no place to run and was too tired and battered to feel fear—thought that, perhaps, she would never know it again.

But when the assault craft's hatches opened, instead of letting forth attack teams of Triumviroids, it yielded her own 15th squad, along with Nova, Musica, and a bunch of clones.

"Damn it, Phillips!" Angelo Dante was seething. "I'd like

to see you make a better landing with an XT ship! We walked away from it, didn't we?"

"All I said was," Sean replied in a blasé voice, "that I could do better with boxing gloves on. Hey, Dana! You made it!"

The refugees stayed back, but her squadmates and Musica and Nova clustered around her, along with Marie Crystal and Dennis Brown. She blinked at him. "How did you find me?"

"Picked up your voice transmissions from the escape capsule," Angelo said. "But then, all of a sudden, the engines and all the systems quit. We had to land on emergency power."

"Ya shoulda let Marie and Dennis take over," Sean snorted.

But Dana was shaking her head. "No, Angie couldn't help what happened. It's the Protoculture—there was nothing he could do." Angelo looked at her strangely, not used to having her defend him.

There were still Protoculture power supplies on Earth, she knew, outside the radius of effect of the wraiths' transformation. Enough to animate mecha for a transition period. But there would be no new Matrices, no new sources.

"The war's over, Lieutenant," Bowie told her happily. "The enemy mecha stopped fighting, and the clones just want peace."

"That's . . . that's great, Bowie." He didn't understand why she sounded like she was about to start bawling. People noticed the Pollinator, but hesitated to ask about it. They saw the huge Flower that had been Zand, but they were used to seeing the triad plants by now, and even such a huge one was far down on the list of topics of discussion.

"Where's Zor?" Musica inquired timidly, fearing to hear the answer.

Dana pointed to where the mushroom cloud of spores and petals still rose up and up, funneled into the higher atmosphere, sent on their appointed way by those strange winds. "He died trying to save Earth."

Musica was shaking her head slowly, looking at the pink

petals and tiny spores that filled the sky like a blizzard. "But in vain. Now the Invid come. Oh poor, poor Zor!" Bowie slipped his armored arm around her.

Nova drew a deep breath and declared, "Well, then! We've got to get back and report to whoever's in interim command! We have defenses to set up, plans to make—" She looked a little funny acting military with the infant still in her arms.

But Dana was shaking her head, too. "You do what you have to. I'm through with war." She already saw where her new course lay.

She had beheld something greater than herself, greater than the Human race or any other corporeal race. She understood at last the Vision that had filled her dreams all her life. She knew that there was no way to oppose or derail the Shaping, though there was much more suffering and strife ahead. She recalled that magnificent, infinitely sad Phoenix of racial transfiguration, and the recollection took away some of her sorrow.

"What d'you mean? You think you can hide from what's coming?" Nova snapped. "There's nowhere to run, Dana." The 15th and the others were looking at her worriedly, too, afraid that what she had been through had pushed her over the edge.

"What's going to happen on Earth will go beyond armies, beyond Protoculture," she told them calmly. "The next Robotech War will be the last, but I've had enough. I'm going to find my parents, and my sister. They're with a group that includes Admiral Hunter and Admiral Hayes, who've parted ways with the original SDF-3 expedition. They're trying to establish a new, positive force, the Sentinels. I'm joining them."

Everybody was babbling at once, but Angelo Dante held stage center by dint of his overwhelming voice. "Even if you weren't crazy, Dana, there's no way to get there! All the Robotech Masters' starships were blown to smithereens, and Earth ain't got no more." He looked toward the flaming remains of Monument City and Fokker Base. "And ain't likely to for a long, long time."

The Pollinator let out a playful yip and he reached out unconsciously to pet the thing, barely aware that Polly was there.

Dana puzzled for a microsecond, but her new powers offered up the answer at once, like some unfailing databank. "Before too long, a senior officer named Wolfe will arrive with another expedition, carrying word from the SDF-3, like Major Carpenter's ships did.

"By then, I'll be ready with the fuel and charts and everything else I need to take one of his ships and find my family and the others. Any of you who want to come are welcome."

They didn't have to ask if she meant to get the starship by legal means; the world was in ruins and all chains of command shattered. All the military certainties were swept away.

And, somehow, nobody thought to scoff at her, not even the aloof, skeptical Nova. The way back to what they had known was shut to them forever; within seconds they were all telling her she could count them in. All save one.

"Wish you the best of luck," he said, then shrugged a little. "You follow your own instincts, Dana, but somehow I figure my place is here. I think Earth's gonna need me."

She accepted that, knew that special knowledge was given where it was needed, and that she was far from unique in that regard. "If it's what you want, Louie."

Louie Nichols gave his patented clever-funny smirk. "There's still a lot of things I want to know, and I can only find 'em out *here*. And besides, well—don't laugh!—but maybe I've got my *own* part to play." He adjusted the big, dark tech goggles self-consciously.

Nobody laughed. There would be months, perhaps years, of preparation yet—in a world half in ruins—and only Dana had any coherent idea of what was to come. But somehow there was, on the crest of the little hill, a feeling very much like what the sundering of the Round Table must have felt like.

ATAC squad 15 (Hovertanks) turned to get the refugees formed up for the long hike back to Monument City; the assault ship would never rise again. There were already the pairings of Bowie and Musica, Sean and Marie. And now, Nova Satori stayed close to Dennis Brown; the looks they exchanged spoke eloquently.

Dana, sitting on a rock, was stripping off the armor that she hoped never to have to wear again. The spores still drifted everywhere. A sudden loneliness had come over her; there was so very much to do yet, and no one could possibly share her knowledge and her responsibilities—no one could ever understand her longing. She let go a long breath.

Something blocked the low, orange rays of the sunset from her. Angelo Dante stood there, stretching and scratching, having ditched his own armor, wearing a pack made up of most of the usable things he had managed to scare up in the assault ship. The weight of it didn't seem to bother him. He was adjusting his rifle sling.

He didn't seem to have a care in the world. "Lieutenant —Dana—you're still callin' the shots. I got 'em ready; you move 'em out."

Before she knew it, she was on her feet, arms thrown around him. About her had spun the symmetries and vectors of the Second Robotech War; she alone had the powers of mind that would let a leader perform the job she had to do now. But her nineteenth birthday was still three weeks and three days away.

Angelo patted her back and spoke more softly than she had ever heard him. "There, there, now, ma'am: we can't *all* be sergeants. But as officers go, I've seen worse than you. Dana, all we need is someone to show us the way."

She knew he didn't mean the way to Monument; the flames would do that. She surprised herself as much as him by pulling his head down to her and kissing Angelo Dante hard.

Then she let him go, took the sidearm from his belt and stalked off to the front of the disorderly mob while he was still recovering and turning to glower at the ATACs, who had seen what happened but kept discreet silence.

Dana saw that the 15th had gotten all the emergency supplies and lights, water and rations from the assault ship and even from her own little escape capsule. She tucked Angelo's pistol into her belt and noted with approval the order of march, weakened or older refugees surrounded by stronger ones who could help at need.

Not that she thought there would be much call for it; the route was pretty straightforward and unobstructed, and the clones who had been so lethargic before now seemed somehow more vital.

She was about to call for a start when there was a little yipping sound nearby. Dana had put Polly down while stripping off her armor; she had assumed that he had disappeared. But he was practically sitting on her feet.

"Polly. In for the distance, are you, hmm?"

The Pollinator showed her a red postage stamp of tongue. She looked back to see that the 15th had the refugees formed up for the march. Angelo winked and gave her a look she hadn't seen from him before. She wondered whether or not she would, at some point, return it; she had a feeling she might.

Later.

First Lieutenant Dana Sterling, 15th squad, Alpha Tactical Armored Corps, gave hand and voice signals, and all the rest began moving. The Pollinator fell in to waddle along beside.

ATACs and TASCs, GMP and clone refugees followed her down the slope and the Pollinator capered around her feet, as darkness came across the sky. They looked for her to point the way.

The following chapter is a sneak preview of *The Invid Invasion*—Book X in the continuing saga of ROBOTECH!!

Somewhere a queen was weeping ... her children scattered; her regent a prisoner of the bloodlust, at war with nature and enslaved to vengeance.

But dare we presume to read her thoughts even now, to walk a path not taken—one denied to us by gates and towers our senses cannot perceive, and perhaps never will?

Still, it must have seemed like the answer to a prayer: a planet newly rich in the flower that was life itself; a profusion of such incredible nutrient wealth that her Sensor Nebulae had found it clear across the galaxy. A blue-and-white world as distant from her Optera as she was from the peaceful form her consciousness once inhabited.

And yet Optera was lost to her, to half her children. Left in the care of one who had betrayed his kind; who had become what he fought so desperately to destroy. As she herself had. . . .

All but trapped now in the guise that *he* had worn, the one who lured the secrets of the Flower from her. And whose giant warriors had returned to possess the planet and dispossess its inhabitants. *But oh, how she had loved him!*

Enough to summon from her very depths the ability to emulate him. And later to summon a hatred keen enough to birth a warring nature, an army of soldiers to rival his—to rival *Zor's* own!

But he, too, was lost to her, killed by the very soldiers her hatred had fashioned.

Oh, to be rid of these dark memories! her ancient heart must have screamed. *To be rescued from these sorry realms! Garuda, Spheris, Tirol. And this Haydon IV with its sterile flowers long awaiting the caress of the Pollinators—this confused world even her Inorganics could not subdue.*

But she was aware that all these things would soon be behind her. She would gather the cosmic stuff of her race and make the jump to that world the Sensor Nebula had located. *And woe to the life-form that inhabited that world!* For nothing would prevent her from finding a home for her children, a home for the completion of their grand evolutionary design!

News of the Invid exodus from Haydon IV spread through the Fourth Quadrant—to Spheris and Garuda and Praxis, worlds already abandoned by the insectlike horde, worlds singled out by fate to feel the backlash of Zor's attempt at recompense, nature's cruel joke.

The Tirolian scientist had attempted to foliate them with the same Flowers he had been ordered to steal from Optera —an action that had sentenced that warm world's sentient life-form to a desperate quest to relocate their nutrient grail. But Zor's experiments had failed, because the Flower of Life proved to be a discriminating plant—choosy about where it would and would not put down roots—and a malignantly loyal one as well.

Deriving as much from the Invid as the Invid derived from it, the Flower called out from Zor's seeded worlds to its former guardian/hosts. Warlike and driven—instincts born of the Robotech Masters' transgression—the Invid answered those calls. Their army of mecha and Inorganics arrived in swarms to overwhelm and rule; and instead of the Protoculture paradises the founder of Robotechnology had envisioned, these were planets dominated by the beings his discoveries had all but doomed.

And now suddenly they were gone; off on a new quest that would take them clear across the galactic core.

To Earth . . .

Word of their departure reached Rick Hunter aboard the SDF-3. Admiral again (the schism and subsequent rebellion behind him), Rick was in the command seat on the fortress bridge when the communiqué was received. Thin and pale, a war-weary veteran of countless battles, Rick was almost forty years old by Earth reckoning; but the vagaries of hyperspace travel put him closer to twenty-five or two hundred and seventy, depending on how one figured it.

The giant planet Fantoma, once home to the Zentraedi, filled the forward viewports. In the foreground Rick could just discern the small inhabited moon called Tirol, an angry dot against Fantoma's barren face. *How could such an insignificant world have unleashed so much evil on an unsuspecting galaxy?* Rick wondered.

Rick glanced over at Lisa, humming to herself while she tapped a flurry of commands into her console. *His wife.* They had stayed together through thick and thin these past seventeen years; although they had had their share of disagreements, especially when Rick had opted to join the Sentinels—Baldon, Teal, Crysta, and the others—and pursue the Invid.

Who would have thought it would come to this? he asked himself. A mission whose purpose had been peace at war with itself. Edwards and his grand designs of empire . . . how like the Invid Regent he was, how like the Masters, too! But he was history now, and that fleet he had raised to conquer Earth would be used to battle the Invid when the Expeditionary Force reached the planet.

Providing the fleet reached Earth, of course. There were still major problems with the spacefold system Lang and the Tirolian Cabell had designed. Some missing ingredient . . . Major Carpenter had never been heard from, nor Wolfe; and now the Mars and Jupiter Group attack wings were preparing to fold, with almost two thousand Veritechs between them.

Rick exhaled slowly and deliberately, loud enough for Lisa to hear him and turn a thin smile his way. Somehow it was fitting that Earth end up on the Invid's list, Rick decided. But what could have happened there to draw them in such unprecedented numbers? Rick shuddered at the thought.

Perhaps Earth was where the final battle was meant to be fought.

Ravaged by the Robotech Masters and their gargantuan agents, the Zentraedi, it was a miracle that Earth had managed to survive at all. Looking on the planet from deep space, it would have appeared unchanged: its beautiful oceans and swirling masses of cloud, its silver satellite, bright as any beacon in the quadrant. But a closer look revealed the scars and disfigurations those invasions had wrought. The northern hemisphere was all but a barren waste, forested by the rusting remains of Dolza's ill-fated four-million-ship armada. Great cities of gleaming concrete, steel, and glass towers lay ruined and abandoned. Wide highways and graceful bridges were cratered and collapsed. Airports, schools, hospitals, sports complexes, industrial and residential zones... reduced to rubble, unmarked graveyards one and all.

A fifteen-year period of peace—that tranquil prologue to the Masters' arrival—saw the resurrection of some of those things the twentieth century had all but taken for granted. Cities had rebuilt themselves, new ones had grown up. But humankind was now a different species from that which had originally raised those towering sculptures of stone. Post-Cataclysmites, they were a feudal, warring breed, as distrustful of one another as they were of those stars their hopeful ancestors had once wished upon. Perhaps, as some have claimed, Earth actually called in its second period of catastrophe, as if bent on adhering to some self-fulfilled prophecy of doom. The Masters, too, for that matter: the two races met and engaged in an unspoken agreement for mutual annihilation—a paving of the way for what would follow.

Those who still wish to blame Protoculture trace the genesis of this back to Zor, Aquarian-age Prometheus, whose gift to the galaxy was a Pandora's box he willingly opened. Displaced and repressed, the Flower of Life had rebelled. And there were no chains, molecular or otherwise, capable of containing its power. That Zor, resurrected by the Elders of his race for their dark purposes, should have been the one to free the Flower from its Matrix is now seen as part of Protoculture's equation. Equally so, that that liberation should call forth the Invid to complete the circle.

They came without warning: a swarm of monsters and mecha folded across space and time by their leader/queen, the Regis, through an effort of pure psychic will. They did not choose to announce themselves the way their former enemies had, nor did they delay their invasion to puzzle out humankind's strengths and weaknesses, quirks and foibles. There was no need to determine whether Earth did or did not have what they sought; their Sensor Nebulae had already alerted them to the presence of the Flower. It had found compatible soil and climate on the blue-and-white world. All that was required was the Pollinators, a missing element in the Robotech Masters' equations.

In any case, the Invid had already had dealings with Earthlings, having battled them on a dozen planets, including Tirol itself. But as resilient as they might have been on Haydon IV, Spheris, and the rest, Humans were a pathetic lot on their homeworld.

In less than a week the Invid conquered the planet, destroying the orbiting Factory Satellite,—an ironic end for the Zentraedi giants who inhabited it—laying to waste city after city, and dismissing with very little effort the vestiges of the Army of the Southern Cross. Depleted of the Protoculture charges necessary to fuel their Robotechnological war machines, those warriors who had fought so valiantly against the Masters were forced to fall back on a small supply of nuclear weapons and conventional ordnance that was no match for the Invid's plasma and laser-array superiority.

Even if Protoculture had been available to the Southern Cross for their Hovertanks and Veritechs, there would have been gross problems to overcome: the two years since the mutual annihilation of the Robotech Masters and Anatole Leonard's command had seen civilization's unchecked slide into lawlessness and barbarism. Cities became city-states and warred with one another; men and women rose quickly to positions of power only to fall even more swiftly in the face of greater military might. Greed and butchery ruled, and what little remained of the northern hemisphere's dignity collapsed.

Though certain cities remained strong—Mannatan, for-example (formerly New York City)—the centers of power shifted southward, into Brazilas especially (the former Zen-traedi Control Zone), where growth had been sure and steady since the SDF-1's return to devastated Earth and the founding of New Macross and its sister city, Monument.

Unlike the Zentraedi or the Tirol Masters, the Invid were not inclined to destroy the planet or exterminate human-kind. Quite the contrary: not only had the *Flower* found favorable conditions for growth, but the Invid had as well. The Regis had learned enough in her campaign against the Tirolians and the so-called Sentinels to recognize the contin-uing need for technology. Gone was the blissful tranquillity of Optera; but the experiment had to be carried forth to its conclusion nonetheless, and Earth was well-suited for the purpose.

After disarming and occupying the planet, the Regis be-lieved she was more than halfway toward her goal. By utiliz-ing a percentage of Humans to cultivate and harvest the Flowers, she was free to carry out her experiments uninter-rupted. The central hive, which came to be called Reflex Point, was to be the site of the Great Work; but secondary hives were soon in place across the planet to maintain con-trol of the Human sectors of her empire. The Regis was to let humankind survive until such time as the Work neared completion. Then she would rid herself of them.

There was, however, one thing she had not taken into account: the very warriors she had fought tooth-and-claw on those worlds once seeded by Zor. Enslave a world she might; but take it for her own?

Never!

ABOUT THE AUTHOR

Jack McKinney has been a psychiatric aide, fusion-rock guitarist and session man, worldwide wilderness guide, and "consultant" to the U.S. Military in Southeast Asia (although they had to draft him for that).

His numerous other works of mainstream and science fiction—novels, radio and television scripts—have been written under various pseudonyms.

He currently resides in Dos Lagunas, El Petén, Guatemala.

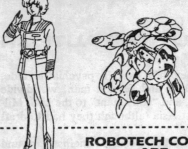